VALENTINE & HOPEWELL

HE WALKS

PAST MY

HOUSE

Amanda Hopewell.

TIGER ◆ DIAMOND ◆ PRESS

First published by Tiger Diamond Press 2023

Paperback ISBN: 978-1-7394404-0-4
Printed and bound in the UK by Biddles Books
Limited, King's Lynn, Norfolk
Cover Design Nick Castle Design 2023

ABOUT VALENTINE & HOPEWELL AND THE STORY BEHIND THE STORY

Charlotte Valentine and Amanda Hopewell 'met' virtually on Instagram in 2021 and decided to collaborate together on a writing project. *He Walks Past My House* began life as a series of alternately written live daily posts. Encouraged by the response the story received, they continued to write and post until it became a full-length novel.

Charlotte studied Law and worked in corporate life before leaving to study for her MA in Literature; this inspired her to write creatively herself. She has previously published a novel and a collection of short stories.

Amanda has been writing since she was eight. She has an MA in Theatre: Writing, Directing & Performance and is an author, playwright and music artist. She has previously published plays and a poetry collection.

ALSO BY CHARLOTTE VALENTINE

The Cerberus Affair
Late Night Shots

ALSO BY AMANDA HOPEWELL

Amanda Hopewell: Plays One
Amanda Hopewell: Poetry One

From Charlotte V:

In memory of Pudsey and Zeke, who were by my side throughout the writing of this book and who showed me the power and joy of unconditional love.
And for Alex, who is the light of my life.

From Amanda H:

Thank you to my mum, Cheryl Greenwood, for being an amazing woman and always allowing me to follow my dreams.
And in memory of Colin Greenwood. I completed the book, Dad.

HE WALKS

PAST MY

HOUSE

Chapter 1

SANDIE

Today should be my wedding day, the happiest day of my life. But my fiancé decided he had somewhere better to be.

A week ago, he made his cold, matter-of-fact announcement. 'I'm moving to number 12.'

Then he picked up his favourite pair of socks from the bedroom floor, threw them into one of his bags, and without even saying sorry or goodbye, he walked out of the house and across the road. I watched my life implode like a scene from a silent movie, as a gaping hole opened up inside my chest cavity.

The night before he left, we'd been as intimate and connected as two people can be, wrapped in each other's arms as we discussed our future together.

'This is beautiful, Garrie.'

'Just like you, my darling.'

A wave of contentment washed over me. 'I want to feel like this forever.'

'Me too.'

'Hold me tight.'

'If I hold you any tighter your brain will pop out and you might forget who I am.'

I laughed. 'I don't think I'll ever forget you, Garrie.'

'You're my everything, Sandie. I'm marrying my perfect love.'

The way he said those words stirred every fibre and emotion in my body. Sometimes in life, there are moments that stay with us, when we take an internal snapshot, so we never lose them. That was one of those moments, when I was neither in the past nor the future. I was right there, sinking deep within myself and allowing my emotions to wrap around his. I think that's what heaven would feel like, a combination of contentment and intensity far beyond physical attraction.

'I can't wait to marry you.'

'We're going to be perfect together, Sandie.'

I closed my eyes and smiled as images of that perfect future danced across my eyelids.

But now he's gone. And I'm alone; desolate and diminished on the sofa, when I should be standing next to him, glowing with excitement in my wedding dress.

As the clock chimes 2:30 p.m. I stare again at the vows I'd expected to be saying now. Lines I'd rehearsed until I was word perfect, the ultimate expression of my feelings for him.

I promise to honour and cherish our love together, to dedicate myself to your happiness...

I can't read any more. Tears distort my vision as the salty droplets fall onto my handwritten notes and the words merge. I scrunch the paper with the full force of my anger and toss it into the silent void of the home we so recently shared. I stare at my lifeless phone, desperate for it to light up with a call or a message from him. Anything to explain why he changed his mind so abruptly about our plans, and me. But its stony silence catapults the emptiness inside me further into darkness. There's been nothing from him since the single text message he sent after he walked out of my life.

Forgive me, Sandie, but I'm with Emily now. One day you'll understand.

Understand? How can I understand something that came out of nowhere and hit me like a sledgehammer? I had no idea Emily was anything more than a neighbour we hardly knew.

The day after he left, I stormed across the road carrying the weight of my pent-up anger. The familiar landscape of my neighbourhood felt like a desolate plain as I banged on her front door and shouted through the letterbox.

'I know you're in there so you might as well open the door. Do you remember me, Garrie? I'm Sandie, your wife-to-be. The woman you once lived with in the house you can see through your new bedroom window.'

Neither of them showed their faces.

'I know you're inside and I'm out here angry and hurt, Garrie. You owe me some sort of an explanation.'

Tears started to flood as my emotions made their bid to escape. I was surrounded by the rest of the world's comfortable normality, yet I felt like a stranger in its midst. Beautiful houses with high arched windows and cream city brickwork. Homes filled with people's dreams; every façade representing a family and a future. I glanced across at my house, its Victorian brickwork basking in the late summer sunshine, where my life was about to be so different from the one I'd assumed. Garrie had turned my world upside down.

I shouted at him one final time. 'Fine, have it your way, your loss. If you can't even face me and own what you've done, you're a coward.'

I straightened my shoulders and walked back towards the sanctuary of my home. I mustered up my inner strength and told myself to stay away from them; to put loving, and losing, down to one of life's lessons. I loved him, maybe more than I should have done; and now it's over.

I thought I could make myself accept it, but today I can't deal with his cruel silence. He should have the decency to give me some kind of closure instead of shutting me down as if I'd never existed. I type a message.
You've broken my heart, Garrie. How can I ever understand this?

Silence.
I deserve an explanation.
Silence.

Can you imagine how I'm feeling?

Nothing comes back and the pain of this total abandonment is suffocating. I'm left wondering how it all fell apart. I pull myself up from the sofa and walk to the window, surprised my legs support me. I look across at number 12 and torture myself with thoughts of what's happening inside. I know the fabric of love is fragile and yet I never saw the stitches break.

My anger erupts, and I grab the antique vase that was Garrie's first gift to me and hurl it at the wall. It shatters into pieces, like my heart. I want to yell at him and tell him how badly he's hurt me, so I call his number, but it diverts to voicemail. Fury and tears collide as I fire words at his profile photo on my phone screen.

'Garrie, what the hell's going on? Why won't you speak to me? Today should have been our special day and instead, I had to tell everybody the wedding was off. How do you suppose that felt?' I pause to take a breath. 'I didn't call the hotel by the way. That was in your name, so it's your problem. But I want the fifty per cent back that I paid into your bank account. None of this is my fault so you needn't think I'm going to be out of pocket.'

Then I scream with frustration into the silence of his inbox.

'I hate you.'

Chapter 2

EMILY

I snuggle into Garrie's chest as he wraps his arms around me. I can hardly believe he's been here almost a week, and he's mine. I've wanted him from the moment we locked gazes across a crowded bar and instantly we were the only two people there; the passion in his eyes told me he felt the same way.

But I wasn't prepared to keep seeing him in secret, and finally I sent him an ultimatum text.

I want you, and I want this, Garrie. But I won't wait any longer. Tell her now, or we're over.

It worked. An hour later he appeared at my front door with a big smile on his face. 'You look gorgeous, sweetheart.'

'I'm not exactly dressed up.'

'You don't need to be. You're perfect the way you are.'

'How was everything when you left? How was Sandie?'

'Sandie will be OK; she's strong. And she has her studies to focus on. It wasn't easy to walk out, but love has no boundaries, Emily.'

I fell into his arms. 'Are you here to stay, Garrie?'

'You know I am.' He nodded towards one of the bags he'd brought with him and smiled. 'My favourite socks are in there. Where they go, I go.'

I giggled and hugged him closer; he has such a thing about his socks. 'I'm so happy, Garrie.'

I know I should feel guilty about Sandie, but I didn't know they were together until it was too late. I assumed the man I'd fallen in love with was single because that's what he led me to believe. When he told me about Sandie, I was shocked, but he also told me things weren't working between them anymore and it was me he wanted. I never meant to steal another woman's fiancé, but Garrie made me feel special and I hadn't felt that for a long time.

I look across at his suitcase still sitting in the corner of our bedroom; I know there's a package inside it for me. I caught a glimpse of silk ribbon when he was unpacking, but he refuses to let me open it yet. I look up at him and he's grinning.

'I know what you're thinking, but no peeking until we wake up tomorrow. It's our one-week anniversary and it's going to be a special day. One you won't forget.'

I give him a playful poke in the ribs. 'You know the suspense is killing me. At least give me a clue about what it is.'

'I've told you, sweetheart, it's a surprise. And you're going to love it. But let's get some sleep.'

His eyelids close, but like a child at Christmas I want to know what's inside the suitcase, so I try to keep him awake. I reach out to the Tiffany touch lamp on my bedside table, and it casts an instant warm glow over his face.

'It's almost tomorrow now. Let me open it.'

'When we wake up in the morning. Now go to sleep.'

I brush my lips against his cheek and whisper. 'I think I'm in love with you, Garrie.' He's on his back and I wrap myself around him and kiss his neck. I can't believe how strongly I feel about him after such a short time. 'I can't sleep, Garrie.'

He opens his eyes and looks into mine. 'I've never met anyone like you, Emily.'

I giggle as I reply. 'You don't completely know me yet.'

He strokes my hair and caresses my face. 'I feel like I've always known you.'

I feel a rush of overwhelming tenderness for him. 'That's how I feel. We've connected so quickly.'

'Some people are mean to be together in life.'

'Do you believe that Garrie? That we're somehow drawn together by a universal power?'

'I believe fate guides us towards certain people.'

'I'm not sure what I believe about fate. There are billions of people on the planet so fate would have a big job on its hands.'

'Maybe we were top of fate's list.'

We laugh, but the truth is I do feel drawn to him by some irresistible force. With his looks, he could have picked any woman in the bar that night, but he chose me. The first thing he said was, 'You've got my attention.' He never took his eyes off me all night; an entire room of attractive women but I was the only one that existed for him.

'Garrie…'

'Yes, sweetheart?'

'I feel bad for not feeling more guilty about Sandie.'

'I know what you mean.'

'I should feel terrible that I've taken her fiancé.'

'You haven't taken me, I'm here of my own free will.'

'I know but…'

He slides his finger gently over my lips. 'Shhhh.'

His touch sends shivers down my entire body. 'I've fallen for you so hard, Garrie, and I don't ever want to lose you.'

'You're not going to lose me; I feel the same. OK, so open the package.'

'Really? Now?'

'Yes, now. I want you to know how special you are.'

I jump out of bed and open the suitcase. Garrie watches for my reaction as I pull the ivory meringue dress from the white tissue paper that protects it.

'Garrie, it's gorgeous but…'

'It's yours.'

'What are you saying?'

'I think you know, but now isn't the time for me to ask that question. You deserve to be asked properly.'

'Oh, Garrie, I can't believe this is happening. And it's a beautiful dress.'

'Almost as beautiful as you. It belonged to my mother.'

As he speaks, I contemplate the awful thought that this was going to be Sandie's dress, but Garrie somehow reads my mind.

'Sandie didn't like it when I showed it to her. She said it was old-fashioned.'

'No. It's vintage and it's perfect.'

'It's yours, sweetheart.'

'Does this mean what I think it means, Garrie?'

'You know it does.'

I'm spinning in a whirlwind romance, and I've never experienced anything like it. He's bought me the most stunning wedding dress and now I'm certain he's planning to propose. It all feels too good to be true. He buys me flowers, gifts, gives me compliments and makes me feel more special than I've ever felt before. I've become addicted to his attention, and I can't get enough of him.

He closes his eyes, and I can see he now needs sleep. I stroke his face, loving every contour of it. He knows nothing about my past and I want to keep it that way. This is a fresh start for me, a blank canvas. It's my chance to wipe the slate clean. The past and future are only ever illusions, anyway. The present is what matters and the only thing that truly exists. And right now, Garrie excites me and makes me feel passion I haven't felt in a long time.

I'm sorry, Sandie, but I'm not giving that up. Garrie's mine now.

Chapter 3

SANDIE

It's bittersweet that Garrie's living across the road because he walks past my house every morning. I tell myself I shouldn't wait at the window to catch a glimpse of him, but I do. His lean, athletic stride is a drug that distorts my reality for a few brief moments, and I allow myself to imagine what it would be like if he was still mine and Emily never existed. But suspended reality doesn't last long before the harsh truth intrudes on it. Because Emily is all too real and there's no getting away from the fact that Garrie chose her over me, and that cuts deep.

I look across at her house. It has the same triangular shaped loft window as mine, the same rectangular patch of grass and the same crimson red front door. The only difference is that she's got a garage and I haven't. She's got brown hair and I'm blonde. She's possibly a little taller than me, but she wears stilettos so it's difficult to tell. I don't know much else about her.

I know every detail of Garrie's early morning rituals. He slides a pair of freshly washed socks onto his feet, grabs a cereal bar and walks to his car. He drives to the corner of Desmond Street where he parks and takes the path down towards the train station. He catches the 7:45 a.m. which gets him into town twenty minutes before work. He walks towards his office, checking his phone messages, and grabs a large latte from his favourite coffee shop; one of the small independents. That's where we first met. I served him a skinny latte with a biscotti and by the time he was paying his bill he'd got my phone number. A week later he took me to France; a moment of impulse, he called it. We had our first date in Calais - a cheap ferry across the channel, continental lunch, a bottle of champagne and back home again. Three weeks later he proposed. I guess that's what the romantics mean by love at first sight.

I lived with his daily routine for three months. That's how long it's been since we moved in together and our names were engraved into a solid oak cheeseboard that still sits on my kitchen table. *Garrie & Sandie*, both names without the usual *y*. We used to laugh about that. As if fate had brought us together because we shared a missing consonant.

I thought we were perfect together. People remarked on how happy we looked and how we finished each other's sentences as if we thought in stereo. It was like I'd found the mirror image of myself in a man. Now I realise I should have known it was too good to be true; it all happened so fast. I hadn't even met his family or friends; they were names on a wedding list. A wedding that was planned so he could step across the street and jump into bed with Emily and her perfectly spelled name.

I only spoke to her once, at our housewarming party. She arrived, accompanied by a flamboyantly large houseplant and an annoying giggle, and proceeded to swoon over my interior design skills and "what I'd done to the place".

'Did you choose these wall coverings?'

'Yes, they're Nina Campbell.'

'You've got a good eye for detail. I love the way you've matched the cushions and chairs. I wouldn't know where to start.'

'Thank you, I love pretty pastels.'

Now I know she was secretly swooning over my fiancé while pretending to love my wallpaper choices.

I'm back at the window again, waiting for my early evening fix of Garrie through my overpriced net curtains. I had them custom-made, a beautiful washed-out mauve that matches perfectly with the decor and gives me some privacy. It's strange because it hurts to see him and yet I've got into the habit of looking for him. I'm studying for a master's degree in English and my desk is in front of the window, so in an odd way, Garrie helps to keep me on track.

I sit at my computer and have the perfect view of the street outside. A large oak tree blocks the sunlight until late afternoon and a beautiful old-fashioned lamppost sits neatly against a backdrop of willow trees, flower beds and shrubs. I used to love the view but now I'm too preoccupied to notice it.

I look down at Ms. Perfect's houseplant that refuses to die despite my best attempts to kill it off. I took it to the charity shop earlier, but the woman said they don't accept living plants. So, it's back in my house next to the window. A Monstera Deliciosa, flourishing with healthy fenestrated leaves; a reminder that life goes on even though my world seems to have stopped.

Garrie's late tonight and number 12 is in darkness so Emily must be out too. I wonder if he's met her at the coffee shop after work, and they're sitting at his usual window seat while he tells her about his day. Jealousy rears its ugly head, but I try to stifle the life out of it before it spreads. Even though it's my place of work, I still loved sharing moments like that with him. It's a small French style coffee shop with chalk board menus, freshly baked delicacies, bookshelves and vintage teapots. Garrie used to tell me stories and make me laugh. Those are the moments that stick with me, the small things that are actually big things. They are the hardest memories to erase.

I walk to the kitchen, cradling my now lukewarm coffee and stare at the oak cheeseboard, another reminder to stir up my emotions. I wish I could have a word with my brain and tell it to clear its memory bank. I pick up the knife, enjoying the coolness of the smooth steel. I run my finger lightly over its serrated edge then press its forked tip into the flesh of my palm until two indents appear. The knife still glints with newness. It has never been used.

At least, not yet.

I place it back onto the cheeseboard, pick up my phone and hit Judith's name. She's my co-worker at the coffee shop and she's been working extra hours so I can take some time off to sort myself out. She should be on her break now and I want to talk to her.

'Hey, Jude.' I sing it as soon as she answers and before she can speak. It always makes her smile.

'Hi, Sandie. I was just thinking about you. You alright? Sorry, stupid question.'

'I'm a mess Jude, to be honest. Thank you for covering my shifts; you're a wonderful friend. It's not fair to you, but I honestly don't know what to do with myself to get past this. I was on cloud nine planning a wedding and now look at me. I can't believe what he's done.'

'It's no wonder. Take all the time you need. Don't worry about me, I'm happy to have the extra hours.'

'Have you seen him?'

I hear her catch her breath. 'Yes. He's been in. Left not long ago, actually. But you need to focus on you, not them…'

'Was he with her?'

'You're better off without them, Sandie.'

'Just tell me.'

'Yes, he was.'

'Did they look happy?'

'Stop tormenting yourself.'

'Jude, I need to know.'

'She looked happier than he did. I went to take their order and she was making a performance of twirling a ring on her finger. I almost wanted to punch her and wipe the smug look off her face.'

'What did it look like?'

'The ring? Bit flashy for my taste. Blue, sparkly. Shaped like a hexagon.'

'What? That sounds like the ring he was going to give me. He told me it had been passed down in his family and it would be mine on my wedding day.'

'Oh God, Sandie, I'm sorry. But I wouldn't put anything past the bastard after what he's done. Even giving her a ring that he'd promised you. And to think she was sitting there, showing it off.'

'I don't understand any of this, Jude. I never even saw it coming. I'm normally observant so how the hell did I miss the signs?'

'Sandie, there's something else. And I don't know how to tell you.'

'Say it, Jude. It's not as if things can get much worse.'

'They're married.'

The two words consume me, and I deflate like a punctured balloon.

'Sandie? Are you there? I'm so sorry. This is brutal, I know.'

I take a breath. 'But they can't be married. It's too soon. They couldn't have thrown a wedding together that quickly. There are legalities to sort.'

'I heard them talking about it. It was last Saturday.'

'What?' I scream. 'No! That was meant to be our wedding day. He wouldn't do that to me.'

'I could hardly believe it either and I didn't want to tell you, but it's better than hearing it from someone else. You must want to kill him.'

'I don't know what I want to do. It's one punch after another. I'm devastated.'

'You shouldn't be on your own with this, Sandie. I'll call round later and keep you company.'

I barely hear her last words as images of Garrie and Emily swim across my eyes and I drown in the realisation of what's happened. How long had he been planning all this?

'Jude, I need to do something. Stay on the line.' I run upstairs to the spare room and fling open the wardrobe. I need to see my wedding dress; touch it and prove I'm not going mad. That this was once real, and I was going to be a bride.

But there's an empty space where it should be.

'Jude? I was wrong earlier. This did get worse. Much worse. She didn't only steal Garrie. I think she stole my entire wedding.'

Chapter 4

SANDIE

I open my front door and Jude is standing there.

She gives me a bear hug. 'You're better off without him, Sandie. He doesn't deserve you.'

I almost collapse into her. 'I'm so pleased you're here, Jude.'

'You can't be on your own with this. I've brought wine.'

She cracks open her bottle of supermarket red and makes herself comfy on the sofa with a large glass in her hand before launching into full anti-Garrie mode.

'I know it sounds a bit "told you so" but I've never trusted the bastard. He's too much of a charmer.'

'I used to love his charisma, Jude.'

'I don't think I'd call it charisma, Sandie. He's a flirt. He even tried it on with me once.'

'Did he?'

'I don't know where he thought that was going, but I soon put him in his place. He asked for my number. It was before you came to work at the coffee shop.'

'I really liked him, Jude. I was on cloud nine when he asked for my number.'

'He's good-looking, but the trouble is, he knows it.'

'I fell in love with him.'

'Well, now you know what a bastard he is, you can fall for someone else.'

'I wish there was a button, and I could turn my emotions off.'

'Remind yourself what he's done, and you'll soon find the off switch.'

Jude haphazardly fills her glass, and it splashes onto her work uniform. She's rushed straight here from the coffee shop on a mission to make me feel better. She tops my glass up and makes herself even more comfortable by kicking off her shoes.

'Forget him and move on. Find someone who won't be such a shit.' I love the straight-talking simplicity of Jude. 'You're a strong woman, Sandie.'

'My mum always encouraged me to be.'

'But you've got such a soft heart. It's lovely, but it can leave you vulnerable.'

'Maybe. I think I developed that sensitivity when my dad left. I was young when he walked out and left mum to cope with things. I struggled to understand why he would leave us without ever coming back. He made promises that he broke and sent a few gifts but that's about it. Mum got over it, but I always felt I could have done something to make him stay. I guess that's why I try so hard and feel responsible in relationships. I try to hold on to things that matter.'

'But Garrie doesn't matter.'

'My brain knows that, but I need my emotions to catch up, Jude.'

'You need to learn how to kick out the bad rubbish.'

We both laugh at her words, but she's right. 'Like my mum did. She struggled after dad left but she got past it, rebuilt her life, and became a successful businesswoman. It's because of how hard she worked that I'm living in this lovely house. She bought it as an investment and it's a perfect base for me to focus on my university course. That was the deal.'

'Your mum's great, Sandie. And she's right; you should focus on finishing your master's and get yourself a damn good job. You're so smart and it's in your blood to become a success, and you should move on from this whole Garrie saga.'

She tips the wine bottle, gives it an exasperated shake, but nothing comes out. 'Damn. I think that's my cue to leave but you must call me any time you need some sense knocking into you, and a reminder to find yourself a new model.'

I give her a hug; at least she's put a smile on my face. And I know she's right, I need to stay positive, accept Garrie's history, and focus on my future.

Chapter 5

GARRIE

I'm visiting my daughter, Katie. I walk from the entrance along a dimly lit corridor with grey walls. A place like this needs colour, I always think that every time I visit. Anything to make it feel less cold and clinical. Maybe a painted tapestry of bright flowers on the walls, or a scenic landscape to give the impression that the world exists. I wonder if my daughter knows there's something beyond these walls, a future that's bright and achievable.

I walk into her private room and take a seat next to her bed. It's very basic, but there's a small window so she can see the sky, an indication of the passing of time. The walls are the same cool grey as the corridor, but she's got pink bed sheets and a few cuddly toys. I slide my fingers into hers. I squeeze gently and stare at the vacant expression in her eyes. She never looks at me. Not now. She used to when she was younger. When she wanted to know things. She had limited communication skills, but she was an inquisitive child, always smiling and trying to understand things.

The nurses are friendly, so she's warm, safe, and well looked after. I always bring chocolate for her. We're not supposed to but there's a nice woman on the reception desk. She does the usual safety checks and gives me a smile. It's a mutual agreement between us. Just some of Katie's favourites to brighten her day.

I unwrap one of the bars and pop a square of white chocolate into her mouth. 'Is that nice?'

She goes through the chewing motion with no change in her expression. I think she's enjoying it, but I don't know.

'White chocolate was your mum's favourite, Katie. She could never go to the supermarket without buying some.' I smile at the memory. 'I miss your mum, Katie. She was the most beautiful woman in the world.'

I look for some indication that my daughter knows who I am. Deep down I believe she does. Sometimes I think she knows everything.

When she first came here, I didn't know what to do about everything that had happened. My head was all over the place. People indulged me for a while, but they didn't understand. I'm sure they dismissed most of what I said as the ramblings of a distraught father trying to make sense of a situation. They told me it was the best place for my daughter in the circumstances and given 'how she was'. They said I needed time to grieve the loss of my wife, that Katie could come back home once I felt stronger, but I knew that would never happen. I was too heartbroken.

I look at her now and wonder what she sees. She used to be such a happy little girl with curly hair, a permanently infectious giggle and the same sapphire blue eyes as her mother, my beautiful wife, Annabel. But Katie's always seen the world differently and that made her unique. We struggled to deal with it, but Annabel did everything she possibly could to help her progress. She threw herself completely into the role of mother and full-time carer, and life became very different.

Until I saw an advert in the local newspaper offering children's tuition and said we should give it a try. I saw it as the perfect opportunity to give myself and Annabel some quality time together. She agreed and started taking her to lessons. That's when Emily came into my daughter's life. It was wonderful at first because Annabel would take Katie to lessons every day and she started to make progress. I never saw Emily, but Annabel used to tell me what a lovely person she was, and how they were becoming good friends. I was happy because I was starting to get my wife back, but things went horribly wrong between her and Emily. The lessons stopped and it was heartbreaking because the sparkle disappeared from Katie's eyes and Annabel became even more protective of her.

As Katie eats another piece of chocolate, I wonder how much she remembers about the day that changed her life and mine, because it was the day Emily ruined everything and became my worst enemy. I loved Annabel so much, but I couldn't protect her and now Katie exists in the vacuum of this place. I can never forgive Emily and I need to make her pay.

I hold Katie's hand for a while and sing to her; *I Don't Want to Visit the Moon*, by Sesame Street. It makes me smile because I used to sing it to her as a baby and her mum always laughed at my terrible voice as she told me to shut up. I wonder if my little girl recognises my voice now.

'Oh, Katie, I wish you would speak to Daddy. Nothing's going to hurt you; not anymore.'

Chapter 6

EMILY

It's midnight, Garrie's just got home, and something is different about him tonight. He's in a strange mood; cold and unloving, virtually ignoring me and offering no explanation about why he's so late. Apart from a muttered, 'Don't know why you waited up. You should have gone to sleep,' he doesn't speak to me as he gets ready for bed. He seems preoccupied as he climbs in next to me and turns over.

I run my fingers down his back, but he doesn't respond. 'Are you OK, Garrie? You've hardly spoken to me since you got in.' He says nothing, but I don't give up. 'Anything you want to talk about? How was work today?'

I know I'm babbling, but I feel uncomfortable about the atmosphere between us tonight.

'Everything's fine, Emily.'

'You don't seem fine.'

'For God's sake, go to sleep. I'm tired. It's been a long day.'

'But you're home so late and I had no idea where you were.'

'Something came up. For God's sake, it's not a big deal. Why do you always have to make an issue out of everything?'

I don't know why he's being so sharp with me. 'I'm not making an issue out of it. But I was worried when I didn't hear from you. I mean, we're a proper couple now, and...'

He spins round to face me. 'As if I could forget. It's all you bloody talk about. Is that what this is all about? I must account to you for my every move?'

I shrink back from the anger that flashes in his eyes. I've no idea where it's coming from. I've never seen him like this. 'I'm only trying to be supportive, Garrie.'

'No. You're questioning me, Emily. You don't have the right to do that.' His tone is almost venomous. He circles his finger over my mouth as he spits words out at me. 'And you shouldn't attack me through those beautiful red lips of yours, no matter how tempting they are.'

Attacking him? I'm asking a perfectly reasonable question.

I feel his hot breath against my skin as his hands cup my face. 'Anyway, I'm bored with the questions now. Were you disappointed because I wasn't here earlier to give you attention?'

He pulls me closer as his hands begin a slow journey down my body.

For the first time ever, I cringe from his touch and push his hands away. 'No, Garrie. This isn't what I want.'

'But you've got my complete attention now, and it's what I want.'

'No, Garrie, please. Let's sleep. We can talk in the morning.'

He fires his next words into my face like bullets. 'I wanted to sleep, but you wouldn't let me. And now you decide to change your mind? I thought you'd be begging for my forgiveness, not rejecting my advances. You should be showing me how much you love me.'

'You already know how much.'

'No, I don't. You've even got a photograph of your ex-husband downstairs. What's that about?'

'It's a photo I've had for years and it's not on show. It's with some things from my old house.'

'Get rid of it.'

'It's you I want, Garrie.'

He ignores me and continues his tirade. 'You're to blame for all of this. You're supposed to trust me.'

His anger is in complete contrast to the man who so recently arrived at my front door with his belongings and a loving smile. I want that man back.

'Your love should be unconditional, Emily.'

This is relentless. I feel like I'm stuck in a moment I can't climb out of. 'For goodness sake, Garrie, it is.'

'Tell me I'm the best you've ever had.'

'You know you are.'

'Look at me and tell me, I need to see you mean it.'

'You're the best I've ever had, OK.'

His voice softens. 'Right answer. I forgive you, darling.' He kisses my head and repeats the words in a soft whisper against my ear. 'I forgive you.'

I'm stunned. I have no idea how to respond. I don't understand why I need be forgiven but if it stops this unexpected onslaught from him, I'm willing to go along with it for now and keep quiet. Anything to make this stop so I can sleep.

'My beautiful lady.' He strokes my face and I look at him in relief because at least his anger has subsided. 'You're so important to me, Emily; the most important thing in my life.'

I'm taken aback by another sudden change in him. One minute I feel as though he's got me hanging from the gallows, and the next, he puts me on a pedestal in a golden crown. But tonight, I don't feel like being his queen. He's upset me and I want to sleep. I lay my head on the pillow instead of his chest as he whispers into my ear, 'Don't worry, darling.'

I close my eyes and I'm about to fall into a gentle sleep as I'm lulled by the gentle tone of his voice. 'I'm here, my love.' He's so quiet that it's barely audible as he pauses over each syllable. Then he sighs in contentment as his arms and voice caress me.

'Annabel.'

The name I hear hits me like a close-range bullet splintering on impact; it shatters me. Confusion and disbelief shock me into numbed silence. I've been catapulted to a place I don't want to be and into a memory I don't want to face. I'm scrambling to get away from the thoughts in my head that threaten to overwhelm me.

Garrie's earlier anger has been replaced by a tenderness I have never witnessed. His expression is peaceful as his head sinks into the soft duck-feather pillow, and I hear his breathing deepen as he falls asleep. I try to move but I'm as limp as a ragdoll, my body sapped of energy. I want to escape from this bed, and from the man next to me but I don't have the ability to separate myself from the name I just heard. Did he really say it, or is my mind playing cruel tricks on me? I honestly thought the flashbacks had stopped and I was getting better, but those familiar waves of nausea rise up from my stomach and I claw at the bedsheets as I'm plunged into the nightmare of my past.

I'm floating, looking down at myself. I'm in a different bed and another man is holding my hand. I'm crying for my Annabel. She's all I can see and feel. The beautiful baby daughter I had wanted so much. A life that was cruelly snatched away before it even began. I'm staring into the scene and reliving it all over again. Facing the fact that I'm no longer complete. Because the day I lost my beautiful baby is the day I also lost the part of me that would allow me to ever be a mother.

I've tried so hard to begin a new life and repress the memories that continue to haunt me. But one whispered word from Garrie and everything comes flooding back to overwhelm me. I've never told him about Annabel because I still can't bring myself to talk about it. Nobody in my new life knows. So maybe I imagined him saying her name, a memory triggered by the turmoil of his anger towards me.

I've no idea why my questions caused such a dramatic change in him. It felt like I was being punished and I never want to see that side of him again. I need calmness in my life, so I'm not drawn back to my dark place, and to a memory I try so hard to keep buried because it's too painful to remember.

It's an image I keep shrouded in fog so I can't see it or speak its name but it's there; it's always there, waiting in the wings.

Chapter 7

SANDIE

Garrie is in a hurry this morning, trying to escape the late-summer rain. It's one of those sudden cloud bursts on a warm day. I watch him vanish out of sight before I decide to work on my essay about the work of John Keats. I glance up to see Emily dragging her rubbish bin out of the gate before she reverses her car out of the garage. The rain bounces frantically against her car roof as she speeds off down the street.

They're obviously getting on with the normality of life, while I'm still reeling from the news about their wedding. We made beautiful plans for our special day, and he gave it all to her. I want to heal and move on with my life, but I feel my insides have been ripped out. Can you ever get over something like that? I think every relationship leaves an imprint that changes you in some way. Garrie taught me what it feels like to be loved but he also showed me that love is fragile and can slip away like sand. I wish I could fall out of love with him and forget he was ever in my life, but I can't flick a switch and turn off my emotions as he seems to have done.

I spend the rest of the morning writing about the form and structure of a selection of poems including the famous *Ode on Melancholy*. A very apt poem by Keats that asserts we should live each day as if it were our last.

I save my essay, snap the laptop shut and stare out of the window. Pent-up fury rises up in me again as I look across at number 12. I wish I could follow Jude's advice, accept I'm better off without Garrie, and move on. But I can't. Not until I can understand why Garrie airbrushed me out of his life. I want answers and I want to vent this toxic anger.

There's only one place I can do that, and before I know it, I'm standing outside number 12; squinting through frosted glass to catch a glimpse of Garrie's new home. The home he clearly prefers to the one he had with me, and I want to know why. A thick-pile rug extends across the hallway and a selection of tiny photographs, artwork and purple hydrangeas give a glimpse of the life that should have been mine. I stretch my neck further, ignoring that it's customary to knock the door before checking out the décor.

'Do you want something?'

I spin around to see Emily behind me. I notice she looks pale and tired as I try to think of something to say.

'The hallway looks amazing'.

It sounds pathetic, but they're the only words I can find. I've been imagining this moment, when I could at last be face-to-face with the woman who stole my life. I had it planned; the perfect script etched word-for-word onto my brain so I could give an Oscar-worthy performance. Instead, I'm standing in front of my nemesis and feeling exposed, stupid, and tongue-tied. Normally, I would be quick to react and tell Emily exactly what I think of her; walk away from the whole sorry saga, head held high, and leave them to get on with it. But this post-Garrie Sandie is a woman on an emotional rollercoaster. I'm too much of a hurt mess to find the right words for the other woman in front of me.

Emily raises her perfectly arched brows; her face has "you're crazy" written all over it. Finding me peering through her front door has temporarily wrong-footed her into silence too, but finally, she speaks.

'Something tells me you didn't come here to check out my hallway. What do you want, Sandie? If you're looking for Garrie he's not here.'

'I didn't come to see Garrie. I know he's at work. I came to see you.'

'So that you can yell at me again through my letterbox?'

'I don't want to yell, Emily. But you're the one that's stolen my fiancé, remember.'

'I didn't steal him, he walked out freely. It was his decision.'

'I came here because I thought we might at least talk.'

'About what?'

'About the fact you stole him and my wedding. That's low, Emily, even by your standards.'

'By my standards? Who the hell do you think you are?'

'Now who's yelling? I haven't come here to argue, Emily.'

'I didn't steal your wedding. Garrie wanted us to have a ceremony and since he'd already paid for the hotel…'

'Correction. We paid for the hotel between us. He still owes me fifty percent that I paid in advance.'

'You'll have to speak to him about that.'

'I would if he'd pick up his phone or reply to a message.'

'He obviously doesn't want to. He's told me how difficult things were becoming between you.'

'Difficult?' I've no idea what Garrie's told her. 'Things weren't difficult, Emily. In fact, I thought they were perfect.'

'Clearly, he didn't think so.' She pauses for a moment. 'Look, I know it must be hard on you that your relationship didn't work out, but you need to stop spying on us.'

I take a step back. When did I go from being the innocent woman scorned to the guilty party in this whole fiasco?

'Excuse me? I'm not spying on you.'

'I know you've been watching us. Those fancy new nets you've put up aren't fooling anybody.'

'I can assure you I didn't put them up to spy on you. They're for my privacy.'

'Garrie thinks the whole thing's funny, but the thought of it creeps me out and you need to stop.'

'I'm sorry you feel like that, but I'd like to talk.'

She bends to pick up her shopping bags. 'I must get this lot inside.'

She fumbles for keys, and that's when I notice she's not wearing her wedding ring. She puts one of the shopping bags down, so I swoop in, and my fingers squash between the plastic handle, a spit-roast chicken, and a pack of dog food.

'I can manage the bags, Sandie.'

'Don't worry, I'm not about to attack you with a cooked chicken. I'm here for some answers. I was supposed to be marrying him, remember?'

I step inside her house with the carrier bags.

'Take your shoes off.'

I take her words as permission to stay. One less bag to carry seems to have temporarily triumphed over her desire to see the back of me. I let my toes sink into the hall rug and imagine Emily's life as Mrs Paisley-Jonas; I always did love Garrie's surname. I follow her into the kitchen and we both deposit our bags on the worktop. Emily looks across at me with a slightly softer expression.

'There really is nothing else I can tell you, apart from…I never meant to hurt you. We fell in love, and I didn't know he was with you when I met him.'

'He never told you?'

'Not at first, no.'

'Where did you meet?'

'At the Tanet Bar, in town.'

'He never goes there.'

'He obviously does, because that's where I met him.'

As she talks, I glance around the room. There's a plaque on the wall. *Emily and Garrie* in fancy lettering; no surname. There are a few items from the wedding day scattered on a side table. A blue garter, one of those silver plastic lucky horseshoes, and a wedding card. Only one card? I wonder who it's from and why there aren't more. And the blue topaz wedding ring is there, glistening in the sunlight. The ring that should have been mine.

Emily's already unpacking bags and in a moment of impulse, I ask if I can use the loo.

'You only live across the road. Why don't you go and use your own?'

I know she wants me to leave. But I want to see that card.

'I'll be quick.'

I don't give her a chance to reply. While her back is turned, I grab the wedding card and slide it underneath my jumper. I cross the hallway, close the door, and read.

To Emily and Garrie,
Congratulations on your wedding rehearsal,
Can't wait for the real thing!
Liz xxx

A rehearsal? So, they're not officially married. The news gives me a moment of pleasure, but it's soon replaced by fury. She stole my day and my dress for a practice run. I'd like to take their hideous name plaque and smash it into pieces. The words I've read are playing on a loop inside my head, and I need to get out of this house because I'm not sure I can trust myself if I don't.

In angry disbelief, I put the card back exactly where I found it. Emily's too engrossed in rearranging her fridge shelves to notice. I'd love to push her inside it along with her shopping, but instead I head to the front door.

As I walk out of the kitchen, I realise this house doesn't feel like a home; there's no warmth to it. It's too meticulously ordered; impersonal, almost clinical. The only thing giving it life is the puppy that's chased after me, ears pricked up and watching my every move. I bend down to make a fuss of the dog when I spot a photograph on a side table. It's half-hidden behind a porcelain teapot and some envelopes. It's Emily, but not with Garrie; another man is holding her hand. Her left hand.

And they're both gazing at a solitaire diamond on her ring finger.

Chapter 8

EMILY

The flowers are bigger than Garrie's head. An elaborate bouquet of African Daisies, the symbol of fidelity. He knows I love them. I told him when we first met, and he's remembered. But it's going to take a lot more than a bunch of flowers to forget the appalling way he treated me. I'm concerned about it and I can't allow myself to mellow at the sight of his exorbitant expression of affection.

He's returned from work with a spring in his step.

'For you, my darling.'

He plants a kiss on my cheek as I admire the Osteospermum petals. They're beautiful, but I can't tell him that, not today. And I decide not to tell him about Sandie's surprise visit, either. I don't have the energy to get into a dialogue about it right now.

'I'll put them in a vase.'

He looks like the man I fell in love with but I'm not feeling it. He's behaving as if his strange mood swing never happened.

'Let me run you a magnifique bath before dinner, my darling.'

He raises his right hand on cue with his debatable French accent. He obviously has no idea how much his behaviour last night shocked me and stirred my emotions; and now he's love-bombing me with fanciful words, flowers, and a fragrant bath. His over-the-top display of affection is unnerving; I can't forget what he did and what he said, and I watch him hesitantly as he continues with his gushy comments.

'A bubble bath and candles. Just how you like it sweetie-pie.'

I don't bother to smile, and I retreat to the kitchen to search for a vase.

The sun is still high enough in the sky to cast light and shadow onto the kitchen floor, and Ginger chases a moving reflection as my watch sparkles against the sunlight.

'Silly dog, there's nothing there.'

She stares at me with her bright inquisitive eyes and there's something about her innocence that puts things into perspective. 'If only you could talk, Ginger. You're such a little thing in this massive adult world but I'd sooner be in your world right now.'

She wags her tail excitedly and runs for her smelly toy, but I find it first. 'This is mine, Ginger.'

I laugh as she chases me around the kitchen, and I dangle the toy above her head. Her tail wags with excitement; she loves to play. I give her the toy and kiss the top of her head as she tilts it from side to side enjoying my affection. Dogs appreciate the smallest gestures.

'Bath's ready.' I hear Garrie's voice shouting down the stairs and it pulls me out of my simple little doggy world. I don't want any confrontation today, so I respond accordingly.

'OK, thanks, won't be long.'

I smile down at Ginger who is chasing another shadow on the wall, running at it and barking. I give her a dog treat, place the flowers in their vase onto the windowsill and make my way towards the sanctuary of the bathroom.

Garrie leaves me alone and I lock the door as I breathe in the scented steam because this is my space. I wipe condensation from the mirror and see the tiredness of my eyes staring back. I immerse myself in the water and close my eyes against threatening tears as I sink further into the warm cocoon of fragrance. I scrub my skin until it hurts as I think about my Annabel.

I would give anything for her to be here right now.

Chapter 9

SANDIE

I can't stop thinking about the photograph I saw inside Emily's house, of her with another man. I'm guessing it was her ex-fiancé or husband. I wonder what Garrie thinks about that. He always said it was important that I'd never been married.

'I want to be your first and only.'

'You are, Garrie. I've never been married, or even engaged.'

'I couldn't be with you if you'd ever promised yourself to another man.'

I used to think it was beautiful that he wanted us to have complete and undivided love. But the shock of him leaving me for Emily has made me question everything.

The couple at number 18 are hosting a barbecue tonight, but I'm not invited. It's another consequence of the Garrie and Emily show. It seems I've morphed overnight from welcome neighbour and dinner guest, the fun half of a romantic whirlwind, into the awkward singleton who'd throw the place-setting symmetry out and weep into her wine glass.

'Of course, we'd all love you to join us on Saturday, Sandie but…erm…it would be a bit difficult, wouldn't it?'

I've heard that sentence or similar too many times recently. I've not only been abandoned by my fiancé but also by the people in my own neighbourhood. I close my windows to avoid the sound of glasses clinking and the aroma of over-barbecued sausages. I hate the thought of Emily giggling and blushing when everybody tells her what a great couple she and Garrie make. I suppose it's a social nicety; they used to say it to me.

I want to scream down the street, 'She stole my fiancé and my wedding. And it wasn't even real.' But they'd think I was crazy.

My phone pings into the void of my Saturday evening. It's a message from an old school friend.

Reunion party next Friday and you're coming! We're not taking no for an answer. You need to put all this Garrie stuff behind you. Tons of great guys out there delighted you're single again. Message me back!!

The thought of another man in my life makes my insides lurch, but she's right that I need to stop moping around, so I hit reply.

Think I'll steer clear of men for a while but count me in for the reunion. It'll be good to see everybody. X

There's a message from Jude too, asking if she can call round after work. I send her a thumbs-up sign. Her brand of cynical humour is exactly what I could use tonight, and I want to give her the news that the 'wedding' wasn't official, in person. I can imagine where she'll go with that snippet. In the meantime, I need a distraction from the revelry at number 18. I want to see that rehearsal for myself; I wonder if they took any photos.

I open Facebook and type in Paisley-Jonas. I'm looking for Garrie even though I know he doesn't really do social media. He always says life has enough complications without adding digital ones to the mix. Sometimes I think he's right, but on this occasion, I'm hoping to find him. He's not there but my eyes are drawn to the only account with his surname.

EMILY PAISLEY-JONAS

I can't believe it. They're not officially married and she's already on Facebook using the surname that should have been mine. And as I might have guessed, she's posted photographs.

'You bitch.' I grip my phone with anger as I scroll through images that torment me. The two of them with her bridesmaid, in the hotel we'd booked. I wish I'd cancelled it now. And she's wearing my dress. Apparently, it was from the Riki Dalal Collection and was his mother's. I didn't like it when he first gave it to me, but it grew on me. To think he took it and gave it to her, so she could use it for a rehearsal. I wish I could cut it into a thousand pieces, to make sure she can't wear it again.

And of course, she's flaunting the blue topaz ring he'd promised to give to me the day he tried to balance on one knee in the middle of the coffee shop. I wonder if that's how he proposed to her, too, in between Jude and the condiment station.

There's even the light-up marriage sign he'd ordered for us, from eBay.

'Damn you, Garrie. You airbrushed me out and got them to change my name to hers on that.'

Each photograph is a flawless image of perfection. Emily glows, with her long shiny brunette hair cascading in waves, and whimsical forest flowers adorning her temple. I snap my phone shut. I can't handle him looking so ridiculously happy with her when he should have been standing next to me wearing that perma-grin. My blood starts to boil, and I scroll my contacts for the hotel's number. Garrie still hasn't given me the fifty percent I paid so I think they need to know what's going on.

'Oh hi, can I speak to the manager please?'

'Yes, speaking.'

'I'd like to...'

I hesitate at the thought of having to explain everything.

'I'd like to know if there's anything left owing on the Paisley-Jonas wedding reception account from last Saturday.'

'Is this Mrs Paisley-Jonas?'

I should have anticipated that question, but I manage to mutter an uncomfortable 'Yes.'

'No problem, I'll check on the system for you. And congratulations, of course.'

I cringe at the word and overpowering thoughts of Garrie and Emily flood my brain.

'Everything's fully paid.'

I put the phone down without replying. I'm not even sure what I hoped the call would achieve. But I don't understand why Garrie went through with that expense for a rehearsal, or why his conscience didn't eventually kick in and tell him it was wrong. I remind myself to chase him for my share of the deposit.

I hear the noise from number 18 getting louder, even with my windows closed. And I realise I'm wrong about the void; that's not where I am at all. I've fallen down a rabbit hole, like Alice in Wonderland. And everybody here is quite mad.

Except for me.

Chapter 10

EMILY

Garrie left early for work today and there's a note on the kitchen table.

You were fast asleep my darling, so I didn't wake you. Just want to tell you how beautiful you are. See you later, baby. Love you. Garrie xx

Garrie's an expert at flowery words and gestures, and since the other night I've been getting his perfect man performance. He's even suggested we head to Paris for our honeymoon when we finally make things official. I can't reconcile this behaviour with the man who looked at me so differently recently; his pupils narrowing to two laser beams of fury that burned into my skull. And how he moaned the name Annabel, his voice caressing each syllable. I've tried to convince myself I imagined it; but the siren's continuous call in my head tells me I didn't and refuses to let me forget.

I scroll to my favourite photograph from our wedding rehearsal on my phone. Garrie's good looks, charm and charisma fill my screen and his loving expression reminds me why I fell for him. At the rehearsal, hotel staff kept telling us what a beautiful couple we were, and the waitresses couldn't take their eyes off him. He relished the attention and I felt like the luckiest woman alive that day; the first time I've felt like that for so long. Yet in one night, and with one whispered name, Garrie's left me confused and tortured again.

I pull on my neck scarf because there's a chill in the air today and I've asked Liz to meet me at the park. She's the one person I trust and she's the one link I have between my past and my present. Ginger starts barking at me to pay her some attention.

'Yes, Ginger, you're coming to the park. I trust you too, Ginger. You listen and let me speak. You don't judge, not like humans, we all think too much. Even the tiniest thing activates the amygdala in the brain.'

Ginger looks up at me, moving her head from side to side, as if weighing up my conversation with her.

'Here, let's put your lead on.' She waggles her bottom and saunters across with excitement etched across her face. 'That's how I feel, Ginger. I always love seeing Liz, and I'm sure she'll have some doggy treats for you.'

I leave the house, and soon Liz and I are sitting in the park sipping takeaway coffee while an exhausted Ginger lies between us.

'You look tired, Em. Talk to me; I can see something's wrong. I know you didn't call me to spend my work break walking Ginger. What's going on?'

'It's happening again, Liz. The flashbacks; drowning in dark memories. I hate feeling like this, and I hate burdening you with it. I really thought I'd got myself back on track and had the constant thoughts about my past under control. Now I feel it's coming back to haunt me again.'

'You've been doing great, Emily. Don't be hard on yourself.'

'I thought Garrie was the answer.'

'And you don't anymore?'

'I thought he was the miracle cure.'

Liz smiles. 'I don't think any man can be a miracle cure.'

I give her a weak smile. 'And yet, since meeting Garrie, I haven't suffered a single flashback, until recently.'

'That's good progress. You were having them every day.'

'I know. But I don't want to go back down that slippery slope. I don't want to have another breakdown.'

'You're not going to. You must keep moving forward and not let one bad day push you back. Focus on the teaching.'

'Hell, I've just seen the time. Little Lucas will be arriving for his lesson in thirty minutes. Did I tell you how cute he is?'

Liz laughs. 'Several times. Come on, I'll walk part of the way with you. Means I can skip the gym tonight. How's the tutoring going by the way? Enjoying it again after the break from it?'

'Liz, I love it. It makes me feel alive again. Like I'm doing something useful that I'm good at. And children are such a good distraction from all the adult complications.

'And the certificate helped?'

'Yes, it makes everything more professional. I know I don't need to be a qualified tutor to work from home, but it helps to have something official on the wall.'

'You mean a fake certificate downloaded from some dodgy internet site?' She throws her head back with laughter.

'I hang it on the wall before students arrive and remove it again before Garrie gets home.'

'You make me laugh, Emily. But I'm glad it's giving you purpose. Are you still planning to study and qualify one day so you can teach in a proper school?'

'Definitely. The dream is to work full-time in a primary school.'

'It's a great idea and you must do it. Martin always said you'd make a wonderful teacher.

'I know. He was always so supportive. He took me to a few open days at a local university and encouraged me to apply, but I never got around to it.'

'He was a good husband.'

I feel tears welling up as I remember Martin's soft, calm voice and how he cradled me to him when I was mad with grief. 'I miss him, Liz. I can't believe the way I treated him. I drove him away. How did I let myself lose such a wonderful man?'

'Because life gets in the way sometimes, things change, and we decide we want different things.'

I nod but say nothing. I can't allow myself to dwell on it. We've reached the park gates and I give Liz a hug before she heads back to her office, and I head home.

Chapter 11

SANDIE

I'm in the supermarket, aisle five, and I spot Garrie. He's alone, there's no sign of little Miss Perfect. He's got one of those small baskets that slides along the floor and it's full of crisps, chocolate and cake. He's paler than normal and I catch myself wondering if he's eating proper meals at Emily's. I know it's ridiculous, but after loving him so much it's difficult to switch that off. It's a thin line between wanting to kill him or hug him. But that's how emotions work; the heart tells you one thing, and the brain tells you another. Love is like feeling the sun from all sides, beautiful, bright; an all-consuming fire that overpowers the body and mind. Ours lit up the sky for a while but now I stand in the shadows.

We're in the deli section, but he hasn't seen me. I'm sandwiched between a stack of green crates and the Spanish tapas. I consider making an appearance. It would be the first time we've spoken since he left. But his phone rings.

'Hey sweetie.'

It's been so long since I heard his voice and I'm fixed to the spot, my ears trying to clear a space in the tympanic membrane. His familiar voice is like a musical symphony that stirs emotions and brings back memories. I want to hear more of his conversation but I'm being accosted by a woman determined to get the Spanish chorizo from the top shelf. That's when I hear it; the words are crisp and clear.

'Daddy will be back again soon.'

I don't know what I expected to hear but it wasn't that. My insides start to churn, and I step back, oblivious to my surroundings after hearing his words. I lose my balance as I collide with the green crates and a shelf stacker.

I wince at the sharp pain in my foot and an icy sensation against my face. I open my eyes and I'm confronted by a large bag of frozen peas and a woman towering above me, clutching a packet of sliced luncheon meat.

'Are you OK?'

I feel fuzzy but I'm aware I'm in the supermarket, and Garrie was here. Something happened that threw me off balance and I try to prise myself up, but the movement makes my head spin faster.

'Don't move, dear. Hold the peas against your face. You had a nasty fall.'

Pain from my foot shoots through me like an electric shock. I feel a pair of strong arms around me, and I know they belong to Garrie. I can't help but breathe him in; the man I hate for what he did to me. But I'm with him for the first time since he walked out, and the feeling of familiarity is intoxicating. His strength envelops me as he lifts me to my feet.

'Sandie, what happened?'

Words tumble out of my mouth from the rush of conflicting emotions at the sight of him. 'It was a shock seeing you, Garrie. And hearing you have a conversation with…' I pause for a second…'

'Go on.'

I can see he's waiting for an answer but after recovering from my fall I'm a little apprehensive about causing another involuntary response in my nervous system. But he keeps staring at me until I have no choice but to say something.

'You were talking to your child on the phone.'

Garrie raises his eyebrows. 'Oh, you heard.'

'Yes. And I wish I hadn't. It caused me to faint. What more can you possibly throw at me, Garrie? You never told me you were a father. You knew I wanted us to have children in the future, and you couldn't bring yourself to tell me you already had a child. We were supposed to be getting married, but you changed the subject whenever I mentioned having a family. Something else you hid from me. I'm beginning to wonder if I ever really knew you at all.'

He stares down at his feet, as if he feels uncomfortable. 'I should have told you about my daughter, but it never seemed to be the right moment.'

'I would have loved her, Garrie. You know how much I love children.'

'I know, and in time I would have told you.'

'Why didn't you?'

'Now isn't the time or place, Sandie; we need to get you home.'

'I'm upset, Garrie.'

'And you're in pain; your ankle's starting to swell. Hold on to me.'

I push him away and try to stand, but my leg gives way and I fall against him. I'm in far too much pain from the throbbing in my foot to argue against his insistence as he half-carries me to his car and helps me into the back seat. He's the first to break the awkward silence as he starts the engine and adjusts his rearview mirror to look at me.

'How are you feeling now?'

'It hurts but I'll be fine, Garrie. I want to get home now and put some ice on this. I was a bit shaken, that's all.'

'I kind of guessed as you were lying flat out in aisle five.'

He laughs, and without thinking so do I. The whole situation is farcical, and I find myself laughing a little too long.

'I've always loved your laugh, Sandie.'

'Don't even go there, Garrie. We're over, remember? Because you didn't love my laugh enough to stay with me.'

'It wasn't like that.'

'Seriously, Garrie, let's not talk about any of it. I'm in too much pain with my foot right now.'

I stare out of the window as we pass the rest of the journey in silence. It's one of those situations where there's too much that needs saying, and sometimes things are better left unsaid when you're unsure of the outcome.

We drive past trees that have been there since I can remember. Old oak trees remain true to their roots; they sit there while life goes on around them. They never wilt or wither. They stay strong through the seasons. The land around them has been built on, but they remain untouched. Our neighbourhood is one of the new ones and the houses went up quickly. I can remember it being a flat piece of land until one day the gates were open to a new village.

As he drives toward my house, I notice his quick glance across the road as he helps me out of the car and leads me to the side gate, away from the prying eyes of Emily. I'm instantly irritated by it.

'Frightened of being seen playing the Good Samaritan? Don't worry, Garrie. I've got this from here. I'd hate to cause trouble in paradise.'

He tightens his grip on my arm and turns to face me. 'Don't be silly; I'm getting you inside. And no, this is not my good deed for the day. It's about a lot more than that. You're still the one, Sandie.'

I swallow his words, but it's impossible to digest them.

'Don't play with me, Garrie.'

'I'm not.'

'I mean it, don't even go there.'

I have no choice but to let him help me because I don't dare put any pressure on my foot. And my body responds to his closeness in the same way it always has. It's an untamed attraction, a bodily instinct that makes me want this man despite everything. It's irrational, but chemistry is such a powerful thing. The memory of a particular touch triggers a cocktail of endorphins, dopamine and oxytocin that sets your body on fire. I know how it works and right now I can't escape it. I wish I could tell my heart and body to stop responding to him and catch up with the logic of my brain. But neither of them is listening.

We wade our way through the thick bracken and overgrown nettles that lead to the back of my house. We make it to the gate and Garrie does what he always did when we were together. He strokes my hair as I fumble to open the lock and an instant wave of electricity pulses through my veins. I don't tell him to stop because I don't want him to stop. I desire his touch.

'Ouch, I think a stinger got my leg. It's not my day.'

'Ice will help that too. I'll sort that when we get in.'

Now my leg and foot both hurt, but a leg full of stingers is better than facing Emily's glare. She'll be watching out for Garrie's arrival home, I'm sure; I've seen her do it enough times. I'm not proud of it but I realise I'm enjoying the idea that I'm now deceiving her.

Once we're inside the house he helps to bathe my leg and places a cold compress against my foot. His masculine hands are gentle against my skin and with every touch, I'm allowing myself to enjoy the sensual pleasure.

'Help me upstairs, Garrie. I need to lie down.'

He leads me upstairs and helps me onto my usual side of the bed.

'Anything else you need?'

'Sit with me, Garrie.'

He slides onto the bed next to me and the arousal I feel is undeniable. We link hands and I know it's a moment of passionate foolishness, but his touch stimulates my sexual desire. I've missed this type of intimacy and closeness. He slides towards me, and I pull him closer. Our lips press together, and I know this is the point where I should stop what's about to happen, but my body is already over-run with hormones. The juxtaposition of familiarity and unfamiliarity makes me kiss him with a longing I've never felt before.

I've got so many burning questions but now isn't the time. I'm in bed with the man who stirs my emotions like no other. I'm about to abandon myself to the enjoyment of him. A purely physical encounter of animalistic passion. I tell myself it doesn't mean any more than that. There needn't be any consequences. The anger I feel towards him turns into raw, uncontrollable passion as his fingers slide over my skin and every nerve ending starts to tingle. I catch traces of his favourite Aventus Creed aftershave, and I breathe it in, allowing the heady aroma to exude deeply into my lungs. It stirs my senses as he moans into my mouth and pulls me closer.

'You're so special to me, Sandie.'

I don't say it back. I mustn't. I'm taking what I need and nothing more. This is the same man who told me only weeks ago that our love was unbreakable hours before he walked out on me. It's temporary madness but I'm going to enjoy the hunger of our sexual encounter. I close my eyes as my body tenses and becomes fully consumed. At this moment the world outside doesn't exist.

≈ ≈ ≈

When I open my eyes it's dark. I'm wrapped in his embrace, and I bury my head in the thick hair of his chest. He's relaxed and sleeping so I listen for the sound of his heartbeat. Tears prick my eyes, but I blink them away because I can't allow myself to be fooled by this beautiful moment. I return to my side of the bed because I've had my fix of Garrie and that's as far as it goes. When he wakes up, I'll tell him to go home. The silence is pierced by a discordant ringtone. It isn't mine, but I don't recognise it as his either. He must have changed it. This one is shrill and insistent. He opens his eyes and I feel his body tense against it.

'You should answer it, Garrie.'

He mutters 'Damn' under his breath and reaches down into a pocket of his discarded jacket. His finger slides across his mobile screen and he drops the phone back on top of his crumpled clothes.

'Why can't she ever leave me alone?'

It's more a statement to himself than a question to me but I answer anyway. 'Because you're hers now. She'll be wondering where you are.'

He relaxes on the bed. It seems he's in no rush to walk back into the meticulously ordered atmosphere of number 12. 'She'll have to wonder.'

'One moment of passion doesn't mean I want to get back with you, Garrie.'

He stares at the ceiling deep in his own thoughts, but he doesn't reply.

'It was wonderful. But it can never be what we had before. You really should go.'

Finally, he seems to have heard me. 'I don't want to go, Sandie, but I will. I'll take a quick shower first if that's OK.'

He walks into the bathroom, and I hear the water running and the familiar sounds of his routine as he washes away all traces of me before he goes home. I feel the intensity of his presence without him saying a word. After his shower, he leaves a trail of footprints along the carpet, as he always did, because he doesn't dry his feet. It makes me half smile because I always hated that when he lived with me but now there's something comforting about it.

His phone lights up again; he's put it on vibrate. He picks it up and types a message; I'm certain it's not a love message but a few words to stop Emily from asking questions. He stares at the phone with a pained expression, and I see his face change.

'You need to get dressed and go, Garrie.'

The bubble has burst, and our brief interlude is over.

'It's been fun, Garrie. But don't misunderstand what this was; a purely physical encounter, nothing more. It doesn't change anything and there is no us.'

'Please, Sandie…'

I put my fingers to his lips before he can say any more. 'No, Garrie. It's time for you to go home.'

He throws on the rest of his clothes and leans in to kiss me, but I turn away, so his mouth only brushes my cheek. Then he leaves. I hear the backdoor close and I limp to the bedroom window. I watch him walking towards number 12 carrying his supermarket bag and I see Emily standing on her doorstep. My stomach does somersaults as he disappears inside, and I think about what I've done.

I hop downstairs, trying to keep the weight off my foot. My ankle needs ice and without the distraction of Garrie to take my mind off the pain, I need a painkiller. I feel alone now he's gone, but I don't regret what happened. The sex was amazing, and I only hope I haven't sparked a fire I won't be able to control.

I can't allow myself to get burned again.

Chapter 12

EMILY

It's 8 p.m. and Garrie's not home yet. I told him I was planning a nice meal for us, so I find it rude that he didn't let me know he was going to be late and took forever to respond to my messages. His unpredictable behaviour and mood swings are disturbing. So are his disappearing acts, but I've asked Liz for advice, and she's suggested I download a tracker app. She probably thinks I'm making too much of this, but she understands why I'm unsettled by his secrecy.

Now all I need is access to his phone when he's asleep so I can set it up; next time he's missing in action I'll know exactly where he is. Hopefully, it will put my mind at rest, stop me worrying, and we can get on with our lives.

I look out of the window and see him walking towards our house with his shopping bag. I open the front door and give him a welcome home smile I don't really feel.

'Everything alright, Garrie? All OK at work today?'

'Yeah. Crazy busy. But I got a lot done.'

I feel I'm treading on eggshells. I want to ask him where he's been, but I don't dare risk a repeat of what happened the last time I questioned his movements.

'Shall I put the kettle on?'

'I need to get changed first. It'll help clear my head. Work pressure.'

I take a deep breath and tell my brain not to blurt anything out that I might regret. I give him my sweetest smile. 'I'll make you a coffee when you come back down.'

I don't think he hears me because he's already halfway up the stairs. He doesn't seem to be the slightest bit interested in telling me what's happening at work, or what kept him. I had one conversation with him this afternoon. I messaged him with a reminder to pick up puppy food for Ginger on his way home, and he called me from the supermarket. The conversation lasted ninety seconds and I could barely hear him over the PA system announcing 3 for 2 offers, let alone get any hint he wasn't coming home until much later.

Worse than that, to go completely AWOL; with no explanation, and every phone call and message from me ignored. If he got called back into work, why didn't he let me know? It's as if he disappears into a world of his own where I don't exist, and it's none of my business where he goes, or why.

And now he's back, muttering about work pressure, and carrying on with life as if the bit in between didn't happen. I hear him singing upstairs in the bedroom as he's getting changed.

'Relight my fire, your love is my only desire.'

His mood's changed again and his happiness springs off the floorboards. Work pressure obviously didn't affect him that much.

'Relight my fire, 'cause I need your love.'

I'm angry about yet another disappearing act but I'm going to give him the benefit of the doubt, one more time. We haven't been together long so maybe he needs some space to process our new relationship and our wedding plans. And maybe he truly is under pressure at work.

I call upstairs. 'I've missed you, Garrie.'

'Missed you too, sweetheart.'

'I haven't missed your singing though.'

'I thought that's what you loved about me.'

I try to dismiss my angst and prepare the table for dinner. I'll behave as though everything is normal, but I'll also be on my guard.

≈ ≈ ≈

I watch Garrie flip the steaks for me while I'm crumbling feta cheese into a Greek salad. I still feel deeply attracted to him despite the recent red flags that have made me question our relationship, and I can't take my eyes off him. I'm riding an emotional rollercoaster and he's at the controls. It's been that way since the first time we met; his magnetic power was instant. When he looked at me, and his eyes lingered a little too long on my mouth, I knew he felt it too. We were random strangers that fate had thrown together on adjacent bar stools, but it seemed fate had a plan for us. Now I wonder what fate has planned for our future.

I sprinkle virgin olive oil on the salad, as he waves the meat tongs at me, and takes a bow. 'Two medium rare steaks, as madame requested.'

'Perfect timing, chef. Let's eat outside, it's such a lovely evening.' I smile as I carry our food to the table.

He stretches his arms wide. 'You look beautiful tonight, Emily. Come here, sweetheart.'

He's in such a playful and loving mood this evening. I feel his lips trace down my neck and my body tingles with excitement. I tilt my head back as he pulls my hair, and our tongues slide against each other in a moment of pure lust. His fingers slide over my breasts, and I allow myself to succumb to his seduction. The evening breeze is chilly, and I feel it against my skin as he slides his hands underneath my dress and the intensity of our lovemaking builds until I'm begging for release. I want to freeze this moment forever.

I lie on the cool grass, the sexual energy replaced by silent contentment. I could easily fall asleep, but Garrie is already on his feet as Ginger comes bounding towards us licking her lips and wagging her tail. The silence is broken by my laughter as I realise, she's been busy trying to demolish our steaks while we've been too preoccupied to notice.

'I think Ginger approves of your cooking. But salad obviously isn't her thing.'

He takes the dinner plates and what's left of the food inside, as my head sinks deeper into the soft grass and I bask in the afterglow of Garrie's lovemaking.

'I'm taking a shower before bed. You got me all hot and bothered.'

'Save some water for me.'

I stare across at his masculine silhouette in the kitchen doorway as Ginger chases him with her dog toy. I stretch my body in satisfaction, my fingers lengthening towards the sky as I yawn and breathe in the scent of summer.

The upstairs window is open, but I can't hear Garrie's usual shower singing. I close my eyes to hear the rustling of leaves and birds singing. I feel something next to my leg and realise it's Garrie's phone on vibrate. After our beautiful evening, I feel a twinge of guilt about my plan to fit the tracking app, but then the phone lights up. A thin strip of light flashing a message. Curiosity gets the better of me and I'm intrigued to find out who it's from. I glance up at the open window, grab the phone and read the message notification. I swipe down to see the full message but realise the phone's password protected. I try to think what his password might be.

'What the hell are you doing?'

I'm paralysed with guilty embarrassment. He runs outside, fury etched on his face as he lunges at me and snatches the phone from my hand.

'I'm sorry, Garrie.'

'Haven't you heard of trust, Emily? It's something that couples feel when they love each other.'

He walks away and I'm mad with myself because I let curiosity get the better of me. The only reason I need access to his phone is to connect the tracking app, so I don't know why I got distracted by a text message. What makes it worse, it was from his mum.

Garrie, when are you coming to see me?

That's all I could see; a normal message but it was a surprise. Garrie never talks about his mum or any of his family. The one time I asked, he changed the subject, wearing an expression that warned me to shut up. And now I know what can happen when I push him too far. His eyes turn black, and I see a different Garrie. I wonder if his mum ever sees that side of her son.

I walk into the house and he's dunking a teabag into his Coldplay mug.

'Garrie, can we talk?'

He wordlessly pours the cold milk and ignores me.

'Garrie.'

He raises his hand to silence me.

'Don't say anything, Emily; you'll make this worse. If it could be any worse.'

I move towards him, but his tone turns even angrier. 'Don't come any closer, or I swear to God …'

I freeze. I don't know what to do next. I feel guilty, but angry too. Surely, he can understand why I felt the urge to look. Especially after his recent disappearing acts. Any woman would want to know where the hell her man goes when he disappears without warning.

'Garrie, I get you're upset. I was wrong to look at your phone. But I wasn't spying on you, even though you're so secretive. Where do you keep disappearing to?'

'I don't keep disappearing, Emily. I've got a life beyond you.'

'But you could at least have the decency to let me know when you're going to be late home or staying away somewhere.'

'I'm not telling you my every move.'

'I'm not asking you to.'

'But you decided to snoop on me because I screwed up a dinner arrangement?'

'It's not like that, Garrie. And why didn't you tell me you have a mother?'

He looks up and spits his next words through a distorted grin. 'Newsflash, Emily. Everybody has a mother. Not that I know anything about yours, or much else about you for that matter, but I don't go snooping on your phone.'

His words snap me out of my guilt. How dare he turn this on me?

'Firstly, I repeat, I wasn't snooping. And secondly, I've told you there's nothing to know about my parents, Garrie. They're both dead. And I barely remember them.'

I fight away the emotion that bubbles underneath the surface at my lack of family. Dead is such a dark, final word; a word that leaves you with nowhere to go. Just memories of familiar faces and happy times. At least, I suppose that's what most people have. But not me because I no longer have any family. I try to think of happy times from the past, but they always become clouded by painful memories, so I try not to go there.

I turn my back on him and make my way upstairs, grasping onto the stair rail to secure my balance.

Garrie ignores me for the rest of the evening and sleeps on the sofa.

Chapter 13

GARRIE

I could barely wake up this morning, but that's hardly surprising; making love to two women within hours of each other was bound to have an effect. I've finished work early, and now I'm on my way to Sandie's. After messaging her repeatedly, she finally agreed to see me.

Plus, I needed to escape the interrogations from Emily. It makes me smile when she keeps trying to check up on me because she's got it into her head I'm up to no good. The look on her face yesterday was hilarious when she saw it was a text from my mum. If only she knew what I'm scheming; but she'll find out soon enough. She's the one that destroyed my happiness so now I'm going to destroy hers.

I've parked my car out of sight and I'm almost at Sandie's back garden gate. She's cut the weeds back, so I've got easier access and she's sitting on her garden bench in a floral dress and sun hat. I look across at her and see the image of beauty. She has soft delicate features and the most natural feminine simplicity in her appearance. She's the woman I want, and I'm determined to convince her I'm worth waiting for despite what I've done but I know it's going to be an uphill struggle to make her understand.

Leaving her to move in with Emily hurt her badly, but Sandie was never part of the plan. I met her out of the blue and it was bad timing. She was serving in the coffee shop, and I was mesmerised by her. Her blonde hair was pulled into a ponytail, and she was wearing a black apron and balancing a tray full of coffee cups, but I was captured. She's the first woman I've wanted since losing my wife, and I know I'll have to tell her the truth about Emily soon.

But I need to wait until the time is right. First, I need to put the demons to rest. Then I can make a new life with Sandie.

Our sexual encounter implies she still wants me. When we were in the throes of passion, she surrendered to me completely and I could feel her desire. She yearns for me; I know she does. I hope when she finds out the truth, she'll be able to forgive me, but I'm not convinced she will. I need to work hard if I'm to get her back.

'Thanks for letting me come round, Sandie. I had to see you.'

'Don't get your hopes up, Garrie.'

'I can't help being irresistible.'

'I'm serious; what happened the other day doesn't change anything. I need to get on with my own life, Garrie. Not live on the outskirts of yours.'

'I still want you, Sandie.'

'Because we fell into bed with each other it doesn't make me forget that you destroyed our future together.'

'I did something I had to.'

'You moved across the road to live with another woman.'

'I don't love her, Sandie.'

'It didn't take you long to get fed up with her. You've beaten your own record, Garrie.'

'I've never loved her.'

'Then why?'

'I have my reasons and I will tell you as soon I'm able to.'

'I've no idea what the hell that means. But I bet you're saying the same to her across the street.'

'I'm not, believe me.'

'Why did you give her my wedding dress and have a wedding rehearsal on the day that we should have got married?'

'Sandie, I know what it looks like, but I promise I'm not going to marry Emily.'

'You keep going back to her. Does she have some kind of hold over you?'

I feel my forehead crease at her question. I don't know what to say and I see her searching my face for clues. 'I never meant to hurt you, Sandie.'

She looks down at her hands. 'But you did. And we both know you'll be back across there tonight.'

'But it won't be for much longer, Sandie. I'm going to walk away from her.'

'Like you walked away from me?'

'No, it's not like that. I'll explain everything to you soon. I promise.'

'And that's supposed to make it all OK? I don't think so, Garrie. I think you should go.'

She twists her fingers together in anger as she presses me for an answer. 'Who the hell is she, Garrie?'

'She's someone I hate.'

'But you're living with her, for God's sake.'

'Because I have no choice.'

'She's hardly holding you prisoner.'

'That's what you think. But she is, Sandie. Not physically, but metaphorically she has my mind and body shackled and bound to her.'

'In what way? This isn't making any sense, Garrie.'

'I can't tell you at the moment.'

'I want you to leave.'

I know I must respect what she's saying, but I rest my hand gently on her shoulder before I leave. 'I will go, but I'm never going to give up on us.'

'There is no us, Garrie.'

'I know how it looks and sounds but I'll do whatever it takes to make things right between us.'

I feel Sandie slipping away and I'm desperate to tell her I'm playing with Emily. She means nothing; she's a puppet and I'm pulling all her strings until I'm able to pull them so tightly she's unable to breathe.

Chapter 14

EMILY

I'm waiting for a student to arrive for her maths lesson. Her name's Martha. She's a bright girl; only twelve but she already knows Pythagoras' theorem. I'm not convinced she needs tutoring, but I love her company. The truth is she understands more than me, but I don't let her know that. I move on to another topic when I don't understand something and look it up when she's gone.

I open the front door to let her in and notice Sandie's no longer planting seeds in her front garden. She was there earlier kneeling on one of those garden mats but didn't bother to look up. She has such a pretty garden with perennials, roses and tiny shoots peeping out of the soil; a stretch of colour that draws your attention. She seems to be getting on with her life and I think she's stopped spying on us.

Martha's as energetic and bubbly as ever. She's so inquisitive and she loves to ask questions. We both enjoy her visits. I have a surprise for her today. Last week she told me she collects bracelets and showed me a long line of them on her wrist, so I've made one for her.

Her face lights up when I hand it to her. 'It's for you, do you like it?'

'It's so pretty, Emily.' She raises her arm to display the multicoloured beads. 'My mum thinks bracelets are silly.'

'I think they're great.'

She smiles and I watch her slide the new bracelet onto her wrist. She takes out her maths book and opens it, but I have other plans.

'Not today, Martha. Let's do something different. I've got another surprise for you.'

She seems nervous, but we've only known each other a short time; I'm still a stranger. I pull a large cardboard box from underneath the table and give her a reassuring grin. 'Trust me, you're going to like this.'

Her eyes widen as she cautiously opens the box. She squeals with delight when she sees what's inside. 'You've bought me a rabbit? I've been asking Mum for a rabbit, but she keeps saying no because she'd have to look after it when I'm at school.'

'I know, you told me. That's why I wanted to surprise you. You must give him a name.'

'You've bought him for me?'

'He'll have to stay here but you can help to feed him and take care of him.'

'Yay, I've got my own rabbit.'

I've always wanted a rabbit myself, so when Martha mentioned how much she loves them I decided to get one. I'm not sure I've done the right thing letting her believe he's hers, but she seems so happy. Seeing her smiles of joy makes me happy, too.

The rabbit jumps out of the box and hops around the living room leaving little currant trails behind him. Ginger's too scared to go anywhere near him and runs under the table to watch from a safe distance.

'So, what should we call him?'

'Hoppy. I'll call him Hoppy.'

I grin at her. 'Hoppy it is.'

It's hardly an original name but it fits. We take him into the back garden, and together we set up a hutch with fresh straw, carrots and drinking water.

'Can I feed him when I come to lessons?'

I smile at her excited expression. 'Of course. It can be our secret.'

She throws her arms around me and gives me a hug. 'I love you, Emily. And I love Hoppy.'

It's funny that the smallest things can be such big things for children. Her happiness seeps into my consciousness and I smile back at her. I wish I could have had the chance to do simple things like this with a child of my own.

≈ ≈ ≈

After her mum collects her, I scoop up the rabbit droppings before Garrie gets home. He sent a text earlier and didn't mention me looking at his phone so I'm hoping his anger's worn off. I relax on the sofa and pour a glass of Prosecco. I'm getting my life back on track and I'm proud of myself. I haven't had any dark thoughts since my flashback on the night Garrie lost his temper with me.

Ginger picks up her lead with her teeth and carries it towards me, so we take each other out for a walk. She sniffs every lamppost, so we don't get far but I observe life in the street. It's busier than usual with children, dogs and people milling around in the sunshine. I'm about to head home when I spot Garrie coming out of the alleyway that runs towards the back of Sandie's house. I pull Ginger back and observe from a safe distance, hidden behind a privet bush. He walks quickly in the opposite direction from our house and disappears out of sight.

I contemplate what I've seen. Garrie would have no reason to use the alleyway unless he's been to visit Sandie, via the back garden. I stare across at her house but can't see anything. I make my way home with tension in my heart and confusion in my brain as Garrie's car appears and speeds past me. He waves, so I smile and wave back.

But there's a whirlwind in my head and I need time to think.

Chapter 15

SANDIE

Something unexpected has happened, and it changes everything. I should have guessed sooner because my dates are usually so regular. I put being late down to stress, but I decided to take a pregnancy test and it was positive. I'm shocked because the timing's awful, but I'm also thrilled. Maybe my hormones are in overdrive but it's the most beautiful feeling in the world, even under these circumstances. I almost can't believe it, but the test is sitting on the coffee table and every time I glance at it the news is confirmed. I'm having a baby. This must have been Garrie's parting gift before he left me for Emily.

The television's on and I'm body popping to a car advert. This one always gets me; I love the rhythm. But I don't need an incentive to make me jump up and dance; I already feel so alive because of the new life inside me.

Garrie's texted constantly since we spoke in my back garden. He made it clear he wants to rekindle our romance, but I made it equally clear there's no chance of that. I can't allow him to crawl underneath my skin again. But now those two lines on the test kit keep staring back at me and I've agreed to see him again. I don't know how I'll find the words, I'm still processing this discovery in my own head, but I must tell him about the baby. I've no idea how he'll react, but I no longer want to completely push him away. I want my child to have a father.

But I'm not prepared to take him back just because we slept together. I obviously sent him mixed signals so it's important I make that clear before telling him about the baby. It was passionate and sensual, and I won't let myself regret it. I certainly won't feel guilty about responding to being wanted. I'm a woman, I have needs, and sometimes it's easier to have those met by someone who already knows exactly how to meet them. I felt that familiar tingle as soon as he touched me, and I would have happily let that moment last forever.

It's strange that in the midst of passion, you can be so in the moment that even the most hurtful things can fade into insignificance. Part of me suspended belief, as if the last few weeks had never happened. But reality was waiting in the wings because all good things come to an end. Flames burn brightly until we watch them wither away into the wind; lovers burn deeply into our hearts until the passing of time separates us. We are left with nothing but memories of beautiful things that can no longer be touched.

When Garrie left my bed and went back to her at Number 12, I felt it was the end, my moment of closure as I whispered, 'Goodbye Garrie.' It was my final fling after trying to dampen down the flames of physical longing I'd felt for so long. But the embers are still smouldering and the fact that he's only across the road makes it worse. I can't risk being tempted by him again, and I've been thinking about renting a flat in the centre of town.

He's coming to my house again tomorrow, and that's when I'll break the news to him. I've made the decision to let him back into my life, but I'll be clear with him about the ground rules.

Chapter 16

GARRIE

My phone rings for the second time in five minutes as I'm getting off the train. It's Mum's next-door neighbour; he's been a friend of the family for years. I hit connect as I scramble to get past the rush hour crowds with my briefcase in one hand and phone in the other. I head towards the station car park.

'Hold on mate, I can't hear you.' Why do phones always ring in the most awkward places?

'I think you need to come over, Garrie. It's your mum. I found her lying on the kitchen floor; she must have passed out and fallen.'

It's always the same conversation, and I could do without it. I'm supposed to be seeing Sandie in literally ten minutes.

'I'm heading to the car now and I'll drive straight there. How is she?'

'She was out cold but she's in her chair now, and she's more alert. But she's asking for you like she always does when she's …you know …' His voice tails off.

'Yeah, I know. She's not easy to deal with when she's like this, so thanks for everything you've done and for letting me know. I'll be there as soon as I can.'

I end the call. Shit, I really don't need this today. But it's hardly the first time it's happened, so I'm not surprised. Mum started to drink a bit too much, too often, years ago. And it got worse after Annabel died and Katie's condition got worse. Mum wouldn't stop crying and I was too numb from my own grief to be able to deal with hers. We replayed the same conversation every time we spoke.

'My life will never be the same without Annabel. She was the perfect daughter-in-law everybody dreams of having.'

'And the perfect wife, Mum.'

'She certainly cured you of your wild ways. I hope you're not planning on going back to them now she's gone.'

'For God's sake, Mum, not this again. I can barely get through one day at a time.'

'You'll have to keep going for Katie's sake. And why you've put her in that awful place, I don't know. She needs her family. When am I going to get to see her?'

'I've told you why. She doesn't even recognise me most of the time, Mum. She's almost catatonic and she needs specialist attention and care. Things I can't provide.'

'Annabel would hate the idea of her child being somewhere like that, with strangers. She was such a perfect mother.'

It was incessant. The same attack on me every time I visited until eventually, I couldn't face seeing her. I needed my time and space to grieve for my wife. And I wished for a mother who could help me, but she couldn't; any more than I could help her. She found her help in a bottle, like my father used to before he flew into his drunken rages whenever it suited him. They were usually aimed at my mother whose main concern was to protect my younger sister. And he started lashing out more at me, until I was big enough to hit back. Mum's a borderline alcoholic, she has days when she can't cope, and it sends her over the edge. Today is obviously one of those days.

I start the car engine and angrily crunch the gear stick into reverse. Everything's caving in on me and I need to be in too many places at once. I've still got Emily onside for the moment and she'll be irritable if I get home from work late. I don't give a damn about her, but I need to give her enough attention to keep her sweet. Sandie finally agreed to see me today, but because of Mum I'll have to keep her waiting and she'll feel let down again.

In frustration, I reverse into a lamppost and slap the steering wheel with both hands as if it's to blame, before speeding off down the street. I've no time to check the damage to the car. I need to calm down. I'll phone Sandie to explain everything as soon as I've checked on Mum. I can't give her any more reasons to be upset with me.

Chapter 17

SANDIE

Garrie should have been here by now. He sent me a text to tell me he was leaving work early and is bringing my favourite cake with him. I've decided to make food - a Waldorf salad, one of my signature dishes and one of Garrie's favourites. I'll pour lemonade for me and wine for him because I want him to be calm when I tell him the news about the baby. My phone lights up with a message and my heart begins to pound with nervous anticipation as I assume it's from him, but it's from my friend, telling me the reunion has been cancelled.

Half an hour later I still haven't heard anything, and I'm left in a state of limbo where I vowed never to venture. How have I become "the other woman" who sits and waits, casually dismissed if an arrangement needs to be cancelled? My hormones fire into action and I'm determined to stay strong. I know my worth and won't let him bring me down again. The thing that really hurt when he walked out was that my own expectations were shattered. When someone you love causes that, it shows you they're not the person you thought they were, and that's a painful discovery. It's like mourning the loss of someone who wasn't there in the first place.

I won't let him destroy my expectations for our baby. I want him to be a father but only if he's going to step up to the job. I never got to know my own father because he walked out when I was young. I treasured the few occasions when he sent me letters and gifts but what I remember the most are the times when he made promises, built up my hopes and never delivered on them. I will never let that happen to my child.

Most of all, I need Garrie to start levelling with me about what the deal is with Emily. I'm done with this incessant 'I can't tell you yet' nonsense.

I look out of the window but there's no sign of him. He's now more than an hour late and I'm not waiting any longer. I lock the doors and close the curtains, change into my most comfortable PJs, and scroll through Netflix as I munch my way through the Waldorf salad and sip lemonade. I go for a nap and my head flops onto Garrie's pillow. The clean, masculine smell of his hair from when he was last here permeates it. Perhaps because I'm pregnant, it stirs the ache of missing him. But hormones be damned; furious disillusionment and disappointment kick in, and I punch the pillow in despair. I should be sharing this pregnancy with him. How did everything go so wrong and become such a crazy mess?

So much for him trying to convince me he doesn't love Emily and he's going to move out of number 12. Whatever's going on between them in that house is a mystery to me, and I hate being excluded from it. It's about time Garrie let me in on the secret. I know she was staring at me while I was out planting sunflower seeds. She thinks I didn't realise, but I could feel her eyes boring into my back, and it made me uncomfortable. It seems the watcher has become the watched.

And Garrie's let me down again.

I hate what I'm about to do, but I'm angry. I start punching a message to him into my phone.

Chapter 18

GARRIE

Mum's sitting in her chair with a knitted blanket over her legs, dunking a digestive biscuit into a mug of tea. She's been complaining to me ever since I arrived so she must be recovering. It's always the same one-sided conversation.

'You don't visit enough.'

'I do visit.'

'A son should check up on his mum.'

'I'm always checking up on you.'

'I'm the one that gave birth to you…'

Under my breath I mutter 'Yeah. Lucky me.' I see her mouth moving and I nod in the right places, but I'm not listening to her; it's another of her regular speeches I've heard too often. I reach for my phone to check my notifications; the usual several missed calls from Emily which I ignore, and a message from Sandie.

Garrie, please tell me what's going on. I'm trying to be understanding, I really am. But I need to know what's so important that you've missed our time together. I really wanted to see you today.

Her last sentence surprises me because she was so angry when we spoke in her back garden. She pretty much threw me out and told me we'd never have a future together. Now she seems truly disappointed I'm so late for our meeting today. Maybe she's thought about everything, and she's changed her mind. Maybe I'm starting to win her round. I'm about to send a reply when I see she's typing another message. My heart skips a beat and I wonder what I'm about to read.

This might be a long message, but I don't want that last line about wanting to see you to be misleading. I meant what I said in the garden. There's no "us" in the way you'd like there to be. Too much has happened. But I need to tell you some important news. It changes everything. I didn't want to say this in a text message but you're not here. You let me down again and you've left me with no choice. You need to know…I'm having your baby.

My emotions change in the blink of an eye. I stare at the words on my screen as my head plays mental charades. *Baby.* One word, two syllables. Four letters that tilt my world further on its axis.

'It would help if you could leave your phone alone for a minute.'

I spin around to confront my mother's challenging look. Her tone is even more aggressive than usual; it's always the same until she sobers up.

'I do have a life and a job, Mum.'

'And as usual your things always come first. Been the same ever since you were a kid; always wanting your own way. Thinking you were more important than everybody else and we should all dance to your tune. The same way your father thought.'

'Oh, I really got lucky in the parental lottery, didn't I? A womanising drunk for a dad and a cold "couldn't-give-a-shit-about-my-kids" mother.'

'I did my best for you. But you never listened to anybody; always thought you knew best. You were a cocky little sod then and you're the same now.'

I don't answer. I need to get out of here. I can't deal with any more of her verbal attacks after reading Sandie's message.

Her neighbour raises both eyebrows. 'What is it, Garrie? You look like you've seen a ghost.'

If only I could tell him, I have. An image of my darling Annabel dances before my eyes. The day when we sat holding hands all those years ago, both transfixed by the test kit she was holding. Minutes had felt like hours until we hugged each other when two vertical blue lines told us it was positive.

Today's news ought to make me happy, but it doesn't. Another woman I love is carrying my child and it feels like history is repeating itself. I'm going to have to tell Sandie some things I didn't want to tell her yet. But I don't have a choice now; this forces my hand.

There's one problem. I have no idea where to start.

Chapter 19

SANDIE

I can't believe I've blurted out perhaps the most important news I'll ever tell anybody, in a text message. But once I started typing, the momentum of my anger kept my fingers flying over the letters. With some regret, I slide under the duvet as if I'm hiding from Garrie's reaction and within minutes, it arrives. Waves of nauseous anticipation crash through me.

I'll be with you as soon as I can, Sandie.

I stare at the emotionless message. It gives me no idea where he is or why he isn't here. And worse, no idea how he feels about what I've told him. Another message lands.

I'm at my Mum's. She had a fall but she's OK. I'll message you when I'm leaving.

His mum, another area of his personal life he never shared with me. Why didn't I see all these red flags before? We were so intimate; why did I choose to ignore all the important things I didn't know about him? I check the time; it feels late, but it's only 7 p.m. My personal body-clock's gone haywire recently. I'm a bundle of nerves as I start to get ready. I want Garrie to be as excited about this baby as I am, but maybe that's unrealistic in the circumstances. Or perhaps he is but was too preoccupied with his mother to show it. I suppose I'm about to find out.

I can't decide what to wear; indecision seems to be hormonal too. I settle on the one pair of skinny jeans that still fit me and my favourite T-shirt. My phone pings again. *Leaving in ten minutes. Let's meet at the coffee shop in half an hour.*

The coffee shop? I'm surprised he wants to meet there and not here at the house. We haven't done that since he left me for Emily. But I don't have the energy to argue, and at this point, any conversation's better than no conversation.

I look in the mirror. Thinking about Emily makes me decide to up my game. I throw on my sparkly beads and blingy trainers and do my ten-minute make-up routine before grabbing my leather jacket. I check the mirror again. I think my look's about right for a meeting with the father of my child.

I pass Emily's house on my way to the bus stop, but I don't get a chance to glance inside because the bus comes speeding down the street. I wave my arms and quickly jump on. All the seats are taken so I hold on to one of those stringy poles that make it impossible to stand up straight. My phone pings yet again as I get to the stop opposite the cafe.

I'm inside waiting for you.

Dammit, I feel under more pressure. I'd hoped I could say hi to Jude and update her before he arrived. Instead, I'm clumsily stepping into the coffee shop, trying to squeeze past two screaming children as I see Garrie waving at me. He looks as awkward as I feel; this whole situation seems surreal.

'I got your usual.'

'Thanks.'

I slide alongside him at his usual window seat, with Jude's surprised expression peering over the counter at us. I shrug my shoulders at her, hoping my gesture communicates 'I'm as surprised as you are…I'll update you later.' She doesn't know about the baby, and I can't imagine how she'll react when I tell her. But, for now, I need to concentrate on Garrie's reaction.

He's twirling a spoon in his latte, and I have no idea where to start this conversation. I never imagined I would be back here with him, and certainly not as a mother-to-be. I want him to be a father to my baby, but if I'm going to let him back into my life, I need some answers. I want us to get to know each other properly if we're going to be parents together. I don't think we did that the first time around. We rushed into things and allowed passion and romance to take over. We got caught up in the whirlwind of marriage plans and commitment. Perhaps we really were just two names on a fancy cheeseboard.

But the stakes are higher now; we have a child to think about and I need to know his feelings about that. He finally stops spoon twirling and looks up from his coffee cup. 'Sandie, I…'

I stay quiet through the long pause until he continues.

'I know we're here to talk about what you told me. It's all I've thought about since you messaged, but first, there are some things I need to tell you.'

'You've picked a strange place to have this conversation, Garrie. Why here?'

He starts spoon-twirling again and I realise he's even more nervous than me. 'I don't know. Guess my head's all over the place. Suppose I felt neutral territory might make all this easier.'

'It's not exactly neutral territory and I'm not sure anything's going to make this easy, Garrie. But talk to me.'

'I've been married before, Sandie. But my wife died.'

I wasn't expecting to hear that, and my insides begin to somersault, but I suppose I shouldn't be surprised he's been married before since I heard him call himself Daddy on the phone. But I never considered the possibility of his wife being dead.

'I'm not sure what to say, Garrie; this has come as a shock. I can only imagine how awful it must have been for you. She must have been so young. When did it happen?'

'A little over a year ago. Losing her devastated me and I get so angry about the unfairness of it.'

He breaks eye contact, and I can almost taste the rawness of his emotions. He squeezes the coffee spoon he's holding until his knuckles turn white and I'm convinced he's going to bend the handle. I decide this isn't the right time to ask him for any more details about his wife's death, but I do want to know about his child. And I need to know how he feels about the one I'm expecting.

'I can only imagine what you went through, Garrie. It must be hard to talk about it, but I wish you'd told me sooner.' I pause and almost reach out to take his hand but decide against the intimacy of the gesture until I hear more. 'But she gave you a beautiful gift. You had a child together.'

He hesitates before he speaks. 'Yes. I have a beautiful daughter.'

'Tell me about her.'

'Her name's Katie. She's got beautiful dark curly hair and blue eyes.'

'Where does she live? Perhaps I can meet her one day, especially now she's going to have a baby brother or sister. Are you excited to tell her, Garrie?' He gives me a blank look in response, almost as if he's not really seeing me. 'Garrie? You need to tell me how you feel about our baby. And you need to tell me now. This is happening. It's for real.'

'The thing is, Sandie. Katie's not…' He stops speaking and stares out of the window into the distance; he seems lost in his own thoughts. I wonder what he's about to tell me when I see Jude waving her arms frantically at me. Behind her, I see Emily striding towards our table. Garrie turns from the window at that exact moment and sees her too.

He mutters, 'Leave this to me' and gets up and walks towards her.

Whatever words they exchange make him frown as she gives her trademark shake of the glossy hair. She places a hand on his shoulder and glances in my direction. I can't imagine what he's told her. I feel like an exhibit being viewed and discussed. My hands involuntarily move down to my stomach. I feel a sudden primeval instinct to protect the life growing inside me.

Jude appears in my line of sight. She's restocking the condiment station and staring at me with raised eyebrows and her "I told you this would end in tears" look. Emily leans into Garrie and whispers something as they both walk towards the door. I jump up from my seat and rush over.

'Garrie? Where the hell do you think you're going?'

Emily spins round and I see the blue topaz ring glinting on her finger and a matching glint in her eyes; she must know I've seen it. 'Do you mind? That's my fiancé you're talking to.'

I square up to her as Garrie says nothing. 'And does that mean you own him? He was talking to me.'

She stares at me with a triumphant smile. 'Actually, yes. It does. And we need to go home.'

I watch in punishingly slow motion as she takes Garrie's hand and opens the coffee shop door. Garrie turns around holding his hand to his ear suggesting he'll call me, and mouths 'Sorry. Trust me.' before he follows Emily through the door.

I glance in Jude's direction. Her expression tells me exactly what she's thinking.

Chapter 20

EMILY

'And what the hell are you doing meeting her, Garrie?'

His face flushes a pale shade of scarlet as he scrambles to get out of the coffee shop door and his eyes dart around their sockets as he tries to locate a reply in his brain.

'Stuck for an answer? It's hardly a trick question. What's going on?'

'Nothing.'

'It didn't seem like nothing. It looked like you were enjoying a cosy chat together.'

'It wasn't like that at all. I was sitting alone drinking my latte when she appeared at my table. I hadn't even noticed her arrive and suddenly she was there, right in front of my eyes.'

'How convenient.'

'She just sat down at my table.'

'And you didn't think to ask her to leave?'

'I did, but she started talking before I had a chance to say anything.'

'Talking about what?' I see him squirm as he tries to invent answers on the spot. 'Must have been an interesting conversation.'

'What? No, it was…' He pauses a little too long. 'I don't remember what she was saying. I was about to speak when you walked through the door.'

'So, if I hadn't walked through the door at that very moment, you were going to tell her to leave?'

'Yes.'

He looks even less convinced by his answer than I am. But I don't care anymore because all my illusions about Garrie are gone. I know he's seeing Sandie; I'm not stupid. First, I see him coming out of the alleyway that leads to the back of her house, then I trace him to the coffee shop and find them together. I'm glad I managed to set up the tracking device because now I can follow his every move remotely. I was only testing it today; it was a bonus that it led me to their secret meeting. He was so visibly wrong-footed when I appeared; I savoured that moment. And Sandie's stunned expression as we walked away from her, after her failed attempt to faze me, was priceless.

I can hardly believe I ever thought I loved him and wanted to marry him, but on that first night I met him at the bar he was the perfect gentleman. I was vulnerable, and Garrie filled a void in my life. Now I realise I don't need him. And I never did.

It was his suggestion that I move to number 12. I told him I wanted to rent somewhere, and he said he knew a good place. He told me it was in a beautiful area and as soon as I saw a photograph of the property on his phone, I fell in love with it.

'It's great, Garrie. But I can't afford to rent something like this.

'I'm an estate agent, so I'll keep a lookout for the right thing for you.'

'I'd really appreciate that. I'd be happy with a one-bed flat or apartment.'

We spent the next few days texting constantly; he consumed my daily thoughts. When he suggested paying part of the rent on the house he'd shown me, so we could be together, I jumped at the chance. I trusted him completely, but he blindsided and deceived me. Now I want him out of my life as soon as possible but first, I need to figure out how I can afford to pay the rent myself. Until I do, I'll play along with his lies because it suits me. He's a terrible liar so I'll enjoy watching him squirm while I make plans. I made a point of flashing the blue topaz ring in the coffee shop because I know it winds him up. I deserve a bit of fun at his expense before I tell him it's over and Sandie's welcome to him.

Teaching is a good distraction; I love it. Martha's doing well and her mum pays for her to come twice a week now. We spend most of the time in the garden with her new pet rabbit, but that's our secret. I print questions off the internet and let Martha figure it all out for herself. She's a bright child, and she always comes up with the answers. Garrie doesn't know about the lessons, and I don't want him to find out. Now he's sneaking around with Sandie it's easier to keep it a secret and it gives me more time to teach. But I don't want to provoke him.

If he wants to marry Sandie, I couldn't care less. But I'm not going to make it easy for him after the way he's treated me. I think Sandie deserves someone better than a lying cheat so hopefully she'll see through him, too. He seems to want his cake and eat it because he's flitting between the two of us. I don't know why he doesn't pick his socks up and walk back across the road to her. He seems to enjoy doing things in secret, but I wonder how long he can keep up with the lies.

'I can't believe she turned up out of the blue like that, Garrie.'

He shrugs. 'Well, she did. She appeared, got herself a drink and sat down.'

'She needs to cut that out. She can't engineer secret little meetings whenever she chooses. You're my husband-to-be and she'd better remember that.'

I enjoy watching him cringe as I say the words. He slides both hands into the pockets of his jeans and tries to look casual, but I see a bead of sweat dripping from his forehead, and I press on with my advantage.

'I'm meeting Liz tomorrow afternoon to arrange the fitting for her bridesmaid dress.'

Not unsurprisingly, his mood improves. 'What time?'

'About three. I'll be gone a while, so I'll pick up some party food on the way home. I thought we could invite some of the neighbours round.'

'OK, good idea. And take as long as you need.'

'There's lots to plan for the wedding, and you know how Liz likes to talk.'

He nods and I can imagine his inner self-satisfaction at the thought of getting rid of me for a few hours. We arrive at the car park, and I notice he's parked his car next to mine. Neither of us says anything as we get into our respective cars, but I can see him in my rearview mirror as I drive home.

I wonder what's going through his mind.

Chapter 21

EMILY

'How could I have been so stupid, Liz? How did I let myself be taken in by him?'

'Don't be too hard on yourself, Emily. You've joined the long line of women who fell for the wrong man. You're not the first and you certainly won't be the last. All you can do is move on and file this guy under shit happens.'

I smile, despite how angry and disconcerted I feel. Seeing Liz today is exactly what I need; she has such a knack of cutting to the chase with a perfect choice of words. We're sitting in a beautiful tea shop in a cobbled street that specializes in vintage clothes boutiques, bookshops and craft workshops. It's a quaint but trendy little place; perfect after our retail therapy. Our vintage dress purchases are sitting on the spare chair between us, as we're served afternoon tea with champagne at our table in the conservatory.

I gaze at the array of indulgent treats in front of us. 'This looks incredible. It's ironic to think we made this reservation to discuss wedding plans for the real event, and now everything's a complete mess.'

Liz raises her glass to me. 'There's no mess you can't get yourself out of. So, let's drink to that, instead of weddings. To taking control, Emily.' We clink glasses. 'Now I'm diving into this food while you tell me what's going on.'

'He's seeing his ex behind my back.'

She almost drops her smoked salmon sandwich. 'He's what? But it's only weeks since he walked out on her for you! What the hell's he playing at? And what's she doing taking him back?'

'I suppose she still loves him. Like I thought I did.'

'And how do you know he's seeing her? The tracker app?'

'Partly. Plus, I've seen them together. But there's more; he's so secretive, and he has terrible mood swings. He disappears, refuses to tell me where he's been, and if I ask him all hell breaks loose.'

'In what way? Jesus, Em. Has he been violent with you? You've got to get the hell out of there. Pronto.'

'Not physically violent, no. But there was one night…I'm almost embarrassed to talk about it.'

She takes my hand across the table. 'Tell me.'

'We were in bed. He'd got home late, I asked him where he'd been, and he totally lost it with me. Told me I was being accusing. He started treating me as if I was some sort of a whore, desperate for him. Liz, it was awful.'

'He's a bastard, Emily.'

'And there's more. He stared at me as though he literally hated me. Then in an instant he'd gone full circle, wanting me to console him and tell him he's the only man I'll ever want. That he's the best I've ever had. Stuff like that. And because I was frightened, I went along with it. I'm ashamed I did.'

'Stop blaming yourself. That was self-preservation kicking in.'

'I guess so. But something else happened, and it freaked me out. He was being all loving again, and he called out a name.'

'You're kidding me. Hers? The ex across the road?'

'Worse than that. At least her name would've made sense. But he called out…' I hesitate, hating being back in that moment. 'He said "Annabel". For a split second I thought I'd imagined it, but trust me, I didn't.'

'And that's the night you had the flashback?'

'Yes. You can imagine everything that came flooding back when I heard that name.'

'I can, of course…and I don't know what to think, Emily.'

'Neither did I; it's haunted me ever since. But he can't possibly know what that name means to me. Nobody in my new life does.'

'And he definitely doesn't know about the baby, and everything that happened around that time?'

'Of course not.'

'And you've never met him before? You're sure?'

'Absolutely sure. Not until that night in the bar.'

'Then, and forgive me, Emily, but either he said something that sounded like her name and your imagination did the rest, which would be totally understandable. Or it's someone from his past and it's an insane, cruel coincidence.'

'Which you think is unlikely. I knew you would.'

'It doesn't matter what I think. And it doesn't matter what name he called out. What matters is you need to get away from him, Emily. You can't stay in a situation like this.'

I nod at her. 'I know. And I intend to end it. I'm sure he wants me gone anyway. But he's acting as if he doesn't. In fact, he's been totally love-bombing me recently.'

'Emily. Whatever he's doing, this is toxic. Trust me, get away from him. Let his besotted ex have him back.'

'I'm biding my time.'

'What? For God's sake, Emily. Why?'

'Because he pays half my rent.'

'No. You can't let him control you because he pays half the rent.'

I stare at the blue topaz ring on my finger, mesmerised by its blue hypnotic depths. I haven't taken it off since I found Garrie with Sandie in the coffee shop. I can tell it gets to him every time he sees it. It symbolises control, and when I wear it, I'm the one with the power.

'Why should I make this easy for him and be the one to walk out? He's the one who should go. But I can't afford to keep the house on my own.'

'Don't let any of that stop you. You can try and sort something out with the rental agent and you can stay with me if you need to; you know that.'

I smile at her. 'I couldn't have a better friend than you. But there's another complication. Garrie's the rental agent, or rather his firm is. So, I need to give myself time to figure this out.'

'I'm not happy for you to stay with him, Emily.'

I pour her another glass of champagne. 'I know you're concerned about me. But can I let you into something? Awful though this is, Garrie's done me a favour.'

'Excuse me?'

'Because this is the first time I've felt in control of my life since I lost the baby, and everything went off the rails. I'm living in the moment, good or bad, instead of being haunted by my past. That's why I won't let Garrie control things anymore. I need you to raise your glass again.'

She does, but with a quizzical look. I clink my glass against hers and give her a grin.

'To me. Being back in control.'

Chapter 22

SANDIE

I'm fuming about what happened in the coffee shop. He walked out with her when we were about to have a serious conversation about the baby. Her presence overshadowed everything, and Garrie jumped to his feet as though his unborn child counted for nothing. He made me feel like his cast off, as I sat alone with tears falling into my Earl Grey.

I've ignored his calls, but his voice and text messages have been full of remorse. Now he's desperate to see me again because Emily's going out. She's apparently visiting her friend Liz today and I know he'll show up at my house as soon as she leaves. But I no longer care what he does or says because I've got more important things on my mind. Whatever goes on between them is their business. She clearly has some kind of hold over him, but he won't tell me what, so I need to stop giving them a second thought and remember Jude's words, "Kick out the rubbish."

I've decided to lose myself in my playlist. Taylor Swift's blasting out of the speakers and her music's the perfect choice in these circumstances. Morning sickness has now given way to the energizing effect of pregnancy, so I decide to dance with my tea mug as my partner. I'm swaying to the music and miming to Taylor's words when my phone's ringtone interrupts the track. I ignore it but it persists. It's Garrie. Eventually I've no choice but to answer.

'Dammit, Sandie, I'm at the door. Can't you hear me? I've been knocking and ringing the bell for ages.'

How dare he. 'No, I didn't. And I'm not sure I'd have come to the door if I had. I'm not really in the mood for the latest chapter of the Garrie and Emily story so I suggest you go home.'

In temper I end the call and my music resumes, but he appears at the lounge window and raps his knuckles on the glass. I'm tempted to close the curtains and ignore him but decide I'd better go to the door before he attracts an audience and I become the neighbours' talking point again.

As soon as I open it, he wedges his foot in the door so I've no choice but to let him in and he marches straight through to the living room and turns the music down.

'I don't know why the hell you're listening to this. Every song is about exes being shits.'

'Imagine that. I wonder where she gets her inspiration from. Maybe I should send her our story; she'd have a field day. And what the hell do you want anyway? At a loose end because Emily's out talking wedding venues and bridesmaids' dresses?'

'You know perfectly well. I came to talk about yesterday. I've tried calling and messaging often enough.'

'Oh, my bad. I'm sorry for inconveniencing you.'

'That's not what I meant. I get that you're annoyed.'

I don't know whether to laugh or throw something at him. 'Annoyed? Trust me, Garrie, annoyed doesn't come close to covering it. We had important things to discuss.'

'I know, that's why I'm here. We can discuss them now.'

'I was ready to discuss them yesterday, until you did your disappearing act. But that's your party piece, isn't it? Leaving me high and dry when you have somewhere better to be.'

'How the hell was I to know she was going to show up? She followed me again.'

'I couldn't care less how she found you. You didn't have to leave with her, but you did. Your choice. It's obvious where your loyalties lie.'

'Sandie, please, it's not like that. I need to explain stuff, but it's complicated.'

'I'm sick of that speech, Garrie. It's wearing thin. You're always "about to tell me something" but it never quite happens. I'm done with it, and…'

I stop in mid-sentence as he turns to the window with shock etched onto his features. 'Shit.'

My eyes follow his gaze and land on the image of Emily peering at us through the window. She's got the perfect view of us in the middle of our heated exchange. We both freeze to the spot and the neurons in my brain are firing in all directions. I'm trying to think of an excuse we can give her, but I remind myself her surprise arrival isn't my issue.

'I must let her in Garrie. And it's your problem to talk your way out of this one, not mine. You figure it out.'

I open the front door and Emily breezes in with a smile. I'm about to open my mouth and say the first thing that comes into my head when she speaks.

'So, this is what you get up to when I'm not around? I heard your music playing when I walked past earlier.'

I look over at Garrie who's clearly thinking of an appropriate response when Emily breaks into her annoying giggle. 'Your faces, they're classic. But don't worry. I know why you're here, Garrie. And I don't mind. It's about time we all put the past behind us. Especially as we're about to get married.' She looks at me. 'I'm sorry I've spoiled the secret; I guess he's asked you to get him in shape for our first dance at the wedding. God knows, he needs some improvement.'

I can't believe what she's saying, but her next words surprise me even more.

'Liz left early to visit her mum so I'm not as late as I thought, Garrie. I've been to the supermarket and got plenty of party food. I've spread the word to the neighbours about coming to us tonight for drinks and nibbles.' She turns her red-lipped smile on me. 'I came across to invite you to join us, Sandie. I've decided it's time we bury the hatchet. And you deserve an invite after being brave enough to dance with my fiancé. Your feet probably deserve a break too.'

'I haven't been dancing with him.'

Garrie opens his mouth to speak, but no words come out and Emily steps into the vacuum of his silence.

'Come over at seven, Sandie. Dress as casual as you like. And don't be too long getting home, Garrie, because I need some help to get everything ready.'

She turns and leaves, almost skipping out of the door. I'm stunned.

I spin round in Garrie's direction, with my hands on my hips. 'Well, that was weird. She didn't seem remotely concerned to find you here. And she certainly isn't acting like a woman who has any inkling that her fiancé's about to leave her.'

He walks towards me, but I push him away. 'No, Garrie. Don't even think about it. You need to go.'

'But I wanted to talk about us. The future. I hoped that's what you wanted. I love you, Sandie'.

'Stop it. The only thing I'm interested in is this baby's future, and I only let you in because you're its father. We have nothing else to talk about. But obviously we can't do it now. So, please take your complications, like you took everything else, and go home. I'm tired.'

'But…'

'No buts. Go.'

'I can't believe she's sprung this party on me tonight. I don't suppose you're going to come over?'

I look at him in disbelief. 'Are you joking? Of course, I'm not. You and your damn party are the last things on my mind.'

Chapter 23

SANDIE

I can't believe Emily's casual invitation to her party. She's never invited me before so she must be up to something. She breezed into my house like a whirlwind and was as cool as a cucumber at what she saw. I don't get it; she's caught us together twice so she must wonder what's going on, but she's acting as though everything is perfect between her and Garrie. Is she in denial or is Garrie playing me for a fool, saying one thing to me and another to her? Perhaps he's promising her a wedding and a future, while professing his undying love to me. Or maybe they're both playing a game and I'm the only one who doesn't know the rules.

I'm trying to focus on my latest course assignment; scrunched up post-it notes are scattered across the desk. But my attention is constantly drawn to the neighbours arriving at number 12; it looks like Emily's surprise party is in full swing.

I imagine her playing the perfect hostess in her perfectly ordered house, giggling as everybody laughs at their tacky light-up marriage sign that should have had my name on it. I wonder how many "Poor Sandie, but these things happen" comments are being made, and the thought of their displays of false sympathy gets to me. I make a snap decision and slam the laptop lid down.

'Screw it. I'll go. That'll shock everybody. Let's see how you cope with this, Garrie.'

Thirty minutes later I'm throwing on a maxi dress and sliding into gold sandals. I grab a bottle of wine from the fridge and head across the road. Number 12's door is open, and I walk in. The first person I see is nosey Linda who stares at me open-mouthed.

'Gosh. This is a surprise, Sandie. I didn't expect you to be here but it's nice to see you.'

'You too, Linda.'

'I take it you're OK with… all this? I mean, since you're here…'

'Of course. All water under the bridge now.' I deliver the most beaming smile I can and hope that's the end of the conversation.

Unfortunately, Linda's not one to let things drop. 'Did Emily invite you?'

I can't resist. 'No, I thought I'd crash the party for fun.'

Luckily, I'm saved from Linda's response by Emily, who rushes towards us looking like she stepped off a fashion show catwalk.

'Glad you could make it, Sandie. Hi Linda. Garrie's mixing cocktails in the kitchen. Please go through and help yourselves, the other guests are in the garden. And there's tons of food.'

I follow instructions and place my bottle of wine on the kitchen side table with a couple of others. I'm confronted with an uncomfortable familiarity as I spot the wedding card where I left it. I see the shocked look on Garrie's face as I walk out to the garden and inhale the soft, calming scent of late-blooming flowers.

I observe Garrie and Emily from a distance and it's like a well-choreographed act; she pours wine for the guests as he juggles two fancy cocktail shakers with his typical flamboyance. Music's playing but Emily's annoying giggle gets louder with every sip of Sauvignon Blanc. I take a glass of wine when she insists and pour it into an empty plant pot when nobody's looking. Ginger wags her tail and tries to investigate the contents, but she's too small to reach it. She seems a bit overwhelmed at all the people in her garden and Emily and Garrie are too preoccupied to notice, so I pick her up and take her inside the house. She darts to her dog basket and wrestles with the cushion as she attempts to pull the stuffing out of a tiny hole before she flops into an instant sleep as puppies do.

Since everyone's outside I make the impulsive decision to head upstairs for a look around. Like the rest of the house, it's immaculate. The type of carpet you're scared to walk on and a beautiful chandelier with crystal droplets hanging from the ceiling. The lingering odour of freshly painted walls pierces my nostrils and I smell the newness of their life together. I'm tempted to go into their bedroom, but I hear the doorbell ring. A few seconds later I hear footsteps and Garrie's voice. I remain at the top of the stairs and tilt my head so I can eavesdrop. I don't make a single movement in case the floorboards creak.

'Is Emily home?'

'She's out in the back garden serving guests.'

'Are you having a party?'

'Yes. Are you one of Emily's friends?'

'I'm Martha's mum. She has maths lessons with Emily, but she can't make it tomorrow. I was passing the house, and I thought I'd drop by to let her know.'

'OK, I'll give her the message.'

'Please tell her I'll phone her to rearrange.'

'OK.'

I hear the door close and re-position myself. My right foot was starting to get pins and needles and it's a relief to be able to flex it. I'm beginning to wish I'd never come upstairs because now I can hear Emily below, so I'm stuck up here a little longer.

'Who was that?'

'Who do you think it was?'

'I've no idea, Garrie.'

'I thought I told you not to bring children in the house.'

'What?'

'I've had the mother of someone called Martha at the door, saying they can't make it here at the agreed time tomorrow. Apparently, she brings her daughter for maths lessons which came as a surprise to me, of course. You already know my feelings about this, Emily.'

'That's why I didn't tell you.'

'I've told you before I don't want children in the house.'

'But you're at work when she comes for lessons. How does it affect you?'

'And you think that makes this subterfuge acceptable?'

'I love teaching, Garrie.'

'You're not qualified.'

'I will be one day. I'm going to teach in a primary school.'

'Maybe. But until then I do not want children in this house. Do you hear me?'

His voice gets colder and louder as he repeats himself. 'Do you hear me? I do not want children in this house.'

'Yes, I heard you. Several times.'

'You know how I feel about children, and I don't want them here.'

I hold on to the stair bannister for support. The smell of paint and the conversation I've overheard have combined to make me feel sick. I've never had a proper conversation with Garrie about children. He's got Katie so I assumed he'd want another child, but he still hasn't told me his feelings about the baby. And now I hear his aggressive outburst to Emily that he doesn't want children in the house. Almost as if he hates children. Does that mean he doesn't want to be a father to mine?

I really can't take anymore today, so I head downstairs; I need to go home to my space. I want its cosy sanctuary away from the crazy maelstrom here at number 12. Garrie is standing at the front door, but Emily's walked away. I can't bear to speak to him, so I head straight to the kitchen hoping he won't notice me. I'll leave through the garden and the side gate.

'Sandie? I thought you weren't coming?'

'I've nothing to say to you, Garrie.'

Chapter 24

EMILY

I make my getaway from Garrie's outburst when one of the neighbours appears, drapes herself around him and slurs a request for another of his special Caribbean cocktails.

I'm in the kitchen, pouring myself a glass of wine and I hear Sandie's voice coming from the hallway. She and Garrie are having a conversation.

'What are you doing here?'

'Emily invited me, remember?'

'I thought it was the last place you wanted to be.'

'I changed my mind.'

'And why were you upstairs?'

'That's the trouble with pregnancy, Garrie. It makes you need more loo trips, and the one downstairs was occupied.'

Sandie's pregnant? Devastation punches me in the stomach. I feel myself crumple at what I've overheard and grasp onto the kitchen worktop as my knees threaten to buckle underneath me. A baby between them. Please God, no.

Breathe Emily. Stay calm. Breathe again. Stay in control.

Each breath I take hurts, as my insides twist and contort with pain. Learning she's pregnant is like a stab to the heart as I imagine the idea of a new life growing inside her. I can take anything else, but not that. I truly hate Garrie more than I've ever hated anyone.

'Emily, I didn't realise you were in here.'

I spin round as Sandie appears in the doorway. 'Aren't you a dark horse?'

'I beg your pardon?'

'Don't play the innocent with me, Sandie. No wonder you've been having your secret little meetings together. How does it feel being the mother of Garrie's child?'

Her face suggests she wants the ground to open up beneath her and she's visibly flustered.

'How far along are you?'

She stammers her answer. 'I'm...not sure. Not until I speak to the doctor. I've only recently found out. Garrie knows but I haven't had a proper conversation with him about it yet.'

'Clearly.'

'What's that supposed to mean?'

'You'll find out soon enough that Garrie doesn't want children.'

'Maybe not with you, Emily.'

'He can't stand children.'

I watch her face as she contemplates my statement. 'I overheard your conversation with him.'

'About children?'

'Yes, I was upstairs. I've never heard him speak like that. I almost felt sorry for you.'

'You don't need to feel sorry for me; I'm a big girl and I can take care of myself. But nobody tells me who I can and can't have in my own home. I wish you the best of luck with the baby.'

She looks sceptical, but I can't wish harm on anyone's unborn baby, even if half of this one does belong to Garrie.

'Garrie's yours if you want him, Sandie. I'm finished with the lying cheat. But if I were you, I'd stay away from him. I've seen his dark side and it's not pretty.'

She ignores me and rushes out of the kitchen and into the hallway. Seconds later Garrie confronts me, glaring in icy silence, arms folded aggressively in a gesture of assumed male superiority. 'Well?'

'Well, what?'

'What have you said to upset Sandie?'

'I haven't said anything to upset your precious Sandie. I've just found out you're going to be a daddy. Congratulations.'

I walk away and leave him to drown in his thoughts and wallow in his own silence.

Chapter 25

EMILY

Garrie hasn't spoken to me all evening since I told him I know about Sandie's baby. I've had to endure his pretentious chatter to our guests and I'm glad they've now left so I can escape to the bedroom and hope he'll do the right thing by staying downstairs. But it seems his arrogance has no limits.

I'm lying in bed and trying to fall asleep when he appears in the bedroom doorway. I feel his eyes boring into my skin and try not to let him stir my emotions, but I'm certain he's determined to provoke me.

He sneers at me. 'You think you've got it all worked out in your pretty little head, don't you, Emily.'

'Leave me alone, Garrie.'

'You think you're so clever, don't you?'

'I said, leave me alone.'

He's clearly got fed up with giving me the silent treatment and now wants some kind of confrontation. I'm scared when his dark presence looms above me. He edges towards me, and I shut my eyes to alleviate the tension. I almost retch at the smell of whisky on his breath as he staggers into bed next to me and finally decides to reply to the comment I made hours ago.

'It's not my fault Sandie got herself pregnant.'

'What the hell do you think you're doing?'

He grabs my hair and pulls me towards him as he slurs his words. 'I'm taking what's mine.'

'You don't own me, Garrie, and you're not sleeping next to me tonight.'

I push his wandering hands away and watch his head flop back onto the pillow. Within seconds he's fallen into a drunken sleep. I'm left seething with anger and no choice but to go downstairs and sleep on the sofa. It's uncomfortable as each hour passes and sleep continues to elude me. I need him out of my house and out of my life.

When I open my eyes, sunlight pierces them through the open curtains. I must have fallen asleep because it's now 8 a.m. I walk into the kitchen to make coffee and find a note from him on the table.

See you soon sweetie xxx

A few scribbled lines on some A4 paper, closed with a seven-letter endearment, and he thinks I'll forgive and forget everything that happened at the party and the fact his ex is now carrying his baby. He gives no explanation of where he is or why he's gone out this early on a Sunday morning. He thinks I'm willing to accept anything he throws at me, but he can think again. I'll use the tracker app to follow him, and I'll confront him. He needs to know he can't come waltzing in and out of my life when it suits him. Rent or no rent, I want him gone, now. I'll pack his bags, kick him out and then decide what to do about the house.

I check the app and he's on the move, heading towards the other side of town. I fill Ginger's bowl with puppy food and message Linda to ask her to give her a walk later. I reverse my car at speed out of the garage, feeling like an amateur detective as I place my phone on the dashboard and follow the app's directions. I glance towards the park and see a few dog walkers and a couple of fathers with pushchairs, presumably trying to calm babies who won't sleep to give their mums a break. It's a life far removed from mine; the beauty and normality of motherhood that I will never experience.

The dot stops moving. I drive until I'm a couple of streets away from the address and park my car; arriving on foot will be less conspicuous until I know what I'm dealing with. It's not a neighbourhood I'm familiar with; identical wall-to-wall terraced houses line the street and the only greenery to be found is the occasional hanging basket.

It's not the sort of place I imagined Garrie to have any association with. He likes big houses with big gardens. He prefers flash cars and designer clothes. He loves the attention that comes from status. But this place is different. Walls are covered in graffiti which at least adds colour to these tired, lifeless streets. I'm getting closer to the dot. I turn a corner and see Garrie's car parked outside a parade of small shops.

A few minutes later he emerges from the florist carrying a vase but no flowers. I hide behind a wall and hope he doesn't get back in his car. He doesn't. Instead, he walks across to one of the houses and lets himself in. Now I'm even more intrigued and decide to face him head-on. I take a deep breath and walk towards the front door. It's one of those old-fashioned ones with the thick glass squares you can't see through, and I wonder what I'll discover on the other side. I knock and Garrie opens the front door, discomfort and disbelief etched on his features when he sees me.

'Emily?'

'Surprise! Aren't you going to invite me in?'

I'm amazed at how casual I sound, as if tracking my fiancé to an address he visits in secret is an everyday occurrence. Garrie is lost for words. I've caught him off-guard, and he hates that. He's a salesman who assumes he can talk his way into or out of anything but now I almost hear the cogs grinding in his skull as he tries to figure a way out of this conundrum; his 'sweetie 'showing up out of the blue.

Eventually, he speaks. 'How did you know I was here? 'Seriously, is that the best his cogs can come up with?

Before I can answer, a shrill voice calls out. 'Is that the delivery man?' Garrie flinches. 'Garrie? Did you hear me? If it's the delivery man tell him my parcel is late. And shut the door, I'm catching my death in here.'

'Coming, Mum.' He stares at me. 'Happy now? Is that the answer you were looking for? Congratulations on your clever detective work, Emily. Maybe you should take it up professionally; add sleuthing to your tutoring responsibilities. It's not as if you're qualified for that either.'

He starts to shut the door in my face, but I'm too quick for him. 'Not so fast, Garrie. We've got things to talk about. Things that can't be put off any longer.' I push past him into a hallway that has the aroma of stale tobacco, cheap perfume, and alcohol. My nose guides me into the living room and towards a woman who I suspect is younger than her appearance suggests.

'Lovely to meet you, Mrs Paisley-Jonas. Garrie never stops talking about you.' I turn to give him a quick, sarcastic smile.

His mother squints at me. 'Mrs who? Have you got my parcel?'

Garrie whispers under his breath. 'Emily, you shouldn't have come here.' He turns to his mother. 'No, Mum, it's not your parcel.'

His mother extends a trembling hand to grip mine, and her face lights up at the sight of the blue topaz ring. 'It's you, Annabel. I couldn't tell without my glasses.' She turns to Garrie. 'Why didn't you tell me Annabel was coming? I thought…'

Garrie cuts across her. 'It's not Annabel. You're getting confused, Mum. I'll get you some coffee.'

He marches out of the room, and I follow him. I heard the name Annabel this time, and his sharp intake of breath as his mother said it. So, I wasn't imagining things; he had whispered that name when we were in the bedroom.

'Who is she, Garrie?'

'Who?'

'Annabel.'

His expression hardens. 'You think you can follow me, waltz uninvited into my Mum's home and start quizzing me?' He always manages to twist things.

'I'm not quizzing you. I asked a simple question.'

'You came here to check up on me.'

'No. I came here to tell you we're finished. And I wouldn't have to follow you if you weren't so bloody secretive all the time.'

'Emily, I'll tell you why I'm secretive, it's because I'm embarrassed. My mum drinks too much.' I follow his gaze across the room to a collection of empty gin bottles next to the bin. 'She got so drunk recently that she knocked her favourite vase off the shelf, cut her arm on a piece of glass and passed out. I bought her a new vase this morning to replace it.'

'You should have told me, Garrie. We could have avoided this.'

'Avoided what? Following me because you thought I was up to no good?'

I realise this conversation is pointless and I turn to walk away. 'There's no point talking any more, Garrie. I can't live like this, and I won't. This is over between us. I'm going home and when you get back your bags will be packed.'

It's a relief to escape the toxic atmosphere of the house. I walk to my car inhaling welcome gulps of fresh air and drive straight home.

Linda must have given Ginger plenty of exercise because she barks her usual welcome at me and immediately falls into a deep puppy sleep. I look around at reminders of Garrie. A jacket tossed haphazardly over the back of a kitchen chair, a single sock in front of the washing machine waiting for its partner. His morning coffee mug left on the kitchen table as usual and now caked with dried coffee because he never bothers to rinse it in the sink. I'll be glad to see the back of all the minor niggles I once found endearing.

I allow myself a ten-minute breather in the garden. It seems inconceivable that a man I was madly in love with a matter of weeks ago is now a man I detest. But I realise it was a temporary madness. Ironically, perhaps something I needed; a brief interlude that's made me realise Martin was a wonderful husband who I regret driving away.

I head upstairs and start hurling Garrie's belongings back into his suitcase, backpack, and a black bin liner. It's cathartic knowing I'll soon be rid of him. He was playing me like a fool, but he underestimated me. My hand slides across my flat stomach, which will never swell like Sandie's. Her baby is Garrie's final twist of the knife, and this cuts deeper than the rest. I trusted him, but he abused that trust; and worse, he's been doing it right underneath my nose while pretending he wanted us to have a life together; to get married. I'm better off without him. The bitter taste of anger rises in me like bile. Garrie doesn't realise what he's done, or who he's dealing with.

But he'll find out that betrayal always comes at a price.

Chapter 26

SANDIE

I'm at my desk when I see Garrie rushing out of number 12. He glances towards my house before disappearing in the direction of his car and I shrink back at the sight of him. I'm adrift, like a boat lost at sea without an engine or navigation system, numb after overhearing his conversation with Emily about children. I wanted him to be a part of our child's life but now I'm not sure.

I scroll through the half-written essay on my laptop until my attention's drawn back to the window. Emily reverses her car out of the garage before roaring off at speed, leaving the garage door wide open. I wonder what's going on in their world even though it's none of my business.

I'm playing with my desk pendulum, enjoying the effect of kinetic energy as I watch the aluminium rod swing back and forth. I need some air and exercise to help me focus on my assignment notes. The road is quiet, but as soon as I step out of my front door Linda emerges from Emily's house with the puppy. She waves and crosses the road towards me so I can't escape her, but I could do without her vacuous babbling this morning.

'Hi, Linda. What are you doing with Ginger?'

She nods in the direction of number 12. 'Last-minute plans, I think. Emily messaged early, asking me to walk the puppy while she and Garrie were out. Not sure where they were going but I think it was a surprise outing. Almost married and can't bear to be apart. I can remember those days.' She laughs her oversized laugh.

My stomach does an angry somersault because I need answers from Garrie. He knows I'm in limbo with a baby on the way, but he's taken himself off somewhere with her. Linda's hand flies to her mouth.

'Oh my God, Sandie. I'm sorry. I'm standing here blabbering on. I forget that you two were…'

'It's fine, Linda; no need to apologise. Some things aren't meant to be, and life goes on. I'm a little preoccupied with a college assignment, that's all. A walk will help me focus.'

Ginger is pulling impatiently on her lead, and I bend down to stroke her, using the dog as a cover to hide my real feelings at the thought of Garrie and Emily together.

I get back home, put the radiators on for the first time this year and make myself a warm cup of honey and lemon. I fire up my laptop and throw all the scrappy pieces of paper littering the desk into the bin before I start another read-through and edit my essay.

As I stare absently into space hoping for inspiration, Emily's car flashes past my window and into her garage. This time she remembers to close the remote-controlled doors. I've heard nothing from Garrie. I look at the clock and make a snap decision. I promised myself I wouldn't message him, but I deserve better than this. I pick up my phone and tap angrily at the letters.

I thought I might have heard from you by now, Garrie. You must know how I'm feeling about your speech to Emily about children. It changes everything.

I decide to add another message.

PS I assume Emily's told you she knows about the baby?

The message sits unread, and I sit in abeyance, waiting for a reply. I commute between my phone screen and the laptop until I turn the phone off to get rid of the distraction. I've had enough of tiptoeing around Garrie's games with Emily. Jude's right; I'm better off without him.

By lunchtime, I've completed my essay. I hit send, relieved it's finally zooming through the airwaves to my course tutor. I rub my eyes against the tiredness of several hours' constant screen time and open them at the exact moment Garrie rushes past my house without glancing in my direction. He lets himself into number 12 and disappears into the oblivion of their home.

He still hasn't replied to my message. I have no idea what's going on behind closed doors, but whatever it is he's not sharing it with me.

Chapter 27

GARRIE

How dare she? I don't know who the hell Emily thinks she is, following me as if I'm some sort of criminal under surveillance and announcing she's ending it. She can forget that because it's not part of the plan. She doesn't get to decide what happens; I do. She walked away from my Mum's house after delivering her speech and I could have killed her. I'd love to have shut her red-lipped smart-ass mouth for good.

But I need her to suffer, and a sudden blow is not the way I want to do it. I've made sure Mum has whatever she needs and I'm sitting in the car with an extra-large coffee while I figure out my next move. I need to keep this situation under control. Two women exactly where I want them and both under my spell. I'm used to being in control; that's how I like things. But my plans have become a noisy jumble in my head. Everything's happening in the wrong order and it's a mess.

I can't keep up this double life much longer. Sandie isn't the 'other woman' type. She's like Annabel; when she loves, she loves completely, with all her heart. She's not a woman who can love but sleep alone in an empty bed. And now there's the baby. She wants me to share the joy of it with her, but I can't, because I want her all to myself. We haven't had enough time together, and despite what she says, I know when a baby arrives, I'll never be her priority again. I thought I had more time to deal with the Emily situation and win Sandie back, but this baby has blown my plan off course.

And Emily is proving trickier than I thought. She was a pushover in the beginning and now she's fighting back. I'm caught between a woman I love, a woman I hate, and a baby on the way that I don't want. The only person who can help me figure this out is Annabel, my dead wife. I close my eyes and see her beautiful face; I know she's watching and listening.

And I'm certain she wants me to bring my plan forward before I lose everything.

'I know exactly what I'm going to do, Annabel. I won't let you down.'

I throw the empty paper coffee cup out of the window and check my phone. There's a message from Sandie; I knew there would be. I decide not to reply. I know she'll be pissed off, but I need to deal with the Emily situation before I face another conversation with Sandie.

I start the engine and head towards number 12. I hear Emily in the kitchen when I walk in; she's playing her music. I slam the door behind me so she can't help but hear it. I almost trip over the bin liner sitting in the hallway next to my suitcase and bag. My favourite sweater is almost spilling out of it. How dare she treat my personal belongings with such contempt.

She's making a sandwich, but she doesn't look around. I stick to my plan; I need to call her bluff and buy myself some time. I stand behind her and talk softly to her. 'Can you do one for me? Been a tiring morning at Mum's and I could do with a hug.'

I'm about to slip my arms around her waist when she turns and pushes me away. 'Don't come near me, Garrie. Just go.'

She's still holding the breadknife and I take a step backwards. Her eyes drop to it, then back at me. 'Trust me, Garrie, it's tempting. But I'd prefer you left. Pick up your bags and make the return trip to Sandie's with them; stop dragging this out.'

'You don't really mean all that, you're being over-emotional. Have you forgotten how recently you couldn't get enough of me? Nobody changes their mind that quickly.'

'They do when they open their eyes and see a lying, manipulative cheat in front of them. Did you really think I was too stupid to see what was going on?' Her eyes sparkle with rage. 'And don't make the mistake of thinking I'm like Sandie because I'm not. She has a soft centre where you're concerned; I don't. She might be prepared to forgive you for cheating; I'm not. And it all boils down to one thing. Simple really. For some reason I think she truly loves you; I don't even like you anymore. Are we clear now?'

'Let me make something clear. Have you forgotten I've got every right to be here? I found this house, and I pay half the fucking rent. So, you don't get to dictate terms to me, Emily.'

'But you don't want to be here. You want to be with Sandie. Do the right thing for once, Garrie, and go.'

I look at my watch. Not long now until I can put my plan into action.

'Don't worry, I'm going. I'll put the bags outside the back door and collect them later. Enjoy the rest of your day.'

She seems temporarily stuck for a response as I drag my belongings through the kitchen.

'Cheer up, Emily, and trust me. You'll get what you want. You'll be sleeping alone tonight.'

I deliver a fake smile as I walk away from her.

Chapter 28

SANDIE

I'm comfort eating my way through a packet of breakfast cereal when I finally hear from Garrie.

I'm sorry. I know we need to talk. Today's been difficult. Long story. Don't know what time it'll be, but please wait up for me.

I assume he's still at number 12, but as soon as dusk falls, I close my curtains and avoid looking across the road.

Now it's dark, almost midnight, and I've heard nothing else from him. I'm tired and all I want to do is crawl into bed. I'm tempted to sleep downstairs but drag myself up to my room. I close the window shutters and see most of the houses are in darkness except for Emily's where all the lights are blazing. Whatever they've been doing all afternoon and evening it seems they're still doing it. I'm about to turn away when I see their garage doors open. Moments later Emily's car reverses out and she revs the engine as the garage doors close behind her and she speeds off into the night. I wonder where she's going this late. But I'm too tired to care so I go to bed.

I'm woken by the insistent ring of my mobile. Half-asleep, my hand forages for it on the bedside table and eventually I find it. It's 1:30 a.m. It's him.

'For God's sake, Garrie. I'm exhausted. I need to sleep.'

'I know, baby. And I'm sorry. But please come down and let me in. I need to see you.'

'I can't do this now. Call me tomorrow.'

'Sandie, please. Come downstairs. Emily's left, for good.'

'I actually don't care, Garrie.'

I lie in bed contemplating the prospect she has left him for good. I've reached the point where Emily's actions no longer affect me and that's a good place to be; I can respond to him in a more measured way if I separate myself emotionally. When the doorbell starts ringing insistently, I've no choice but to march downstairs. I see him and Ginger through the frosted glass and I open the door as far as the security chain will allow.

'Garrie, it's almost 2 a.m. Stop this and go home. I'm too exhausted to talk about anything tonight. Whatever you've got to say will have to wait.'

'But where you are is home, Sandie. You're the one I've always wanted. What could be more important than me convincing you of that?'

'No. Your home is at number 12 now. When you told Emily you didn't want children at the house it made me feel sick to the stomach because I questioned your feelings towards our child. You haven't made it clear how you feel about the baby, and I've been desperate to have a conversation with you. You've been doing God knows what all day and you didn't respond to my message for hours. And now you turn up at my doorstep expecting me to welcome you with open arms.'

'I'm sorry. I know I've messed up, but I need you to believe I love you.'

'I don't believe you, Garrie, not anymore. And even if I did, how long before you get fed up with me again and go back to her? You can't play musical chairs with a person's feelings like this. And you certainly can't do it on my doorstep at this insane time.'

'Let me in. Please. Don't make me go back across the road.'

'You should have thought of that before you walked over there the first time. You've told me she's gone so you've got the house to yourself now.' I look down at Ginger's bewildered expression. 'She looks cold, you need to get her inside; and I'm done, Garrie. I'm going back to bed.'

He looks as bewildered as the puppy as I close the door and lean back against it, exhausted.

Chapter 29

GARRIE

Sweat drips down my cheeks as I toss and turn in the murky waters of terror. There's no escape. I taste blood on my lips as I come face to face with the enemy. Her image is as white as pure snow, but her lips are red. Her lips are always red. I don't know whether to open my eyes or keep them shut. I'm hovering somewhere between my subconscious and a reality that frightens me. For a split second I forget that Emily's gone, before relief washes over me when I remember I've finally put my plan in motion and I'm alone in the bed. I wish Sandie was next to me, I should be enjoying this momentous occasion with her.

Sandie makes me feel safe, like Annabel always used to. My beautiful Annabel: I still see the radiance of her smile, as bright as it was on the day we first met.

We were in the park, and I watched her on the swing, tossing her head back and laughing as her friend pushed her. That laugh I came to know so well, and still hear in my mind every day. The sound that made me fall in love in an instant. I walked across to her and made some joke about it being my turn on the swing. She flung her head back again and giggled. After that, I returned to the park every day in the hope that I'd see her again, and a week later I did. She was sitting alone on a bench, and I was on my way to work. I caught her eye and grinned at her. 'Not on the swings today?'

It took her a few moments to recall the memory and she laughed. 'Thought I'd give someone else a chance.'

I sat next to her, and we talked until I was late for work, but it was worth it. She glowed with natural beauty, and I felt as if we'd always known each other. Any other woman I'd ever known was instantly forgotten. This was the woman I wanted.

'Maybe we should do this again over lunch?'

She smiled her agreement and from that moment we were inseparable. I'd found my soulmate; until she was cruelly snatched away from me. That's when I vowed to make Emily pay for what she'd done.

But I've hurt Sandie in the process, and I must win her back. I know she still wants me but she's slipping away from me again and I can't allow that to happen. She's keeping me at arms' length, and I suspect she's only been putting up with me recently because of the baby. My argument with Emily about children has upset her and I need to see her and explain it.

I start to message her, but I change my mind. It's better I leave her to sleep, and surprise her later with coffee and croissants. I must convince her to let me through her door today. She has no idea how much I hate Emily, and I need to find a way to make her understand my actions. I know I've got a mountain to climb to win her back.

She looked beautiful when Ginger and I stood on her doorstep even though she was angry and exhausted. Sandie radiates the same pure joy in her femininity that Annabel did; it's a halo that wraps around her flowing blonde hair and illuminates everything in its sight. She's the only light there's been in my life since my world descended into darkness. But even she can't fully penetrate the despair that's pervaded me ever since Emily destroyed everything that mattered.

Ginger's scratching at the bedroom door; it's time for her walk. As I get ready, I have an idea; I want to take Sandie a gift later. I open Emily's jewellery box and rummage around the contents until I find what I'm looking for. I open the small blue velvet box with a triumphant smile; her favourite pendant which she'll never wear again.

It will look perfect on Sandie.

Chapter 30

SANDIE

I feel more awake this morning. I've slept yesterday's exhaustion away and a warm shower has energised my mood. Garrie's asked if he can visit and I've agreed. Today, I'm ready to face him and listen to what he has to say. I need answers and at least this encounter will be in daylight.

I open the door and he's clutching a bag from our local bakery.

'Warm croissants and coffee for madame. I thought I'd better do something to make up for rocking up at a stupid time last night. Do I get to come in today?'

I want to tell him he's got more than badly timed visits to make up for but decide against it, and the aroma of freshly baked French patisserie is making me hungry. 'Bring them through to the kitchen, Garrie. I'll eat while you talk. You've got a lot of explaining to do.'

We sit at the table, and I take a welcome bite out of the croissant's buttery flakiness. 'Where's Emily? I saw her car driving away late last night.'

He looks surprised. 'You saw that?'

'When I was closing the bedroom shutters, yes.'

'Then you know she's gone. I told her I wanted to be with you. That I'd always wanted to be with you. That you're my future.'

'I won't pretend I'm sorry she's gone, Garrie. But don't assume it makes things right between us; that's not your decision to make. What makes you think I want you back?'

'Because we're meant to be together.'

'Your world is full of madness. Nothing makes any sense.'

'I can explain the madness if you'll give me a chance.'

He stretches his hand across the table to take mine, but I pull away. 'Don't, Garrie.'

'I need you to give me another chance, Sandie. That's all I ask, and I won't let you down.'

'You already did that. You were my entire world, but you walked out of it and never told me why. You still haven't. And I loved you more than anything, I really did.'

'I know, and I want you to love me again, Sandie. You've no idea how much I need that.'

'You made the decision to walk away. But this isn't about us anymore, Garrie. It's about the new life growing inside me and I need to know how you feel about it.'

He walks to the kitchen window and stares out as if he's looking for inspiration. 'I don't know where to start, Sandie.'

'Start wherever the hell you want to, Garrie, but start. I have my baby to consider now, and I need you to be honest with me.'

His shoulders tense. It's the first time I've referred to the baby as mine, not as ours. It seems the implication of that hasn't escaped him.

'It all goes back to Katie, and it's complicated. When Annabel and I got married I thought we had our future all mapped out; I had so many plans for us. Then a few months down the line she started to be sick, and it didn't take long for us to work out that she might be pregnant. I remember us staring at the test stick wondering if those two little lines would appear, and they did. It felt too soon to me, but Annabel was thrilled. I'd never seen her look so happy and that made me happy too. At least for a while. Until everything changed.' He pauses as if he's staring at a memory he'd sooner not see.

'What is it, Garrie? Tell me.'

'Our daughter Katie had beautiful blue eyes, curly hair and the most infectious giggle.'

'She sounds gorgeous.'

'She was. Everybody thought she was the perfect baby, but we soon began to realise something was wrong. She didn't interact or respond like other babies. The doctors confirmed she had physical and mental limitations and wasn't developing as she should; they couldn't tell us what the future might hold for her. And from then on, things started to change between Annabel and me. We hardly got any time together anymore. She couldn't bear to let Katie out of her sight.'

'That's understandable. It's a mother's instinct.'

'But that's why I'm scared now; I can't go through all that again. But I love you so, so much Sandie. You must believe that.'

'Garrie, stop. I understand what you and Annabel went through, I really do. But I'm sure this baby will be healthy. There's no reason to be scared.'

'But I don't want history to repeat itself. I never want to lose you like I lost Annabel. Promise you'll never leave me, Sandie.'

'You're the one that left me.'

'Tell me you'll take me back and love me like you did before.'

'That's a promise I can't make. At least I understand your feelings better, and from now on, no more secrets, please; we need to keep talking until you've told me everything. But I need to be clear with you too, Garrie; this baby's future is a top priority for me. I want my child to have a father, but only if you can accept that.'

He nods. 'I can. I will. I promise.'

He says nothing more. I don't know how he lost Annabel, why he walked out on me, or what the full story is about him and Emily, but at least he's started talking to me.

'Now tell me what happened between you and Emily yesterday.'

'Isn't it enough to know I told her it's over and she's gone?'

I suppose that should be enough, but I want to know more; it's as if being part of their conversation would be some sort of strange exorcism of Emily's spirit. 'It's not enough, Garrie. I need to know.'

'For starters, she followed me to my mum's house. Like some obsessed stalker. As if that's normal behaviour.'

'Your Mum's? Is that where you were going when I saw you leave number 12? I was sorting my workbooks at the desk when you dashed past. I wasn't stalking you.'

A smile flickers across his face. 'I know. And, yes, Mum sounded in a bad way on the phone, so I rushed over there. It was damned awkward when Emily arrived out of the blue.'

I consider his words, remembering he was sometimes secretive when we were together. He certainly never spoke about his mother. 'She was probably worried about you, if she didn't know where you'd gone.'

'That's not an excuse for following me.'

'How did she know where you were going?'

'That's what makes this even worse. She must have tracked me, somehow.'

'Maybe one of those phone apps.'

'Probably. More proof that she's unbalanced.'

He's right, that's not normal, and Emily must have been desperate. But she'd just found out her fiancé had got his ex-fiancé pregnant so her emotions must have been all over the place.

'She was dealing with the shock about the baby. I can't pretend to feel sorry for her, but…'

His response is instant and sharp. 'Don't go there, Sandie. That's how Emily manipulates people; she guilt-trips them.'

'I'm surprised she didn't end things with you. She must have been so angry.'

'I ended it. I told her you're the one I want, not her.'

'And she accepted that and walked out without a fight?'

'She was furious. She couldn't deal with the idea of living across the road from us, so she left.'

'Where's she gone?'

'Who cares?'

'When's she coming back?'

'She told me she isn't, and she asked me to keep Ginger for a while.'

'But you shouldn't have told her we were getting back together, Garrie.'

'I didn't, she assumed that. But it's what I want and I'm going to do everything I can to make you want that too.'

It's my turn to get up and look out of the window. I need to look at the world outside, beyond this house, beyond this emotional intensity.

'Nobody should assume anything, Garrie. I need to think about everything you've said. There's a lot to process. I think you should go home now. Ginger's been on her own long enough.'

'Can I come over later?'

'Not today. I need some space. And I've got coursework to do.'

'OK. But before I go, I've got you a present.'

'No, Garrie, you shouldn't be buying me presents. And you really do have to go now.'

I hear the front door close and look at my watch. He was only here for an hour but I'm swirling with emotion. When he's close to me, I still feel the pull of attraction and he's hard to resist. I walk into the lounge and the houseplant confronts me. An image of Emily seems imprinted on it. I know she's out there somewhere feeling angry and bitter, and her presence continues to haunt me.

Garrie says she's unbalanced, so God knows what she's going to do.

Chapter 31

EMILY

I open my eyes and I'm trapped. I scan my location for some kind of clue, but I don't recognise anything. I have no recollection of what happened in the moments leading up to this or why I'm here. As panic threatens to overpower me, I pull and fight against thick ropes that are cutting into my feet and wrists and preventing me from moving.

I'm confronted by the sound of my internal anguish as sharp pain shoots through my head and forces me out of semi-consciousness. I try to lift my hand to massage the constant throbbing in my temples, but I can barely move. My eyes are open and yet I squint against the unfamiliar surroundings. I'm not in my bed and this isn't my home. Everything feels hazy as I'm catapulted into this state of semi-darkness. I have no idea where I am. Panic rises in my throat at what feels like a nightmare; but the pain in my body is real. I've had enough flashbacks to know that this is reality and I need to stop struggling, take a breath, and calm down so I can find a way to escape.

My hands are numb from being clasped awkwardly behind my back, but I try to wiggle my fingers. Relief that I can move them collides with shock when they make direct contact with the rough rope. Why would anyone want to do this to me? It takes a few moments until my brain springs into action and triggers me to shout at the top of my voice. I'm so dehydrated that the vibration of the sound jars against my cracked lips.

Mixed-up, random thoughts attack my head from every direction as I try to recall my last memory. I was in my house, I'd told Garrie we were over, and I wanted him to leave. He walked out and said he'd be back to pick up his bags.

I remember enjoying my nighttime bath and going downstairs to make my usual cup of milky coffee to take to bed. His bags were outside the back door. I don't remember much after that, but I know I was relieved Garrie was out of my life. I must have drifted off to sleep. And after that everything's a blur, until I woke up in this strange place.

My breath quickens again as I try to absorb my surroundings in the faint light. The room looks old, with misshapen walls, an empty log fire and a wooden floor. I look up at a ceiling heavy with thick, black, character beams. I'm sitting on a traditional green leather sofa and my hands and feet have been tightly tied to its legs. I continue shouting as loudly as my dry mouth will allow but my voice simply echoes back.

I'm engulfed by the sound of silence; I never knew it could be so deafening. I scan the room for clues and see a collection of roughly arranged ornaments on the shelves. The air is musky and damp with suspended dust particles that are highlighted by the weak autumn sun glinting through a small window in the side wall. It's a room that appears to have lost its breath; empty, cold, unlived-in and without love. I shiver and realise I'm wearing the thin nightshirt I wore to bed last night.

I resume my struggle against the ropes while I try to think of an explanation for all this. I told Garrie to leave, but surely, he wouldn't do something like this in retaliation. I'm thinking about those times he changed in an instant and his eyes filled with darkness because he was mad with me. I didn't recognise him in those moments and now I'm wondering if he's capable of doing something this evil. My mind is in overdrive, and I scream into the vacuum of silence as desperation rises in my chest and I taste the acrid flavour of fear.

I'm more frightened than I've ever been in my life.

Chapter 32

GARRIE

It was almost too easy. I had to improvise when she decided to throw me out, but my plan was genius; everything worked to perfection. I left her in the afternoon, looking pleased with herself; she probably thought she'd got the better of me. She knows differently now.

I drove to a town thirty minutes away where I'd be anonymous and bought everything I needed from the busiest DIY store I could find. Back in the car I ran my fingers along the coarse fibres of the thick rope and imagined the imprint they would leave on Emily's wrists and ankles later. When dusk descended, I drove back towards number 12 and parked a few streets away. I walked to the back of the house and crept unseen to my vantage point under the willow tree.

And I waited. I knew exactly what her routine would be. As soon as the bathroom light went on around 10 p.m. I made my next move. It took me ten minutes to sprinkle crushed benzodiazepines into the coffee jar, enough to sedate her, and get back to my hiding place. Half an hour later, right on cue, the kitchen light went back on, and her figure appeared at the sink in front of the window. She filled the kettle and scooped coffee mixed with my perfectly concocted sleeping pill into her mug. It was so satisfying to watch, and I could scarcely believe my own brilliance. When the downstairs lights went off, I kept checking my watch until I could be sure the pills would have worked.

I crept upstairs and found her flat out cold on the bed. Shit. Had I overdone the benzodiazepines? This wasn't the end I had planned for her. But she was breathing, so I could breathe again too. I left her lying there while I went through the checklist on my phone. I brought the bags she'd packed for me back into the house, took them upstairs and unpacked them. Then I packed a few of her things into her initialled suitcase and vanity bag. I switched off her phone and slipped it into my jacket pocket.

Satisfied, I deleted the list and carried her bags to the garage before I went back for her. Getting her downstairs was tougher than I'd anticipated. I hadn't realised a dead weight could feel so heavy; she's such a fragile thing when she's awake. But I got her into the boot of her car, along with her bags and went back into the house for a final check. Satisfied I'd covered my tracks, I took Emily's favourite pink cap and jacket from the coat-stand. Then I remembered the coffee jar. How could I almost have forgotten that? I grabbed it, put it in a plastic bag and replaced it with a new one from the cupboard. I filled Ginger's bowl with some biscuits and headed back to the garage.

With Emily's cap pulled low over my face and her jacket draped around me with the collar turned up I reversed her car out as noisily as I could, as if she was driving away in a temper. Ten minutes from the house I dumped the coffee jar in a public refuse bin and drove Emily to her destination. Getting her inside unseen was easy, and once she was, I sat and looked at her; unconscious, helpless, and totally at my mercy. The days and nights I'd dreamt of this moment and now she's exactly where I want her. I've found a way to get my revenge. I close my eyes and look up.

I've done it, Annabel. I've kept my promise. And I'll make her pay for what she did.

Now it's time to make things right with Sandie. I can't tell her the whole truth, but I must find a version of it that's enough to make her understand. And to forgive me.

Chapter 33

SANDIE

He's standing on the doorstep looking sheepish; an expression I used to find endearing, but not anymore.

'Garrie, you must stop showing up like this. You're not giving me any space to think.'

'I can't stay away, Sandie. I love you; I need to be with you. Let me in and hear me out, please.' He reaches into his jacket pocket and passes a small paper bag to me. 'I brought your gift.'

'I told you. I don't want gifts, Garrie.'

'I saw it and thought it was perfect for you.'

'Why don't you keep it and give it to your Mum? I'm sure she would appreciate it.'

'No. I chose it for you.'

I reluctantly peek inside the bag where there's a small, blue velvet box. 'I hope this isn't something expensive, Garrie.'

He smiles. 'It's something to say I'm sorry for the way I've been acting.'

'A gift won't change anything between us.'

'Can I at least come in for a while?'

'What for?'

'I'll make you some tea while you open your gift. And then I'll go, I promise.'

I step back to let him in. 'You can stay for half an hour. I need to study before I go to work.'

In the kitchen he puts the kettle on as I sit down and take the box out of the bag. I notice it looks a little worn, but I don't say anything.

He grins. 'I knew curiosity would get the better of you. You remind me of Katie at Christmas.' His face distorts for a second as he obviously recalls a distant memory. Then he nods at the small velvet box. 'Go on, have a look inside. I hope you like it.'

'I suppose we're all kids at heart when we get presents.' He's never given me a surprise gift; something I would have loved when we were together, but now I feel awkward about it. I lift the lid and a silver heart stares up at me from a bed of blue tissue paper. The single stone at its centre sparkles in the afternoon sunlight.

'Garrie, I can't accept this. It's too much.'

'Don't be silly. Try it on. I know it'll look perfect on you.'

'It's lovely, but...'

'Not as lovely as you.'

'Stop. That's enough. And no more presents.'

He ignores me, drapes the pendant around my neck and fastens the clasp. My skin involuntarily tingles from the sensation of his touch, and I quickly retreat to the lounge and sit on the sofa.

'You relax, my darling. Here's your tea.' He moves closer and old memories resurface. I'm tormented by the familiarity of him that makes me want to fall into his arms. Emily's departure has made me think about rekindling what we once had and that's terrifying. I know I'm romanticising and imagining an ideal scenario in my head. I'm reverting to the feelings of love we had at the beginning of our relationship, but I remind myself that my internal fantasy of us living happily ever after as a family is not real.

'You're deep in thought.'

'I'm thinking about what you gave up, and wondering why you left me for her, Garrie.'

'I'll spend the rest of my life trying to make things right if you'll let me, I promise.'

'Don't make promises you can't keep.'

'I never stopped loving you.'

'You keep saying, but it doesn't change what you did.'

'It's over with Emily, but nothing ever started with her. I was always in love with you, have been from the moment I met you.'

'That's the part I'm struggling with, Garrie. You were prepared to leave me for someone you say you didn't even love. You broke my heart, and I don't know why you did it.'

'That's why I'm here. It's time I shared some things with you. I didn't meet Emily by chance like she thinks, Sandie; I planned it. She knew my wife and my daughter. I never met her in person, I only ever saw her from a distance, but she was Annabel's friend and my daughter's tutor. And she's to blame for my wife's death.'

My hand flies to my mouth. 'Oh my God, Garrie. But you said Annabel's death was an accident?'

'Yes. But it wouldn't have happened if Emily hadn't got involved in our lives and destroyed us. She's the reason Annabel is dead.' He turns to me with dark, almost venomous eyes. 'I detest her, and I wish she was dead.'

'Garrie, I'm sorry, but I must ask this. What did Emily do, exactly?'

'She turned Annabel against me. And she got obsessed with Katie. Apparently, she lost a child of her own and she couldn't handle the grief.'

'That's the worst loss a woman can experience, Garrie. It's a long grieving process for everybody.'

He spits his response out. 'But everybody doesn't turn into a monster who tries to destroy somebody else's family, like Emily destroyed mine. And I vowed I'd find a way of hurting her like she hurt us.'

'What were you planning to do?'

'I had no idea. I only knew I needed to get close to her and find a way to make her suffer like I did. I followed her routine for a while. And one night I went to her favourite bar in town when I knew she'd be there, and I reeled her in.'

'I knew you didn't normally go to the Tanet bar.'

He spins round. 'What?'

'Sorry, remembering something Emily said. Please, go on, Garrie.'

'When the house across the road went up to let, I saw it as the perfect opportunity to get close to her.'

'You arranged that?'

'It was with our estate agency so it was easy, and it meant I could be close to you, Sandie.'

I walk to the window and look across at the vacant number 12 opposite, remembering how it had felt the day he'd walked across to it with his bags, abandoning me. 'But you left me.'

'Only because Emily gave me an ultimatum. And I panicked. You were never part of the plan, Sandie. I never expected to fall so much in love with you. I was in turmoil; desperate to finish what I'd started and punish Emily, and desperate to spend the rest of my life with you.'

'So why couldn't we simply have got on with our lives, Garrie? Maybe I could have helped you forget about punishing Emily. And two wrongs don't make a right.'

'I wanted to; believe me I did. But I'd made a promise to my wife that I would make Emily pay for what she did. It's the one last thing I was able to do in my wife's memory.'

'But we were getting married, and you should have been able to tell me this sooner. We could have worked through it together.'

'I wish I'd had the courage to tell you.'

He puts his arms round me and I let my head press against his chest. For the first time in ages, I allow my emotions to resurface instead of blocking them.'

'I'm back, Sandie, and for good this time.'

'But what about Emily?'

'She's gone.'

'But where?'

'To stay with an aunt, I think. I don't care.'

'Should I be worried about her? She's out there feeling angry, Garrie. And after what you've told me…'

He pulls me tighter to him. 'You've nothing to worry about. You'll never have to see Emily again.'

'How can you be so sure?'

'I know her. Her pride's hurt: she'll never want to come back here.' He kisses the top of my head. 'And anyway, you've got me to protect you.'

'And what about your revenge plan?'

'I've realised I can't change the past. Nothing will ever bring Annabel back so it's time to focus on the future and the woman I love.'

'And our baby.'

I stroke Ginger's head as she bounds into the bedroom and her brown eyes stare into mine. I wonder what her little brain makes of all this.

'I love you, Sandie.' He presses his lips against mine and I succumb to his advances. I decide not to resist temptation and to let my emotions take centre stage. I'm no longer the woman scorned because he didn't leave me for another woman. He left me because he was heartbroken from losing his wife. Grief can drive people to do strange things sometimes and he needed an outlet for his anger and pain.

Now I'm conflicted because I want the Garrie I once had, the one who hadn't yet done all those hurtful things to me. But it's impossible to completely erase things like that, even after what he's told me; being hurt changes a person. I'm not the same Sandie who once trusted wholeheartedly. I'll always be more cautious and maybe that's a good thing. If I give in to him, I'm at least going into this with my eyes wide open, no illusions, and I'll be on my guard until I can properly trust him again.

He leads me into the bedroom and after thirty-minutes of urgent, but gentle love-making I sink contentedly into the arms of the man I desire, and feel it's where I should be.

'I love you, Sandie.'

'It's too soon for me to say it back, Garrie. I'm not sure I can ever trust you unconditionally like I did before. I hope I can, and I really hope you can prove to me you mean it.'

'I do mean it, Sandie.'

'But it's not going to be easy to come back from all this and I don't know if I can recover from what you did, but I'm willing to give it a try. That's the best I can do.'

'That's all I ask. That you learn to love me again. I need your complete and undivided love.'

'It's going to take time, Garrie. But please don't hurt me, I honestly can't take any more hurt.'

He hugs me closer, and I feel safe in his embrace. I'm willing to give him one last chance.

But one thing worries me, despite his reassurances; Emily has more reason than ever to hate me and my baby. I don't know exactly how she contributed to Annabel's death, or how unpredictable she could be, and I wish I did.

She feels like a dangerous enemy to have.

Chapter 34

SANDIE

I allowed Garrie to stay last night. He's about to leave for work and he walks across to me with a huge grin on his face and plants tiny kisses on my forehead. I breathe in his scent as his lips trace down towards my neck.

'I don't know how I can ever make it up to you, Sandie; I know what I've put you through. But I'll spend the rest of my life trying if you'll let me, I promise.'

'Be truthful from now on. That's all I ask.'

'I love you, Sandie. I'll see you later.'

He keeps saying it, and I haven't felt this happy for a long time, but I can't quite let myself believe this is real. Fear flutters in my stomach when I remember recent events, along with the butterflies I always feel when he's close to me, but I tell myself to stop overthinking and sink back down into my soft feather pillow.

I spend the next hour listening to my favourite music on Spotify, immersing myself in the lyrics of romance, as if every song was written for us. I close my eyes and see Garrie, me, and the baby. Our future is within touching distance, and it excites me.

I eventually pull myself out of bed, slide into my most comfortable dress and gloss my lips before heading downstairs. As I fire up my laptop, I notice two people at Emily's front door; a woman and a young girl who I'm guessing is one of her students. I've seen them a few times when Garrie's been at work. I slip a scarf around my shoulders and walk across the road. The mother seems to recognise me.

'Martha's here for her maths lesson.'

As I approach them, I wish I hadn't, because I have no idea what to say. I simply stammer out a weak 'She's not here.'

'Martha is booked in for her lesson now. Do you know what time she'll be back?'

She looks impatient, and Martha looks agitated as she pushes her face against the front door's frosted glass. My cheeks burn as I remember doing that myself when I first visited Emily's house. Now I feel sorry for this little girl in front of me, and I keep my reply as gentle as I can. 'I think she's gone away for a while.'

Disappointment is etched onto her face when she turns to me. 'She can't have gone. She said she'd be here. She promised I could feed Hoppy.'

Martha's mum tells me about the rabbit, who seems to be more of an attraction to her daughter than the maths lesson. 'When will she be back?'

I say the only thing I can. 'I don't know, but if I see her, I'll tell her you were here. The best thing is probably for you to call her.'

I make a swift exit and go home. I'm about to start work at my desk when I'm surprised to hear a buzzing sound from upstairs. I trace the noise to our bedroom and realise it's coming from Garrie's sock drawer. I slide it open and see one of those old flip phones. Garrie has got the latest silver android one so it's not his. It's vibrating and I flip it open and see the caller ID flashing up on the screen. *Martha's mum.*

I stare at it in disbelief until it stops. I press the home button, but it's secured by a pin. This must be Emily's phone. Why the hell has Garrie got her phone in his sock drawer?

Suspicion floods my brain. I try to suppress it, but I know whenever something out of the ordinary happens I'm going to immediately jump to conclusions like I'm doing now. I replace the phone exactly where I found it and tell myself there must be a simple explanation why it's in my bedroom.

I'll ask Garrie about it when he gets home.

Chapter 35

EMILY

I never imagined I would be in a situation like this; I doubt anybody ever seriously does. Trapped in an unknown house full of shadows that I don't recognise. Soundless apart from the repetitious rumbling of car engines and a glimmer of life through a small window above my eye-line, which gives me some hope of a world beyond this strange building where I'm being held hostage. I've no idea how long I've been sitting here since I woke up, but the light's fading again so it must have been hours and I'm desperate to use the loo.

I look down at the rope that stings my wrists even more, because I've tried so hard to break free of it. I've used energy I should have conserved. I'm mentally and physically exhausted and dizzy from dehydration. I listen for any indication I'm not alone, but there's no sign of life within these walls. Just the occasional creak from an old house that struggles to breathe in the dark. I hate the darkness. It scares me and takes me back to the time I was rushed to Lake View hospital. It was dark that night, too. It's the only time I've ever been as scared as I am now. I shake my head to try and eliminate the images that are now taking centre stage underneath my eyelids. I don't want to relive the worst night of my life, especially not here in this awful solitary confinement, but the memories are too powerful, and they take me hostage.

≈ ≈ ≈

2 Years Earlier

My husband, Martin, has gone to the pub. It's the first time he's gone out for the evening in weeks. We've been told my pregnancy is high risk and I must rest. But I've encouraged him to take a night off for once because he does everything for me, and he needs a break. He wants to protect me, and the baby, and I love him so much; he is a wonderful husband. But I'm happy to have an evening lying quietly on the sofa with some reality TV while he has a few beers with a friend at our local pub.

But disaster strikes. As crippling cramps become more intense, I call him before I pass out with the pain. I lie motionless in the foetal position and remember nothing else until I open my eyes and I'm with Martin in the ambulance. He grips my hand as though his life depends on it and the sound of the emergency siren screams into the late-night emptiness of the city. Everything happens so quickly, but the image of Martin's ashen face is ingrained in my mind as the nurses wheel me away from him. I pray with all my heart that my baby can live instead of me as I fight against a mask that is being placed over my nose, then everything goes black until I wake up and my baby has gone. The doctors have saved my life, but I've died inside.

They're telling me there were complications. A word that is used to soften the blow of something unthinkable. An unbearable situation apparently made more acceptable because complications happen. Complications that will change my world forever.

Martin and I hold hands in silent devastation; this was our last throw of the dice. We wanted to have a baby more than anything in the world and I've lost count of the doctors we spoke to and the amount of money we spent trying to make it happen. We'd almost given up when our miracle baby was conceived and surprised us for five glorious months as we anticipated her arrival into the world. Our baby daughter who I carried long enough for her to have her own identity. And a name. My beautiful baby Annabel. But suddenly she's gone.

I lie in the hospital bed, empty, watching my heart beating on a small screen. I'm too frightened to sleep because I know, when I wake up, I will again have to face the truth of what's happened. And what I've lost.

≈ ≈ ≈

I would have been happy in that moment for my wrists to be tied exactly as they are now. I would have been happy to have never gone outside to face the world again.

Chapter 36

SANDIE

Jude answers my call on the third ring as she always seems to, probably anticipating today's episode of what she calls the "Life with Garrie show."

'Hi. Are you OK? What's the latest on Mr. Wrong? What's he done now?'

I stifle a half giggle. Jude's a straight talker who doesn't hold back on her opinions. I don't think she'll ever stop being suspicious of Garrie and she's convinced he'll hurt me again.

'I know you think I'm mad to take him back, Jude. I'm under no illusions about what he's done in the past and if this was the other way around, I would be saying the same to you. But it feels right to try again. I'm not sure what the future holds, and I can't help having doubts but I'm going into this with eyes wide open, trust me. It's a risk, I know, but one I'm willing to take. If I didn't still have feelings for him, I would walk away as fast as I could in the opposite direction. But he seems to be truly sorry for what he did.'

'I hope you're right, Sandie, and I want my instincts to be wrong about him. I really do hope Miss Red Lips is a thing of the past. I don't want to see you caught up in his issues and their backstory again.'

I'm sitting on the edge of the bed and her words make me glance at the chest of drawers where Emily's phone is nestling among Garrie's socks. I tell myself for the umpteenth time today there must be an innocent explanation, but it continues to niggle away at me.

'I know. But at least he opened up to me about why he did everything he did. None of that can have been easy for him, Jude. Especially for someone like Garrie. You and I might think his behaviour was strange, but he was grieving and confused.'

'God knows he owed you some answers and it was about time he was straight with you. But since it's Garrie you should check the small print too.'

We both laugh and it lightens the mood.

'Do you want me to cover your shifts for the next couple of days? It'll give you chance to spend more time with him if that'll help.'

'You read my mind. Thanks, Jude; you're such a good friend. I'd never have got through all this without you.'

'You know I'm always here for you. I want everything to work out for you, Sandie.'

We end the call and I put an excited Ginger on her lead; I'm late taking her for her walk.

As we pass Emily's empty house, I see the side gate to the back garden is swinging in the brisk wind. Linda appears in a panic.

'Sandie. I haven't seen Emily in the garden feeding the rabbit like I usually do. Do you know what's going on?'

'Emily's away, Linda. And Garrie must have forgotten to do it.'

I see the quizzical look on Linda's face as she considers the combination of evidence at her disposal.

'She didn't tell me she was going away. And what do you mean, Garrie forgot this morning? And why have you got Ginger?'

I'm beginning to wish I hadn't walked the dog this morning. The last thing I need is an interrogation from Linda.

'I'm not sure where she's gone. She told Garrie she needed time away to clear her head.'

'Why would she want to clear her head?'

'She's not with Garrie anymore. They've split up.'

I seem to have shocked Linda into uncharacteristic silence. I almost giggle at her expression as she absorbs that newsflash. Linda doesn't like surprises.

'This is all very sudden, Sandie. I'm surprised she hasn't called to tell me this herself. She always asks me to look after things when she's away.'

'Garrie's been left with Ginger and the rabbit to look after while she's away.' I contemplate telling her we've moved back in together but decide against it.

'I'll give Emily a call later to make sure she's OK.'

I try not to dwell on the image of her call to Emily reverberating through Garrie's sock drawer. She looks visibly flustered as she leans towards the hutch to check on the rabbit. I'm relieved when Hoppy lives up to his name and greets us both through the bars. The food and water bowls are empty, so he's clearly been forgotten.

'Would you mind sorting the rabbit, Sandie? I haven't got time because John's waiting for me. His brother's ill, so we're going to visit him.'

'Of course. Where's the food? If it's inside, I'll need the key.'

She jumps when her phone bleeps with a message. She looks even more agitated. 'It's John. He wants to leave now.'

'Then you must go. Leave this to me.'

She hands me the key. 'Use this but pop it straight back through my letterbox afterwards. And don't forget the alarm.'

'What's the code?'

'It's Emily's birthday, 1509. The rabbit food is in the larder with the hutch key. Now I need to dash.'

I let Ginger off her lead, and she runs straight to a patio chair, curls up on the cushion and falls into instant puppy sleep. It's funny that dogs can jump back into a routine without a second thought. I walk round to Emily's front door and stare at the key in my hand; I feel uncomfortable about letting myself in. This house has made me feel uneasy from the first time I walked into it with

Emily, and now I'm about to walk into it with no idea where she is. I hesitate for a moment, then I slowly turn the key in the lock.

Chapter 37

EMILY

I open my eyes and see a dark figure standing in the doorway. My initial reaction is to scream but nothing comes out. I blink a few times to make sure I'm not hallucinating, but he edges closer, and I see his face clearly. It's Garrie.

'Hello, my sweetie.'

His words penetrate my skin like osmosis. I can hardly move, I'm too scared to even speak, and for a moment I'm convinced I've stopped breathing. Garrie fumbles in the rucksack he's carrying and produces a bottle of sparkling Pellegrino. He lifts it towards my lips, and I cough and splutter as I try to quench my overwhelming thirst. Fear trembles through me as I come face-to-face with the man I once loved. The man I thought I wanted to spend the rest of my life with.

'I desperately need to use the loo, Garrie.'

'Oh, sweetie. You'll have to promise to behave if I give you that luxury.'

I think back to every time he's called me "sweetie". The notes left on the kitchen table, the odd text message when he goes missing. It's not a term of endearment from him; it isn't love. It's a sugar-coated word that's a weapon in Garrie's hands; one he used to sweeten me, so I wouldn't question him.

'Just let me use it before I have an accident, please.'

'Don't worry, I won't tell anyone that you can't hold your drink.'

He laughs and then carefully unties one hand at a time so that he can clasp them both together. It's awkward and embarrassing as he uses his strength to make sure I follow his instructions. He pushes me into the hallway and through a door into a small cloakroom with a loo and a washbasin.

'Don't be long.'

He keeps the door ajar and whistles as if he's enjoying humiliating me. I stare at the walls but there's no escape. I look around for something sharp but there's nothing. I have no choice but to allow him to drag me back to the sofa and tie me up again.

'I don't understand what's happening, Garrie. Why are you doing this?'

He doesn't reply, but wordlessly breaks a KitKat into bitesize pieces and feeds them to me. I want to spit them out, but I accept them. I need to eat something. He clearly doesn't want me to die, at least not yet and I take that as a good sign. I need to appear to co-operate and to appease him, so I force myself to play nice.

'We can get through this, Garrie. Whatever it is we can get through it.'

I don't believe that any more than he probably does but I need to say whatever it takes to find a way out of this situation, and fast. I've no idea what his next move might be or when he's thinking of making it.

His phone rings and I see him hesitate before he replies to whoever's calling. 'I'll be back as soon as I can.'

Then he leaves without any explanation to me.

Chapter 38

SANDIE

I look down at the key in the lock and my fingers freeze; another quarter turn and Emily's front door will click open. Once the alarm triggers, I'll have no choice but to walk into her house and I'm not sure how I'll feel once I do. Nothing good has ever happened to me on the few occasions I've crossed the threshold of this house. I consider abandoning my plan until I hear a car engine and see Linda and John on their driveway. They're busy loading the boot of the car for their journey so I know I must complete "mission rabbit rescue" now. Linda's the type of person who'll check I'm following her instructions, so I give the key its final turn, push the door and step inside. My fingers are poised to punch Emily's date of birth into the alarm keypad but there's no alarm tone. Garrie must have forgotten to set it.

The house is silent apart from the ticking clock in the hallway. I check the security control panel to the left of the door again, but no lights are showing. I have the horrible thought that Emily might be inside the house. Maybe she came back and she's upstairs.

I call out a faint 'Hi, Emily, it's Sandie. I've come to check on the rabbit.' I'm relieved when there's no reply and I tell myself to stop being ridiculous. Of course, she's not here. I haven't seen any sign of her or her car since the night she drove away. *Get a grip, Sandie. Pull yourself together, do what you came to do, and leave.*

I start to question what I'm doing inside her house. I want the rabbit to be OK, and I'm following Linda's instructions, but I'm curious to look around. After everything that's happened, I've become less trusting of

Garrie, and finding Emily's phone hasn't helped. I'm almost ashamed of myself because I'm wondering if he's really told me everything.

I walk towards the kitchen then turn back and lock the front door from the inside and tuck the key into my dress pocket. Surely a quick look around isn't going to hurt while I've got this chance. I start with Emily's kitchen which is decidedly less perfect than on my previous visits. Several overlapping coffee rings have dried onto the normally pristine white island worktop and the mug that caused them is standing in the sink alongside two unwashed plates, and a frying pan. Two half-full wine glasses, one with Emily's red lipstick imprinted on it, sit next to the kettle. The kitchen table is cluttered with paperwork and an open laptop which must be Emily's. She didn't take her phone or her laptop with her. I'm feeling increasingly uneasy about her disappearance and worried that there's something Garrie's not telling me.

I open the larder door and see Hoppy's food, with a key next to it and a little tag that says 'hutch'. I grab it and let myself out of the back door.

'You were a long time.' It's Linda checking up on me as I knew she would. 'Everything OK in there?'

I decide to lie about the alarm not being connected. 'All fine Linda. I've been looking for the rabbit food. I won't be long, and I'll post the key back through your letterbox.'

'Fine. I need to dash.' She sounds stressed but relieved. 'Will catch up when I get back. Thanks for sorting the rabbit.'

I hear their car drive away as I watch a hungry Hoppy munch down his food. I take the water container into the house to fill it and glance around the kitchen again. Linda's away now and Garrie won't be home for hours. I've been handed an unexpected opportunity to explore the rest of the house and learn more about Emily. Ginger is now up to mischief, and I see her through the kitchen window digging up a dried pig's ear that she must have buried in the garden. She bounds into the house with muddy paws and a puzzled look as she places it carefully under the kitchen table. She knows where she is and settles down to munch her buried treasure as if she's never left. I've kept my promise to Martha and made sure the rabbit's safe. There's no reason to stay, but curiosity about Emily continues to get the better of me.

I talk to my baby bump. 'Your mother isn't normally a snooper, little one. I'm doing this for a reason, but we won't tell anyone.'

Ginger is still preoccupied but I talk to her anyway. 'I'll give myself ten minutes to look around. You stay here while I go upstairs.'

I walk out of the kitchen and spot something I didn't see earlier. A mobile phone charger is plugged in next to the sideboard; it must be Emily's. I unplug it and slip it into my jacket pocket. At the top of the stairs, I pause outside Emily's closed bedroom door, debating whether to push it open. Irrationally, I feel she's watching my every move; her claustrophobic presence is everywhere in this house even though she's gone.

A noise from downstairs startles me. I smile when Ginger appears with her tail wagging. My imagination is getting out of hand; perhaps pregnancy heightens all the senses. I look at the bedroom door. I'm here, I should go inside; I may never get this chance again. I push the door open as another sound from downstairs stops me in my tracks. This time it isn't Ginger. She's next to me crying to be picked up and I realise I'm shaking.

My breathing quickens as I hear somebody unlocking the front door and I wish I'd remembered to leave the key in the lock. I lean against the wall wondering what to do. Ginger has run back downstairs and is barking like crazy. I'm trying to listen, but I can barely hear myself think; she's got the loudest bark for such a small dog.

'Hey, Ginger, what are you doing here?'

Oh my God, it's Garrie. I spring into action and leap to the top of the stairs so he can see me.

'Hi. I'm here, too. I needed the loo. Did you forget about the rabbit?'

'What?' He looks totally perplexed about my surprise appearance on the landing and my garbled response.

I try to sound matter of fact as I walk downstairs to join him. 'The rabbit, Hoppy. Nobody's been feeding him.' I see the cogs whirling in his brain. 'Linda gave me the spare key to sort him out today. But you'll need to give me yours for next time because she wants hers dropping back through the letterbox.'

He looks totally bewildered.

'And I've done the washing up.'

'What?'

'The washing up. There were things left all over the place, so I decided to clean it up. Emily wouldn't want it left like that.'

'Right.'

Luckily, I seem to have knocked him off-balance. I haven't given him chance to question why I was upstairs using the loo rather than using the one next to the kitchen. He looks confused but I have a question for him. 'What are you doing here anyway? I thought you'd be coming straight home to me.'

His pause is longer than it should be. 'I was on my way home from work, and I suddenly remembered the rabbit.'

'I guess it's easy to forget with everything else that's happened. Did Emily remind you about the rabbit when she asked you to look after Ginger?'

He sounds flustered. 'I don't think she did. But it was a difficult evening. I don't suppose Hoppy was high on her list of priorities.'

'By the way, I heard Emily's phone vibrating in your sock drawer.'

'I took it off her. After she'd followed me to my mum's house, she eventually told me she'd been tracking me on some app on her phone.'

'Really?'

'There's no way I was letting her keep it so she could spy on me. She'll have to get another phone.'

He grabs my hand. 'Anyway, enough of Emily. Come on, let's go home.'

I reach up to the alarm with my other hand and punch in the numbers so we can escape from this clinical house and get back to our cosy home. He's given me an explanation about the phone, and I need to convince myself there's a logical explanation why Emily didn't take her laptop. Unless I can stop questioning and doubting everything, I'll never be able to move forward and make this work.

Chapter 39

SANDIE

We're home and Ginger is prancing around with her new toy dinosaur, trying to get the squeak out of it. She's never happier than when she's destroyed the squeak in a new toy. Garrie has made a pot of tea and put little biscuits onto a tray and I'm taking a snapshot in my mind of this scene. It's the simplicity of our domestic tableau that makes it so wonderful; we feel like a family, and in this moment, I can hardly believe Emily ever existed. We get snuggly on the sofa, and I drape my new blanket over our legs to take the chill off until the heating kicks in. It's that time of year when it's difficult to decide whether the heating should be on or off. We're both dropping crumbs onto the blanket, but we don't care.

My eyelids droop into a deep sleep in Garrie's arms with Ginger lying between us. I wake up to a loud noise screeching out of the television; it's something on the horror channel. I smile at the sound of Garrie snoring his way through it. That's one thing I would change about him, his horrendous snoring.

I pull the blanket over his legs, kiss him gently on the cheek, and sneak upstairs to bed. Snuggled under the duvet I reflect on my visit to Emily's house. I can't believe I nearly went into her bedroom. Snooping isn't normally my thing, but the opportunity was too tempting. I'm not sure what I thought I might find, but if I decide to look around again, I'll make sure Garrie isn't likely to unexpectedly turn up.

I look over at his sock drawer, thinking about Emily's phone again. But he's given me a reasonable explanation why it's here, so I decide to go downstairs to see if he's awake and wants to join me. Being in bed doesn't feel right without him. But the sofa is empty; he's not there and neither is Ginger.

'Garrie? Where are you?'

I'm greeted by silence.

I call his mobile, but he doesn't answer. I assume he must have taken Ginger for a walk. If he'd woken me, I would have gone with him. I try his number again and this time he answers.

'Sandie? Are you OK?'

'I'm fine. Where are you?'

'Ginger needed to go out.'

'I would have come with you if you'd said.'

'I didn't want to wake you.'

'Try not to be too long.'

He rings off. Three quarters of an hour later he returns. He's wide awake after his walk with Ginger, so we don't sleep. We make love, eat toast, kiss, and drink coffee. But we don't talk much. He seems preoccupied and I've learned Garrie needs to process things in his own head before he shares them; pressuring him inevitably backfires.

I wake up feeling thirsty. Garrie's sleeping soundly so I decide I'll make myself a cup of tea. On impulse I slide Garrie's drawer open and take Emily's phone downstairs with me. I look out of the kitchen window at the fading of summer. The leaves are losing their vibrance and everything looks a little weary. It's the early hours of the morning and daylight has begun to creep in. I plug Emily's phone into the charger, and it works. I leave the kettle to boil as I enter Emily's date of birth and watch the phone spring into life. Four digits and I'm sliding into Emily's digital world. I press the screen to view the messages, but there's hardly anything there; just a few texts from Martha's mum that arrived earlier today. She's certainly persistent.

Martha's upset about the rabbit.

I feel sorry for the little girl and feel compelled to punch in a reply as if I'm Emily.

Hi. Sorry for not getting back sooner. I've gone to stay with family for a while. I'm not with Garrie anymore.

I delete the last bit. She doesn't need to know that. *Sandie has agreed to look after the rabbit and Martha's welcome to come around any time to see him. I'll give you Sandie's number so you can message her. Will be in touch when I can. Emily x*

I think that sounds OK, so I insert my phone number and press send. I immediately worry if I've done the right thing. Maybe I shouldn't have invited Martha to see the rabbit. I've added another complication to the mix but it's too late, the message has already gone.

I check the call log; it's empty, which seems strange because I know her phone rang before the battery went flat. It's been in his sock drawer ever since so the only person that could have cleared the call log is Garrie. I gulp down my last mouthful of tea, unplug the phone charger and run upstairs. Garrie is in the same position as when I left him. I quietly open the drawer and I'm about to put the phone back when Garrie's eyes open.

'What are you doing?'

I jump out of my skin because I'm caught red handed. 'I'm putting Emily's phone back.'

'Why did you take it out of my drawer in the first place?'

My cheeks are on fire, and I realise I have no choice but to come clean. 'I wanted to have a little look. When I went to Emily's I spotted her charger and brought it home. I thought I would give it a try.'

'Why?' He's sitting up now, arms folded, with an inquisitive look on his face.

He's clearly not happy about me rifling through his sock drawer so I raise my hands in the air as if to make a joke out of it. 'You got me.'

He isn't laughing and his eyes narrow in a look I've never seen before.

I stammer an explanation. 'I…I wanted to have a look, Garrie. I thought…' My voice trails off as I realise, I'm not sure what I thought.

'So, what were you looking for, Sandie?'

The guilt I feel at being caught turns to anger. Dammit. After everything he's put me through, I think I'm entitled to be curious about the woman's phone. Especially since it's been sleeping in my bedroom.'

'I don't know Garrie, OK? But you can't really blame me for looking so don't make a big thing of it. Not after everything else that's happened. Surely curiosity is a minor offence compared to what I've been through.'

'For God's sake. She's gone, Sandie. Why can't you be happy about that and leave well alone?'

'I am happy about it. But see what's happening? Somehow, she's still coming between us. All because of a bloody mobile phone. It feels like she's in the room with us.'

He looks down at his hands. His knuckles are white as he clenches his fingers together. He begins to sob, and I move closer to him.

'She destroyed my life, Sandie. She destroyed my entire life. She's the reason I lost my Annabel.'

I know, Garrie, but you can't keep tormenting yourself like this.'

I'm trying to comfort him when we're interrupted by a knock at the door. I kiss him on the cheek.

'Stay there, I'll get rid of them. I'll be right back.'

I open the door to see Martha and her mum standing in front of me.

'Emily's been in touch. She told us you're feeding Hoppy and that it's OK for Martha to come around and help.'

My heart sinks. I completely forgot I'd sent that message and I certainly didn't expect them to be standing at my door when I'm in the middle of an important conversation.

I say the first thing that comes into my head. 'I'm cooking dinner.'

'Oh, sorry, but don't worry. We can wait.'

'No. This really isn't a good time.' I know my tone sounds harsh but they're annoying me. 'Tomorrow, come back tomorrow. Ten o'clock. We can feed Hoppy together.'

The mother looks put out, but I can't afford to care. They leave and I turn around to see Garrie behind me. Caught red handed twice in one day. I don't bother to hold my hands up this time. I simply tell the truth. 'It's Emily's student. She wants to feed the rabbit. I replied to a message from Emily's phone telling her it's OK.'

He puts his coat on but says nothing.

'Garrie, I know it was a stupid thing to do, but I acted on impulse. Where are you going?'

'Out. I can't believe you sent a message pretending to be Emily. God knows what you were thinking.'

As he pushes past me and walks out, I realise I've made things worse. I wish I'd never touched the phone. Garrie's right, I should be happy she's gone so we can get on with our lives. When he comes back, I'll tell him I'll leave well alone.

I watch him disappear down the road and that's when I notice the estate agent's board. Number 12 is up for rent.

It looks like Emily really has gone for good.

Chapter 40

GARRIE

I let myself into the house where I'm now holding Emily hostage; the home I used to share with Annabel, my beautiful wife. Even though she's dead, her spirit resides here and fills every corner. It's the one place I can be at peace, because Annabel's presence somehow finds the temporary pause button in my brain and the images that play on a continuous loop go into freeze frame. For a while, at least, I can pretend it's still our home so that the noise in my head stops and I can think without interference from it. It's Annabel's birthday today so I don't venture into the room where Emily's tied up because I won't allow her negative energy to interfere with this moment and the beautiful memory of my wife.

Instead, I look at the birthday flowers I've arranged. White lilies, Annabel's favourite; symbols of love, purity, and rebirth. I bend down to touch their petals and breathe their scent, and instantly feel the calm, gentle serenity that always surrounded her. She enveloped me in it when she was alive, and she still does. My finger traces her face across the photograph I always carry with me, lingering over her beauty, absorbing her as if I was trailing my fingers across her body, remembering all the intimate moments we shared together. Before she was cruelly snatched away because of the actions of Emily; the woman who deserves to suffer for what she did to my family.

My fingers continue their slow journey across the photograph, caressing my wife's features.

'I love you, Annabel. You will always be my first love and I will never stop loving you. Even though I've found Sandie.'

I've told her about Sandie, and I hope she approves. I hope she's watching all of this and can finally rest in peace now that Emily has been made to pay. If Emily hadn't got involved with our lives, I could have saved our marriage and prevented Annabel's death. I remember the day she told me to find someone else if anything ever happened to her. She whispered it to me as we held each other close and watched dawn break.

'Garrie, life is so uncertain; we never know what the future may hold. But I want you to promise me something. That you'll always take care of Katie. She's special and she needs you. And…

She'd paused to catch her breath. 'And she's always going to need a mother. Someone special. If anything happens to me, promise me you'll find someone. For Katie…and for you.'

I'd pulled her tighter to me, kissed her head and told her I wasn't ever letting her go anywhere. But I didn't fulfil my promise. Four weeks later, my daughter was motherless, and I'd lost my soulmate.

Annabel was dead.

Chapter 41

EMILY

I have no idea what time it is. I don't have my phone and I realise my watch must be on the bedside table at home. I always take it off before I get into bed; the last place I remember being before I found myself wherever I am now.

The hands on the grandfather clock in the corner of this strange unknown room are stuck on 10:15. Like everything else here, time seems to have stopped. At least the small window helps me to distinguish between night and day; the only way I can keep track of how long I've been a prisoner here. I think it's three days. Surely somebody will come looking for me soon.

I'm in hell because Garrie's made me his prisoner and I've no idea what he thinks I've done to deserve it. Surely it can't be because I tracked him to his mum's house. I wanted to know where he was going for days on end with no explanation, like any normal girlfriend would want to know. It's certainly not bad enough to warrant this punishment.

I need to understand what's going on inside his head but I'm becoming more tired and confused. I allowed myself some sleep earlier when my eyes refused to stay open any longer. But I'm forcing myself to stay as alert as possible. I can't allow myself to sink into some sensory oblivion.

I'm sure Garrie expects me to crumple and fold, but I won't. He has no idea how much worse I've endured and survived. I will survive this. And I will find a way to escape. I must keep telling myself that. *Think Emily, think. Think of everything Garrie's said. Everything he's done. Somewhere there must be a clue to where you are and why.*

I still remember nothing about being brought to this place. I can't even remember how many times he's visited. I know he came to the house earlier today, but he didn't come into this room. I heard him mutter something to himself outside the door and I heard his footsteps on the stairs before he left. Perhaps he's coming back soon.

He usually brings water and food that he feeds to me, as if I'm a caged specimen. He only unties me for loo trips and his eyes glint as he does it, as if he relishes degrading me. When his coarse hands slide over mine with the rope, I think back to a time when I wanted those hands to slide over my body. Now I feel the anger in them, his need to deny me my freedom and dignity. He brought Ginger last night, but I couldn't even stroke her. I could only watch two confused brown eyes looking up at me.

I sink back into the sofa, thinking about my puppy, and home, and realisation hits me. I didn't hear his car arrive last night. He must have arrived on foot, with Ginger on the lead. Of course, she was his excuse to go out without making Sandie suspicious. The call he ignored when he was here must have been from her asking how long he would be.

Perhaps I have my first clue. Wherever I am, I may be in walking distance of home.

Chapter 42

SANDIE

Martha turns up precisely at 10 a.m. to feed Hoppy. Luckily, I'm out of my pyjamas and eating the last bite of toast that I've coated in thick butter. I wipe the crumbs off my mouth before opening the door. Martha looks eager and, from the size of the bag she's carrying, her mum wants to go shopping. She doesn't say much apart from "See you later" before she dashes off in the direction of the bus stop.

I look down at the delicately featured twelve-year-old standing in my hallway. She's bursting with energy and impatience to get over to number 12 so she can become reacquainted with Hoppy after her brief separation.

As soon as we open Emily's front door, she reaches up to punch in the numbers for the alarm system before marching into the kitchen. She throws her bag onto the sofa, opens a cupboard, and pours herself a glass of orange juice.

'Do you want one?'

'No, I'm fine, thanks.'

She skips her way into the larder and emerges with the rabbit food and some straw. She's obviously no stranger to this house, but her next words surprise me.

'Want to see my room before we feed Hoppy?' She beams up at me with her massive smile. 'Come on, I'll show you.'

Confused, I follow her into the hallway where she expertly removes a piece of carpet to reveal a small hatch. She opens it, starts to climb down a set of steps towards what must be a basement and beckons me to follow.

'Come on, Sandie. This'll be fun. You'll love it down here. It's a secret place, but Emily won't mind me showing you.'

I'm too intrigued to say no, although the steps don't look too appealing. Martha's tiny frame squeezes through the gap easily but I find it a bit more difficult. When she's on the last step she proudly flicks a switch on the wall so at least I can see where I'm going.

'Do you like it?'

I look around the area I've stepped into. It's bigger than I was expecting, and its walls are covered in brightly coloured paintings and sketches. There's a table in the centre with beads and craft items.

'It's my room, what do you think?'

I'm not sure how to respond but it's clear how much she wants me to like what I'm seeing. 'It's lovely, Martha.'

They're the only words I can muster because I need a chance to process this. Martha has got her own room? I'm sure Garrie doesn't know about it; he didn't want children in the house at all. Maybe this is where Emily does her teaching. I decide to ask.

'Is this where you do your maths lessons?'

She gives me an indignant look. 'Of course not, we do that in the living room. Look, this is how we make bracelets.' She holds up a jar full of coloured beads. 'Will she be back soon?'

She's obviously referring to Emily. 'And why is there a sign outside the house? Mum said Emily must be moving. She's not moving, is she?'

She's full of questions and I feel stupid that I don't have answers. I give her the only reply I can think of. 'I'm not sure. But if she does, I promise I will keep Hoppy in my garden so you can visit to feed him.'

I've no idea why I've said that and remind myself to start thinking more before I speak.

'And what about my room? What will happen to all my things?' Another question that stumps me.

'I'm sure you've got your own room at home, Martha.'

'But it's not like this one.'

I need to get her off this subject, and I'm desperate to escape from the basement. Being in it is making me uncomfortable. 'Let's see what happens. I'm sure Emily will be in touch when she's ready.'

I don't think I sound particularly convincing, but my words seem to satisfy her, and she grins at me. 'OK. Let's go and see Hoppy now. I'm glad you like my room.'

I'm relieved to be back in daylight as I slump into a patio chair, smiling at the enjoyment on Martha's face as she takes Hoppy out of the hutch so he can run around the garden. I allow myself to daydream for a few minutes and imagine spending days like this with Garrie and our own child. But my mind returns to the basement room. It was dimly lit, with a craft table in the centre. Martha loves it but it felt creepy to me. It's a strange thing to do for a student, unless she's a family member, a niece maybe. Discomfort rises from the pit of my stomach because I recall what Garrie told me about Emily's involvement with his wife and daughter.

The front doorbell rings and Martha jumps to her feet to answer it. Her mum is full of thanks and seems to be happy that she got her shopping done. I decide to ask my question as casually as I can. 'Are you related to Emily? I thought I saw a family resemblance.'

Her mum laughs. 'I wish. I'd love to look like Emily. But no; we saw her advert in the newspaper.'

I watch them walk away and tell myself I must make sure Martha never goes into that basement room again. If Emily was still at the house, I would report it, but I don't want to do anything to rock the boat with Garrie. He would probably tell me I'm meddling again, and I need him to keep opening up to me. I don't think he even knows about the basement room so I will keep that up my sleeve for now until I can bring the subject up with him.

We've got Emily's phone so at least Martha's mum can't arrange any more lessons with her. The more I learn about Emily, the more I'm glad she's gone.

Chapter 43

GARRIE

I park five minutes away and let myself in quietly. It's early, so Emily's probably asleep. I don't want her calling out and disturbing me. There are things I need to do alone before I'm ready to face her. I put the food and drink I've brought into the fridge. She looked weak last night so I'll give her more today. I don't want her passing out on me. I want her to be fully conscious for everything I'm planning for her.

She still claims to have no idea why she's here, but she'll crack eventually; I know she will. Not even Emily can keep up this innocent pretence forever, however hard she tries and however many other people she's fooled with it. She doesn't fool me.

I have a few surprises in store for her today. I open the fridge door again and enjoy purposely re-arranging what I've brought in random, haphazard order. How Emily would hate that; everything at number 12 always had to be in perfect symmetry and balance. Not any longer.

Even better, I can taste self-satisfaction as I imagine her reaction when I tell her the house news. It will throw the perfect world she's invented completely off-balance when she finds out her house has been put up to let and everybody's convinced that she's gone. Permanently.

I want to see the naked fear on her face when she realises her situation is hopeless and nothing's in her control anymore. I want her to feel the way her actions made me feel. But I have other priorities here first.

I take off my shoes and head silently upstairs.

Chapter 44

EMILY

Morning sunlight streams through the small window; my daily reminder of the real world beyond this limbo I'm in. I guess Garrie will visit soon and bring me some breakfast. I need it. I'm feeling weaker by the day.

I catch my breath on the thought.
'Visit…breakfast…' Why am I using normal vocabulary to describe any of this? As if it's perfectly natural to receive a social call from a man who drags you unconscious to an unknown location in the middle of the night where he's now keeping you captive. A man you thought was in love with you but who manacled you to a sofa like a butterfly being mounted on a frame, with no explanation.

Waves of nausea crash over me at the prospect of having to look at him when he walks in. I've no appetite for whatever food he brings today, but I'm desperate for a drink; my lips feel like dried parchment paper, and I can barely prise them apart. I can't imagine how awful I must look after four days in the same nightshirt, which now swamps me because I've barely eaten since I got here. I hope today he'll finally do what I've asked him for two days now; bring me a change of clothes and allow me to at least have a proper wash.

As my eyes adjust to the daylight, I hear a noise. I didn't hear Garrie arrive, but he must already be in the house. I've heard the same noise before and it is always moments before he walks into this room. I've finally worked out what is, a creaking stair. He's obviously walking downstairs, and I wonder what he's been doing upstairs and what his connection is with this place.

I force my lips apart to call out to him, and wince with pain. 'Garrie? Is that you? Please, I'm frightened.'

The door flies open and he's in front of me. He isn't carrying anything as he walks towards me. 'Who else would it be, sweetie? This room is our little secret.' His lips curl, in contrast to mine. 'Are you enjoying your stay? I'm so loving having you as my guest. You're really no trouble at all.'

He sits down in the seat opposite. My mouth hurts even more as my dry lips crack with every word. 'Garrie, please. Let me have a drink. And please, tell me what's going on. I don't understand. I don't know who you are anymore.'

'Since you're asking so nicely.' He sneers the words then jumps up, leaves, and returns in seconds with a bottle of water he holds to my mouth. I gulp it down as it spills out of the bottle and my mouth onto the nightdress.

He speaks to me like a parent scolding a small child for being clumsy. 'Now look what you've done. Soaked your only item of clothing.' He puts the water bottle on the table and returns to his chair. 'You can have more when you learn how to drink it properly.'

I stare at the bottle and back at him. 'Didn't you bring me any more clothes? I can't stay in this shirt forever, Garrie.'

He laughs. 'No, I didn't. And yes, you can. It's not as if you're going anywhere or about to have house guests, Emily. You'll stay in what you're wearing.'

I can't believe what I'm hearing. How long is he planning on keeping me here?

'Garrie, please tell me what's going on. You can't keep this up for much longer. People will be starting to look for me. I don't know what you've told them, but they'll wonder why I haven't been home.'

He leans towards me. His expression is triumphant. It frightens me how much he's enjoying this. 'Nobody's coming looking, Emily. They think you've left. Permanently.'

I'm scared, but somehow, I manage to stare him out. I know he wants me to crumble, but I have to stay strong. Whatever he says, I know people won't believe him and I need to convince him of the madness of what he's doing.

'Garrie, nobody will believe I walked away from my home, and Ginger, on an emotional impulse and left it unattended with everything in it. They know that's out of character.'

He sits back in his seat, arms folded in a gesture of superiority. 'But they don't think it was impulse, Emily. Or out of character. I've made sure of that. They think you've thought it through in the meticulously planned way you do everything.'

He pauses as he leans closer towards me. 'Right down to organising the re-letting of the house. The giant 'To Let' sign in the garden is a bit of a giveaway. They're convinced you've moved away. Woman scorned and all that. Get the picture?'

My stomach lurches as I look at him. How can I convince him to stop this?

'Garrie, please, untie me and let me go. I won't press any charges against you, I promise. Take me home and I'll pack my things and go quietly. I'll leave you and Sandie to your new life and I'll never tell anybody about this. You'll never hear from me again.'

He gives me a questioning look. 'Why would I make it so easy for you, Emily? After what you did to my life?'

This again; I have no idea what he's talking about. 'Garrie, I'm sorry. I know how angry you were that I tracked you and followed you. But I was desperate. Please understand I did it because I loved you.'

'You think that's what this is about, you tracking me? Stop pretending you don't know what it's about. Do you need me to prompt your memory?'

He gets up and walks towards me. He leans into me, his face an ugly gargoyle of contorted features as he spits his words at me like venom.

'Well, here's a clue, Emily. ANNABEL. Remember that name? ANN A BEL. Is this clearer now, you sick bitch?'

I shrink back in horror from his twisted expression and the pure hatred in his words. And from the name. How can he know what it means to me?

Annabel.

The name that once brought me so much joy but then so much pain that my subconscious tries to protect me from it. As if it never existed in my consciousness. But Garrie uses it as a stake to pierce through my heart, puncturing the dark place where the imperfect Emily keeps her secrets buried. And his look of contorted contentment tells me how much he's enjoying inflicting this pain.

It erupts through me until my mind and body can't take it anymore. And everything goes black.

Chapter 45

SANDIE

I'm back at number 12, inside Emily's bedroom. Garrie is at work and Linda's away; but I know she'll come sniffing around as soon as she returns. The 'To Let' sign will provoke a whole new set of questions from her. But I'm glad it's there because it's confirmation that Emily really is moving on.

Garrie tells me she spoke to one of his colleagues about re-letting the house. He insists I should forget about her; but not knowing where she is or exactly how she contributed to the death of his wife continues to niggle away at me. It's the reason I'm drawn to this house to try and unlock some of the secrets it holds.

I check the drawer in her bedside table. There are the usual knick-knacks; a few pens, a hairdryer, a bottle of deodorant, nothing of any interest. I open other drawers and cupboards but find nothing; not that I have any idea what I'm hoping to discover, but I'm convinced this house holds clues somewhere. I decide to check out the basement room again. It's only 1 p.m. There's plenty of time for me to have a rummage around.

I take the steps one at a time until I reach the light switch, trying to dismiss thoughts of all those late-night horror movies where strange things happen in the dark. But I'm relieved once the light is on, and I take a closer look at the artwork on the walls. I can see why this room appeals to Martha. She must love feeling it's her own little den and she clearly has a flair for art. Her drawings of animals are stunningly detailed, and I take a moment to observe their beauty.

There's a bookshelf in the corner of the room. It's old and battered but the books are neatly laid out in alphabetical order. Typical Emily. Everything ordered to perfection. There's an old cookery book, some self-help books, a few romantic novels and several books about infertility, childbirth, and pregnancy.

I remove one of the pregnancy books and notice something at the back of the shelf. A diary, clearly deliberately hidden from prying eyes. I feel guilty and furtive, but I must look at it. I open randomly and read.

'The baby's nearly due. This is the best thing that's ever happened to me. Life couldn't be better.'

I flick ahead because my back's beginning to ache and it's time I went home; I'll take the book and the diary with me and read them in comfort. I read one more sentence.

'I've lost my baby.'

The words make my insides ache at the thought of losing something so precious. I think back to the day she learned I was pregnant. It must have felt like the ultimate body punch to her after losing a child of her own. No wonder she wanted to get away.

I'm back at the front door ready to leave when I hear Linda pulling onto her driveway. She and John seem to take forever unloading the car and chatting. The minute they go inside the house I make a quick getaway.

'Sandie.'

I knew it. Nothing gets past Linda.

'Oh hi, Linda. I hope everything's OK with John's brother?'

She ignores the question and points at the signboard. 'What the hell's going on?'

'Emily's not coming back.'

'What? I thought she was just staying with family to clear her head.'

I feel I have no choice but to tell her the truth. 'She found out about the baby.'

'What baby?'

'Our baby. Garrie's and mine.'

I see her facial expression connect to her brain as she stares at my protruding baby bump and tries to process this new information. 'Goodness, it's a good job I didn't go away for a fortnight, I dread to think what I would have come back to. I'm surprised Emily hasn't tried to contact me. I've only had one text from her since she left. I never thought this would be a permanent thing.'

'I suppose she wants a fresh start, Linda. The news about the baby must have been a shock. Although we never meant to hurt her.'

John walks out at the right moment; I need to get away from Linda's inquisition. But she has other ideas. 'Listen to this, John. Sandie and Garrie are having a baby and Emily's not coming back.'

John smiles and congratulates me before he gives Linda an impatient look and nods in the direction of the house. He clearly has no desire to stand and gossip on his driveway.

I return home with Emily's diary and pregnancy book tucked safely in my bag. I've got at least two hours before Garrie gets home, so I make a pot of Earl Grey, give Ginger a piece of rawhide to keep her quiet and put my feet up to read Emily's leather-bound diary. My mother always told me never to read other people's diaries, but I've already gone against her advice, and I need to read more. I clasp my hands together. *Sorry, mother, forgive me.* Then I slide the little tassel that sits neatly against page one, and I start to read Emily's perfectly formed handwriting.

Martin is golden. He's the perfect husband in every way. But there's one thing that will make our lives complete and that's to have a baby. Dear God, let us have a baby.

It's tough to read. Emily clearly wanted a baby more than anything in the world and each page echoes her struggle to conceive. Martin appears to have stood by her every step of the way as they kept trying until they almost gave up hope. Then the following entry appears.

I'm pregnant.

The words leap out at me, and I feel a surprising affinity to the woman who was my nemesis. We are not so dissimilar; at our core we're two women who want to be loved and have a family. Her world must have fallen apart when she lost her child, and I can only imagine her heartbreak after her struggle to conceive.

I'm about to read more when I hear a key in the lock. It's Garrie. I quickly hide the diary and walk into the kitchen to check if the lasagne is done. He walks in and wraps his arms around me. I feel lucky to have a second chance at happiness and I know I must embrace it. After reading Emily's struggles it puts things into perspective and I feel truly grateful. Garrie kisses me passionately as our evening begins and I tell myself to put Emily's diary out of my mind until tomorrow.

Chapter 46

EMILY

I've stopped crying. I'm so dehydrated there are no tears left, and the light at my window tells me it will be a while before he visits with water for me. It's easier to use a pronoun than to bring myself to say his name. Garrie. I never did ask him where the pretentious spelling came from. Maybe it was his idea; I can't imagine his mother coming up with the idea. I thought it was attractive when he told me, now I detest it. And I detest him for what he's subjecting me to in this captive hell. All the love I ever felt for him has morphed into pure hatred and anger. I need to harness the power of my anger to give me the energy to fight my way out of here.

I press my long fingernails into the flesh of my hands until they hurt. One nail is ragged and sharp; it broke when he tied me to the sofa, and it's made my hand bleed too. But pain has its uses; it will keep me focused.

I need to dig deep and find the strong, unafraid Emily. The Emily I used to be and the woman who was fearless until circumstances blew her life off course. I need that person back, free of all the suppressed emotions deep within my veins. I can't allow myself the indulgence of fear; I must dive head-first into shark infested waters if I'm going to beat the man who's imprisoned me.

Think, Emily. What does he know? How much can he know? He can't know about the baby I lost; nobody in my new life knows.

My Annabel. I linger over the sound of her name in my head. I remember Martin looking up its meaning. *Favoured grace.* It was perfect for our beautiful daughter, who I never got to see or hold, but who was a part of me until she was cruelly snatched away.

And now I must live with the injustice of Garrie getting to experience parenthood for a second time. Oops, force of habit. I check myself. *Not Garrie. Him. Remember he no longer has the right to a name.* What is it that allowed him to overwhelm two intelligent women like Sandie and me, so powerfully that we couldn't think straight? I thank God I finally saw through his Prince Charming act, but I wonder how he's managed to convince her to take him back.

I wonder what he's told her about me and where she thinks I've gone. I can't imagine she has any idea he's keeping me captive like this, and I'm sure she wouldn't be going along with it if she knew. It explains him bringing Ginger here, as his pretext for leaving the house at night. I'm sure he's not bringing her for my sake.

I press the ragged nail against the palm of my hand again and wince against the pain.

Stop thinking about him and about Sandie. There's no time to wallow in that. You're his prisoner and you need to keep your wits about you. Focus on what this is truly about.

I whisper the words into the silence of the room. And I remember how he spat his words with such venom into this claustrophobic vacuum hours earlier. The way he taunted me with the name Annabel, staring at my face to see my reaction; his expression of contorted delight at the pain it inflicted on me. My lost child, and by horrible coincidence, my friend.

A woman who shared my daughter's name and whose memory my mind forced itself to bury for so long because I couldn't cope with remembering. A woman whose loss was too much for me to bear so soon after losing my daughter. Another Annabel snatched away from me in a cruel twist of fate repeating itself.

The name he called out that night when I first saw a different side to him; the night he twisted everything and blamed me. The name his mother cried out in surprise when she met me. So, their Annabel is real. But who is she? I wish I knew his connection to that name and what he knows - or thinks he knows - about mine. But he's beginning to show his hand. And perhaps that gives me an advantage I didn't have before. I must tell myself that or I'll give in to the utter desperation of weakness and exhaustion.

I'm determined to stay strong. Next time he visits a different Emily will be waiting for him. I'm nauseous from hunger and fear but I won't let him see that. I can't let him defeat me.

Chapter 47

SANDIE

I'm glad Garrie's left for work early because I'm impatient to get back to Emily's diary. Her words have floated around inside my head since I started reading them. I'm getting to know her. It's clear she had a good relationship with her husband, Martin, and she loved him deeply, but something must have driven them apart. Maybe the grief of losing the baby put too much pressure on the relationship.

There's a photograph of him at number 12; it's the one nestled between the porcelain teapot and a pile of envelopes. I noticed it the first time I visited, and I looked at it again yesterday. I assume Garrie must know all about him. He's handsome, but not in the same way as Garrie. Martin's more polished around the edges; tidy hair, neatly dressed, trousers, shirt, that sort of thing. Garrie's more rugged; coarse hands, a little clumsy. Pretty much throws himself together without much thought but somehow manages to look effortlessly great. A jeans and casual jacket kind of guy; but with expensive shoes. He always buys good shoes. And socks. He jokes that if you get the feet right the rest follows.

I open Emily's diary and once again I'm engrossed in her life story. She maps her pregnancy with precision. She attended every antenatal class, stapled her scans to the pages, and wrote letters to her unborn child. Her words prompt a sudden rush of excitement in me, knowing my first scan is due soon. I imagine seeing our tiny miracle on screen.

Emily writes beautifully. The letters and poems to her baby are exquisite and deeply moving. Her innermost thoughts stretch across the pages. Abruptly the writing changes and darkness hangs over every word. Her earlier eloquent sentences become a fractured mishmash of words randomly thrown together. As I read, I'm sharing in her devastation. The loss of her child; the space inside her body where her precious daughter should be; her feeling of emptiness.

I feel a loneliness that's driving me insane. I still love Martin and I know he loves me deeply, but I'm lost.

I close the diary; I can't read any more. I've invaded Emily's pain enough for one day, and I find myself again wondering where she is and how she is.

I take a warm shower to revive me because I need to get to work. I've promised Jude I'll do the afternoon shift and the distraction from Emily's world will be welcome. She'll want an update on all the gossip, especially since I finally summoned up the courage to tell her about the baby.

She gives me a typical Jude bear hug as soon as I walk in. 'Hi, mummy-to-be. Is a horribly healthy ginger tea in order?' She winks at me; she knows I hate the stuff.

'God, no. A normal tea bag dunked in a mug, please.'

'So, how are you? I can't help worrying about you, even if I do have to admit you're glowing.'

'Must be all the hormones. They make you want to be sick, but they do seem to be good for the skin. And please, try to stop worrying; there's no need. It's lovely that you do, but I'm fine. I know it's been a rocky ride with Garrie, but I am thrilled about the baby.'

'Is that the reason you've agreed to take him back, Sandie? That's what worries me.'

I shake my head. 'No Jude. As soon as I did the test, I knew I wanted this baby whatever happened with Garrie. I'm glad he's back and we're going into this together, but I'd go it alone if I had to.' I give her a broad grin. 'Now, I must tell you a funny story about nosey Linda yesterday. You should have seen her face when she saw the 'To Let' sign on Emily's house. She stood looking at it, waving her arms about. She hates not knowing news before everybody else.'

I mimic Linda's stance and her indignant question, 'What the hell's going on?'

Jude laughs, but there's concern behind her smiling eyes. I know she can't stop worrying about me.

'Seriously though, Sandie, is everything really alright?'

'It's good, Jude. Garrie seems a lot more relaxed now Emily's clearly left for good.'

'He was in here yesterday.'

'Garrie?'

'Yes. Lunch time. He looked a bit…' She hesitates as if she's censoring what she's about to say.

'…preoccupied. He ordered his usual, but he barely finished his coffee. Sat staring out of the window and left half an hour later without saying anything.'

'That's strange; he was fine when he got home, full of energy. We stayed up late playing Scrabble and he kept trying to say I was cheating. We had a laugh.'

She shrugs her shoulders. 'Maybe it was my imagination. Forget I said anything.'

'He even took Ginger for a midnight walk, then we went to bed and snuggled.'

She smiles and holds her hands up. 'I don't need to know the rest. Too much information. But I'm glad everything's OK.'

She puts on her coat, gives me a hug, but turns to me as she walks to the door.

'But stay on your guard, Sandie. Something about him makes me uncomfortable. I have to say that as your friend.'

She sends me an air kiss.

'Catch up with you tomorrow.'

Chapter 48

SANDIE

I'm tired after my shift. I take a last glance around the coffee shop before I lock up. All I want is to get home, have a long soak and put my feet up. I smile down at my bump as I punch in the alarm code.

'You're the best reason I ever had for being tired, little one.'

As I wait for the long beep to tell me the security system is armed, I think about Emily again and the niggling doubts that refuse to go away; curiosity about where she is, and a feeling of unease about what she might do next.

And now this remark from Jude that Garrie was in the coffee shop yesterday, looking preoccupied, leaving his drink barely touched and staring into space. What's he not telling me? Is he hiding something from me or trying to protect me?

I know it will aggravate him, and I'm almost too tired to confront him tonight, but as I walk to the bus stop, I know I must ask him. Emily will never be truly gone from our lives until my doubts are satisfied with some answers.

I watch a young mum holding her baby and collapsing the pushchair in an expert one-handed move before boarding the bus. I help her to stow it in the luggage area and she glances at my bump with a smile.

'Thank you. I'll do the same for you when yours arrives. How far along are you?'

'Only a few weeks. I'm due for my first scan soon. I'm quite nervous.' I glance back at the folded pushchair. 'That manoeuvre must take practice. I haven't a clue.'

She gives me a conspiratorial maternal wink. 'Don't be nervous about any of it. I can tell you from experience that we're all wired to deal with this somehow. Instinct seems to kick in and you make it up as you go along. You'll be fine, trust me.'

I smile back at her and her contented baby as I make my way towards the only other vacant seat. It was a conversation that only a new mother and a nervously expectant one could have; a fleeting, unique bond between strangers who may never meet again. Perhaps pregnancy has thrown my emotions off balance, but ever since I found Emily's diary, I've felt a strange connection with her, too; something I could never have imagined a few weeks ago. The connection's grown stronger with every page I've read. I'd hoped the diary would give me answers, but it's only raised more questions. Why does Garrie blame her for his wife's death? And what was he hoping to achieve by moving in with her? Why did he object so strongly to her inviting children into the house; almost as if he thought it was a dangerous obsession? I remember how I felt in Martha's room. It seemed to be put together with love, and yet something about it made me uncomfortable.

≈ ≈ ≈

Garrie's home. I eat six forkfuls of a prawn risotto, my one seafood indulgence of the week. But I decide I can't hold back any longer and I blurt out the question without looking up from my plate. I don't want to see the expression on his face.

'Garrie, I know you've told me to stop this, but I can't. Something about Emily leaving in the way she did doesn't feel right. And I still don't know the story about you and her, the history you share.'

His response is to turn the TV volume up and ignore me. I put my plate down and turn towards him, but he continues to stare at the screen.

'Garrie, please. Talk to me. We should find out where she is, and we should get her phone back to her. I don't like it being here in our house. I've sent messages pretending to be her and now I wish I hadn't. It was a stupid thing to do and now I'm worried.

He spins round to face me. 'It was worse than stupid, Sandie; it was insane. God knows what possessed you. I only let it go because of the baby, or I'd have said more to you, but please, no more now. Leave this alone and stop thinking about her. You're acting like you're obsessed.'

I'm angry at him. 'How can I leave it alone? You left me for her remember? And I'm getting questions all the time from people asking where she is. How do you expect me to move on when that keeps happening? It's impossible.'

He slams his plate down on the coffee table. 'Christ, Sandie, let it drop. You hated it when she was around but you're not happy now she's gone. Why the hell do you need to know where she is? Haven't you listened to anything I've said about her? Let's enjoy our night without spoiling it talking about Emily.' His mouth sets into a hard, angry line and his next words are barely audible. 'She's destroyed enough already.'

'Garrie…'

He holds his hands up.

'Enough. I'm taking Ginger out. I need air. I don't need this.'

I sit in subdued silence as he slams the front door closed. Exhaustion from our encounter hits me; I need to go to bed. This can't be good for the baby. I drag myself upstairs hoping I fall asleep quickly and that by tomorrow Garrie will have calmed down.

My phone pings with a text from him.

Don't wait up for me. You need to sleep and so does the baby. I'm staying at mum's tonight. I need a bit of space. And I've taken Emily's phone. I'll deal with it like you asked. I know you won't be happy until I do. She mentioned her aunt as she was leaving. I think that's where she's probably staying. I know where she lives so I'll call round tomorrow after work and see if Emily is there. I'll give her the phone if she promises never to track us again.

I stare at his message. I hate the thought of him being anywhere near Emily, but I can't have it both ways. He sends another message.

I'm sorry I shouted. But please let that be the end of it, Sandie. I love you. I'll be back tomorrow.

I text a heart emoji back. And instantly fall asleep.

Chapter 49

EMILY

I wake up startled by a menacing figure in front of me. I gasp for air and wait for my brain to catch up with my eyes. It's dark apart from a narrow shaft of moonlight from the small window. I'm not sure what's worse; waking up to an eerie silhouette or discovering that it's Garrie.

'You were fast asleep, sweetie.'

That word again. My skin shivers at his sugar-coated sarcasm and a familiar tremor runs through every nerve cell in my body. He's trying to throw me off balance, but I won't allow it. I look around the room for Ginger and there she is, innocently wagging her tail as if nothing's wrong. I wonder again what Sandie thinks of his behaviour. She must question why he walks the dog at such strange hours. I can tell it's late by the length of darkness and angle of the moonlight; you get to know these things when you're trying to survive.

'Please let me go, Garrie. If you do, I promise you will never hear from me again. I'll be gone from your lives for good and surely that's what you want. Why are you punishing me like this? How can you hate me this much?'

He reacts with a twisted smile. 'Listen to yourself. Begging for freedom. He mocks my voice "Please let me go Garrie, you'll never hear from me again." You must think I'm stupid, Emily. You'd be out of here and straight to the police.'

'I wouldn't, Garrie. I promise.'

He steps closer and leans towards me. 'Look at your sad little face. Shame it's not so pretty anymore. You could have made someone a good wife if you hadn't allowed yourself to get so ugly.'

He takes a red lipstick from his pocket. It's mine; I recognize the case. 'Put your lips out.' He pouts as a demonstration. 'Come on; lips out for your fiancé.'

Oh God, that word. To think I ever dreamt of being his wife.

He smears the crimson gloss across my lips and steps back. 'See? Wasn't so bad, was it? I might have to kiss that off later.'

The thought of his lips on mine makes me want to be sick but I refuse to give in to the waves of nausea and I won't let him get underneath my skin. He's trying to provoke me and I'm not going to give him the satisfaction of rising to his taunts.

Instead, I gulp down the fizzy bubbles from the bottle of sparkling Pellegrino that he holds to my mouth. I know it's from the back of the fridge at number 12. I bought a pack of sparkling by mistake, and they've sat there ever since. He knows I don't like it and I want to spit it back at him, but I won't give him that satisfaction either. And I need every drop of water I can get if I'm to make it out of here alive.

He steps behind the sofa, and I feel his hand slide down my hair before he pulls it until it hurts. 'Good girl, drinking all your fizzy water. I do want to keep you alive a bit longer.'

Fear hits me like a wrecking ball that's about to crush every bone in my body. My blood turns icy cold, and I whimper in pain at every heartbeat. He isn't punishing me. He wants me dead. I'm at the mercy of a madman.

He jolts my head backwards and whispers into my ear. 'Think back to that night at the bar.'

I cry out as he pulls my hair harder as if he's ripping it from my scalp, but my brain automatically goes where he's told it to go.

'Your lips were sparkling, Emily, exactly like they are now.'

I don't want to remember, but I'm back in the bar. I was sparkling. He could have chosen any woman in that room, but he chose me. God knows I wish he hadn't. I wish I'd never set eyes on him.

'You never realised did you, Emily? We didn't meet by chance. I planned it, but you were too full of yourself to guess.'

I shrink in horror from his words and his naked hatred for me; he's crawled underneath my skin. I thought fate had brought us together. As if we were two random strangers destined to meet and meant to be together. Now he's telling me it wasn't fate at all. He orchestrated it.

'I knew exactly where you would be that night; I'd been watching you for a long time.'

I can barely speak but I whisper a question. 'You'd been stalking me?'

'I guess you could call it that. I knew you'd be sitting on that stool next to the bar; I knew you'd order a Bacardi and Coke with a slice of lime; and I knew your friends would be arriving soon, so I needed to work my magic on you fast and get you out of there.'

I feel beads of cold sweat dripping down my forehead as he runs his fingers roughly across my skin and sniggers.

'Getting all hot and bothered thinking about it are you? You make it so easy for me, like you did that night. You were putty in my hands, and you have been ever since.'

He runs his fingers even more roughly across my lips again and I want to scream at him. But somehow adrenaline kicks in and gives me the strength not to. I'm frightened if I provoke him, he'll kill me right now. Then he delivers his sinister punchline.

'You destroyed my life Emily and now I'm going to destroy yours.'

I swallow back panic as he positions himself so that we are face-to-face. I have to say something to him. 'I don't understand any of this, Garrie. I think you've got the wrong person.'

He lets out a high-pitched laugh before he leans into me. 'Let me make this a bit easier for you and jog your memory.'

He pulls a photograph out of his pocket and holds it in front of me. My heart pounds so fast I almost expect it to explode out of my chest. I recognise the woman instantly and cry out. It's my beautiful friend Annabel; Katie's mother. Memories spin round in my head as Garrie speaks again.

'She was my wife. And this was our home.'

His words cut through me like a knife. Now I know exactly who he is. My past has come back to haunt me, and I'm paralysed as my insides shake with fear.

Chapter 50

EMILY

I'm cold, unable to move, barely able to think. The red lipstick he's smeared roughly over my mouth stings against my dry lips. I try to lick it off, but the sting intensifies as the taste of lipstick becomes the taste of blood. I thank God I can't see my reflection, but my mind imagines I've become a caricature of myself, an ugly gargoyle. And that's how Garrie is looking at me, with disgusted contempt. As if he's staring at a sad, ageing whore using cheap lipstick in a desperate attempt to cling on to her youth.

At least he hasn't killed me yet. But he wants me to feel fear. He wants me desperate and helpless. I realise that's what he's always wanted, and that everything he's done since that night in the bar has been leading up to this moment. Through the brain fog of solitary confinement, I'm able to see clearly now. He wants me to give in, to fall apart and admit I'm broken. The truth is I almost am. I'm hanging on to my sanity by a thread.

He's staring through me without any expression in his eyes. I wish I understood why he's blaming me for ruining his life. If he knows about my friendship with Annabel, he must know how much I felt her loss too. I close my eyes and see her face. The beautiful person who walked into my life like a guardian angel, at exactly the right time, and became my salvation for a while. Annabel, and her beautiful daughter Katie.

I use my last reserves of willpower to blink away tears. If I allow myself the indulgence of crying, I know I won't stop, and Garrie is still gauging my response. The slow descent into cried-out exhaustion and blissful unconsciousness is too tempting to resist. Sleep is the easy way out but it's my only sanctuary since the world seems to have abandoned me. Even the moon has left, taking with it the last shaft of light at my window, and plunging me into total darkness.

I can't fight the tiredness any longer. And if I sleep maybe he'll leave without hurting me again tonight. I close my eyes and allow myself to fall asleep with the face of Annabel in that photograph dancing on my eyelids and etched into my mind.

I'm catapulted into brightness, to a state that rests somewhere between the past and present. I see Annabel bathed in an aura of light; it illuminates her like a halo.

≈ ≈ ≈

18 months earlier
Annabel smiles in between sips of tea as she watches Katie fitting the last of the cut-out blocks into her puzzle.

'Mummy, I made a cat.' She claps her chubby hands in excitement. 'Emily, look, I made a cat.'

We join in with her excitement and clap our hands. It's the first time she's completed this puzzle and it's a sign that her skills are improving. Annabel looks across at me with a big smile on her face.

'Emily, you've made such wonderful progress with her. She loves her time with you. It's helping so much. I can't thank you enough; we were lucky to find you.'

I feel a warm glow overflowing inside me as I smile at them both.

'I'm the lucky one. I love having her here. And after losing my…' I can't bring myself to say the word, but she understands. 'It helps me so much. Martin tries his best. He's wonderful, but he'll never really understand. Sometimes I think he tries too hard. I know he thinks I should stop dwelling on what's happened and move on. He doesn't realise there are some things you can never move on from.'

She touches my hand. 'Of course not. Not completely. Your daughter will always be a part of you. You can only…' She pauses as if choosing her words carefully. '…adjust to things not being quite what you expected.'

She glances over at Katie, and I feel her hand tense against mine. 'Men can never understand what makes us tick, however hard they try. They want things to be black and white and straightforward. Unfortunately, they rarely are.'

Her words strike a chord and I relate to her pain. Finding out about Katie's condition must have been difficult, but I'm glad I can help in some way. I wonder about Katie's father. It must be difficult for him too, but Annabel rarely talks about him, and I decide not to ask.

I'm watching her as she packs Katie's toys away and remembering the first time we met. She called me after I placed a small, discreet advert in the local newspaper offering tutoring services for younger children. When she visited, we bonded instantly, and Katie gave me one of her trademark uninhibited hugs. It all seemed it was meant to be, and they've been coming to my house ever since.

If only Martin could be more comfortable with it. He supports me, but he can't hide the fact that he thinks it's all too much too soon.

He hasn't met Annabel yet, so he doesn't know how special she is and how much our friendship means to me. And it feels like beautiful symmetry that she has the same name as my daughter.

≈ ≈ ≈

A sudden noise cuts across my reminiscences. I have no idea where it's coming from. I open my eyes and I'm back in the darkness of the present, but Garrie is no longer here. The noise stops; perhaps I imagined it. Everything is silent. I'm back in my strange, isolated limbo; a sensory no man's land. I never realised how black the dark could be, or how loud silence could be. Perhaps when you're deprived of most of your senses, the void that remains is amplified.

I wish I'd stayed asleep and in my dream. I want to be back in the light watching Katie giggle in childish delight at her cat puzzle, and with Annabel holding my hand. Instead, I'm remembering how I lost my beautiful friend the day she walked out on our friendship and refused to see me again. The day when I descended into my dark place. Even darker than where I find myself now.

A delayed breakdown after the trauma of losing the baby, compounded by the loss of my friend; that's what the doctors called it. I could barely function beyond stumbling through each tranquilized day. Life was a blur.

And then, the end. Annabel's name above a brief announcement in the paper.

A beautiful wife, a loving mother, tragically taken from us too soon.

Annabel was dead and I dealt with it all the only way I knew how. I locked her away in a convenient compartment in my brain along with my baby. The two Annabels who had come into my life and left with an abruptness my mind couldn't deal with; memories I couldn't bear to recall.

But now Garrie has picked at the lock. Challenging me with that photograph; telling me she was his wife.

He's unlocked all the painful memories I never wanted to face again.

I hear the noise again; it's coming from above me. Footsteps walking across a room; the sound of a chair being moved. Then a small whimper as a furry bundle jumps on my knee and curls up. It's Ginger. And if she's still here, my jailer must be too. The icy fear in my veins returns.

I hear the first creak on the stairs. He's on his way down and I cower into the corner of my sofa with Ginger. When he walks in, I'll pretend to be asleep. I haven't heard the second creak that tells me he's at the bottom of the stairs; he must have stopped halfway down. I hear him speak in a low voice and strain my ears to hear the words.

'Hi Sandie. I woke up thinking about you. I miss you. Sleep well and I'll see you tomorrow. Love you, baby.'

I wonder where Sandie thinks he is. At the sound of his voice Ginger nestles in closer to me; after a few seconds I hear Garrie speak again.

'Darling, sleep soundly. I'll be back soon. I love you.'

That can't have been Sandie; he just told her that. I feel Ginger shaking and a matching shiver of fear runs through me again.

He seemed to be speaking to somebody in the house.

Chapter 51

GARRIE

I don't know what the hell I'm doing but I can't stop. Emily's slithering around inside my head, like a maggot gnawing away at my soul.

When my beautiful Annabel died, I made her a promise that Emily would pay for what she'd done. I had no idea how I'd make that happen, but I knew I had to start by getting close to her.

She'd been friendly with my wife before the accident but, luckily, she'd never met me, so it was easy to watch her from a distance before I made my move. I drove past her house every day, a tiny mid-terrace with beige curtains. I would park at a discreet distance and watch. She rarely came out of the house. She had a crate in the front garden where she would throw bottles of wine and, occasionally, she appeared on the driveway to empty the bin or talk to a neighbour.

But every Friday she'd leave the house at 6 p.m., all dressed up for a night out. She'd walk through the town and arrive at the Tanet Bar thirty minutes later. She always got there early for some reason. At 7 p.m. her friend would arrive, and they'd laugh, drink and talk.

I remember the night I made my move. It was satisfyingly easy. I could hardly believe how quickly it all happened, from meeting her to finding I was making love to the enemy. She was like jelly in my hands. My anger dissipated into sexual energy infused with deadly passion because I wanted to kill her. I still do. But not until I've made her suffer like I suffered. I'm not evil. I'm not the devil. I'm a man who loved his wife with all his heart. She was my entire world, and we were planning the most beautiful future together; until it all got ripped apart.

I lost Annabel because of what Emily did. Her obsessions ruined my life, and now I'm going to ruin hers.

Chapter 52

EMILY

I've closed my eyes and I'm back in the light. Remembering.

≈ ≈ ≈

18 months earlier

'Hey Katie, come here, it's ok.' I clutch her to me and watch her little face as her mother walks away.

It breaks Annabel's heart like it breaks every mother's heart to leave her child with a virtual stranger. But this Katie's third lesson with me, and Annabel can see her progress, so she's started trusting me enough to leave her with me. Katie clings on to her, but I've told Annabel I will keep her safe. I love Katie almost as if she's mine.

Annabel knows her daughter isn't developing like other babies; she can't do things that other children her age can do. At first, she'd hoped it was slow progress, and she'd catch up, but it's more than that. Katie finds things challenging but my lessons seem to help. They give Katie a new stimulus and she responds to me, which gives Annabel a break and the chance to spend some time with her husband. Apparently, he dotes on her. That's what she tells me although she never goes into detail. I don't even know his name. In fact, she is oddly nervous and reserved whenever she mentions him; detached somehow. She's started relaxing and opening up a little more now she can see the progress Katie is making.

'He's such a devoted husband, Emily. A true romantic.'

'He sounds wonderful, Annabel.'

'He is. And I'm so glad we answered your advert. You've made such a difference, to all our lives. Katie seems happier and I get to spend more time with my husband which makes him happy.'

She talks of roses and wine, wonderful evenings spent on their terrace, wrapped in each other's arms. She talks of the day her husband whisked her off to France for lunch. She paints a picture that makes their life sound wonderful.

≈ ≈ ≈

I can hardly believe the man she'd been speaking about was Garrie. The same man who later swept me off my feet but who I now hate.

I always longed for the type of romance that Annabel described. Martin loved me, but he was practical and level-headed; a feet-on-the-ground type of man who didn't go in for grand gestures or outward shows of affection. I knew he loved me deeply in his own way, and I knew how much he wanted us to make a go of things. I wish I could have been a better wife, but I couldn't deal with the grief of losing our baby. I withdrew from him; I pushed him away so I could deal with it in my own way. Breaking up was a horrible inevitability.

I'm thinking too much, but it's the only thing I can do inside this prison where time seems to have stopped. The silent stillness has cleared my head of all the debris, and my memories and thoughts are sharper despite my exhaustion. Perhaps if I force myself to remember those times with Annabel and Katie, I'll find something to explain why Garrie is holding me responsible for his wife's death. Somewhere in my head there's a locked compartment that contains answers. I need to access it.

Ginger is shivering in my lap as we wait together for Garrie's next move. I listen for a sign that he might be leaving, but instead I hear the familiar two creaks on the stairs as he goes back upstairs. I wonder what he's doing, and what he's planning. I fear my time is running out.

I need to escape before he kills me.

Chapter 53

SANDIE

Alternating images of Garrie and Emily assault my subconscious. I'm in that early morning half-awake limbo where dreams and reality are indistinguishable. I reach for the reassuring comfort of Garrie's body next to me and remember he's not here. The coldness of the empty space jolts me awake with a shiver. I listen for Ginger's morning scratch at the door to tell me it's time for her walk and breakfast, but she's not here either. I feel alone and vulnerable.

A ping from my phone punctures the silence and I reach for it on the bedside table. I hope it's a message from Garrie telling me he's bringing Ginger home before he heads to work. I need to see them both, and she'll be confused if she's forced to spend the day with his Mum in a strange house. She's already done enough commuting as a puppy between here and across the street. The ping is a spam marketing text and in irritation I block the sender before blinking back tears of disappointment. It's 7:30 a.m. and I'd hoped for a good morning message from him but there's nothing. I look down at my baby bump and run a protective hand over the growing life inside me as my disappointment turns to anger.

Garrie should be here; with both of us. He needs to stop running away. When he gets home, I'll tell him this can't happen again. It feels too much like the first time he left me for Emily. I never want to feel that way again.

I close my eyes against early morning tiredness, but images of Emily dance into the darkness. Why does she keep haunting me? Why can't I do what Garrie tells me to, be pleased that she's gone, and forget her?

Defeated by the images I drag myself out of bed and into the bathroom and splash water against my sleepy eyelids. I sway with tiredness and early morning nausea and grip the sink until my knuckles turn white. I speak to my image in the mirror. '*Let it go, Sandie. Emily's in the past. Garrie never loved her; he's told you that. It's always been you. Accept that and move on.*'

But I already know the speech and it doesn't work. Garrie's haunted by demons from his past that are somehow connected to Emily, so the demons must be exorcised, for all our sakes. I need to discover the secrets he's keeping from me. And there's only one place I can do that.

I grab a mug of tea and two digestive biscuits to ease the nausea and restore my energy. I don't expect Garrie back until after work, so there's plenty of time for what I have planned. I throw on a tracksuit, sit by the window and sip a second mug of tea. I look over at Emily's house and know what I need to do. A niggling voice tells me I shouldn't, but I ignore it. I need to understand more about Emily's connection with Annabel and Katie, and if the answers are anywhere, they're at number 12. I know exactly where I'm going to look first.

I let myself in and head towards the basement but change my mind as I walk past the kitchen. Through the door I see the photograph collection on the sideboard; elegant silver frames so perfectly arranged, Emily-style. Maybe there's one of her Aunt; the one Garrie mentioned. I realise I've never heard Emily talk about her family. I asked her about them the day we first met, when she came to our housewarming party with the annoying houseplant, but she ignored the question.

I avoid taking another look at the wedding card from her friend for the "wedding that never was". It's still nestling behind the porcelain teapot next to the photograph of her and Martin. I wonder again why she kept it on display and how much Garrie knew about him and about the child they lost? I guess he must have known. The rest of the photographs are of Ginger; there's one of Emily drinking champagne with a friend at a restaurant; and one of her with Garrie. There are no family pictures. I wonder why not.

I also wonder why she didn't take any of her photographs with her when she left.

I consider going to visit Hoppy but decide to leave that until later, when hopefully Linda will be around to see me. Feeding the rabbit is my cover for being in the house. Instead, I do what I came to do and take the steps down to the basement. The child-like room I've entered again feels like Emily's private sanctuary and I'm the unwelcome invader. But she and Garrie have given me no choice; I'm convinced it holds secrets I need to uncover.

I replace her diary in the drawer where I found it and search the rest of the contents again, in the hope I'll perhaps find another one. Another window to Emily's past. I'm convinced she continued her story somewhere, but the drawer yields nothing. If a later diary exists, it's somewhere else.

I look around the room and see a battered toybox in the corner. It has a fancy letter K stencilled on the side. It's open and overflowing with toys and puzzles. I dig deeper into its contents and find a book about tutoring children with learning difficulties. I flick through it. Several of the pages are marked with Emily's scribbled notes and I pause when one catches my eye.

This might work with Katie.

I instantly drop the book on the floor and close the lid on the box.

Chapter 54

EMILY

It wasn't long before I realised there were cracks in Annabel's marriage. She made it sound idyllic at first; the perfect romantic union with a man who was the love of her life, but she started to look increasingly tired, stressed, and preoccupied.

≈ ≈ ≈

18 months earlier

'Do you mind looking after Katie a little bit longer today?'

'Of course not, Annabel. Take as long as you need. Is everything OK?'

She looks uncomfortable at my question. 'My husband wants me to spend more time with him. We had an argument last night; he says I've been neglecting him, and I suppose I have. But I've been spending every minute caring for Katie.'

'Surely he understands.'

'Not really. He thinks she's come between us. He says I've given all my love to her and he's the loser.'

'She's your daughter for goodness sake. It's a different type of love.'

'That's what I told him, but he doesn't believe it. He wishes she'd never been born.'

'He said that?'

'Virtually. Tells me she's been a burden since she arrived.'

'Katie could never be a burden to anyone. She's such a loving child with so much to give.'

'I know. And she never stops smiling.'

'Don't worry, Annabel. I'm always here to look after Katie. If your husband gets difficult, you only have to ask.

I hate hearing how difficult her husband makes things for her, but it means I can spend longer with the beautiful little girl who has become such a big part of my life. Katie makes me happy. A happiness I thought I would never find again. Martin doesn't understand of course; he thinks I'm getting too attached, and he wants me to stop the lessons, but I ignore him. For the first time in our married life, I'm doing something we haven't agreed on; I'm continuing the lessons against his wishes. I make sure he's out of the house before Katie arrives. But he knows, and it's starting to drive a wedge between us. He's becoming increasingly unhappy because Katie is spending more time with me. We should be comforting each other, getting through the loss of our daughter together, but I know I'm pushing him away. I need something he can't give me; a way to fill the gaping hole inside me. Katie gives me that. She allows me to indulge my denial of what has happened to my baby and to my body.

But I worry about Annabel. She looks increasingly tense these days.

'I'm sorry for the short notice, Emily. My husband is being difficult again and wants us to spend the afternoon together without Katie.'

I don't press her on what's happening at home, but I have a horrible sense of imminent disaster, which is hard to shrug off.

Chapter 55

SANDIE

I stare down at the book I dropped. KATIE. A beautiful name that could belong to any little girl. But I'm certain this is Garrie's Katie, and I've just opened her toybox. I look inside at the selection of brightly coloured toys, puzzles, and a pink rag doll which I pick up and instantly recognise. A few weeks ago, I asked Garrie to show me a photograph of his daughter. I'd wanted to go and visit her, but he said it wasn't the right time. The tiny passport sized photograph he pulled from his wallet was the closest I got; she looked happy and pretty with pigtails and a bow in her hair, and she was holding the same rag doll I'm clutching now.

I rummage around further, because I know Katie plays a part in the history between Emily and Garrie.

'Sandie?' I spin round and see Martha in the doorway with a beaming smile on her face. 'The door was unlocked so I came in. Have you fed the rabbit?'

Damn, I can't believe I forgot I'd arranged to meet Martha here today at precisely this time.

'No, I haven't seen Hoppy yet. I was waiting for you.'

'Why are you waiting in the basement?'

It's a good question and I'm not entirely sure how to answer it so I ask her a question instead. 'Do you play with the things in this toybox?'

She frowns at me. 'Emily didn't really like me touching it. It belongs to Katie. She used to have lessons with Emily just like me. Shall we make some bracelets? I can show you how to make them.'

The toybox will have to wait. I turn away from it to look at the neatly labelled packets of coloured beads on the table and smile at how quickly Martha can always change the subject.

'OK, that sounds like fun.'

She gives me a piece of plastic string. 'You need to put one of these on the end to stop the beads coming off.' She hands me a silver clasp.

'Do you enjoy your lessons with Emily?'

She gives me a beaming smile of excitement. 'I love them. Have you heard from her? Is she coming back?'

'Not yet. Does she ever talk about Katie?'

'Sometimes. She used to have a room like this in Emily's other house. It was before she moved here. She told me all about it.'

'What was it like?'

'Katie had her own bedroom.'

The walls of the basement close in on me. I need to escape its dim, artificial light and get back to the daylight. Martha seems to love it down here, but to me it's a dark space that feels like an unhealthy shrine to Emily's obsessions. I'm unnerved that Katie once had her own room like this one too.

I take Martha's hand. 'Come on. It's time we fed Hoppy.'

Chapter 56

EMILY

When Martin eventually left, I was relieved. It hurt at first, but I felt it was for the best. Our world had changed overnight, and I didn't think we could ever be happy together again. The moment my daughter was snatched from my imperfect womb, I became more than a grieving mother. I became a different person. I can admit that to myself now. Here, in this dark, cold room where I'm incarcerated and alone with my thoughts there's nothing to distract me from them. It's strange how solitary confinement brings such clarity and perspective.

With Martin gone I could enjoy my time with Katie without having to explain myself. I still loved my husband and that never went away, but Annabel's little girl had become the true centre of my world. She was the daughter I knew I could never have and every day the bond between us grew stronger and more powerful. All I wanted was to make her happy and see her smile.

I loved buying things for her. Sales assistants would smile at my choices and assume I was shopping for my own child. I did nothing to dissuade them. Her favourite surprise gift was a little pink rag doll with hair the same colour as hers; she took it everywhere. Annabel laughed and said it was glued to her; Katie wouldn't go anywhere without it. I would watch her hugging that rag doll to herself and imagine that she could be my baby. My Annabel, a beautiful little girl with pigtails.

When Katie and I were alone in the house, in the private space I'd created especially for her, I even called her Annabel; whispering it to myself when she was distracted with a puzzle so she wouldn't hear me and get confused.

Somewhere in the recesses of my mind I knew it was wrong, but for a few brief, beautiful seconds I could make myself believe I had my daughter back, and that losing her had been a bad dream. I ignored the voice in my head telling me I was heading down a dangerous road, towards an almost inevitable bad outcome.

I should have listened.

But I chose not to, and that drove Martin away. Cracks appeared in our united wall of grief as he gradually came to terms with what had happened and told me it was time for us to look forward. But I could do neither and I resented the fact that he could. A chasm opened up between us. We had both lost our baby, but I'd lost something he hadn't. He could still father a child; I would never again be able to conceive one.

Resentment took hold of me and spread like an inoperable malignant growth; until Katie came along as my miracle cure. It was Liz who had convinced me to resurrect my dream to teach when she turned up unannounced one Sunday when Martin was playing football and dragged me, protesting, out of the house.

'I've decided to kidnap you for a few hours. You look like you haven't slept or eaten in days, so I'm taking you to lunch. No arguments. I'm worried about you, Emily.'

By the time she'd convinced me to finish the last mouthful of my favourite dessert, she'd got my future planned out. Liz is always a force to be reckoned with.

'You need an interest. And you're so gifted with kids. Nothing can make up for what you've lost but maybe teaching is the best way for you to start coming back from what happened.'

The idea had gradually appealed to me more, and four weeks later I was the proud owner of a framed teaching certificate produced on Liz's laptop, and my ad was running in the local newspaper. I began to feel alive again, filled with some sense of purpose. It's ironic that a plan that had felt so right, seems inexplicably to have led me to this prison cell where Garrie is the jailer.

I wish something in my memory bank could help me to understand why I'm here.

Chapter 57

GARRIE

Ginger pricks up her ears and tilts her head in puppy confusion; she doesn't understand why we're at my mum's and I know she misses Sandie. She wants to be at home; I do too, but I can't face going back to more questions yet. I'm not ready to answer them. I pat her head before she jumps onto my knee, snuggling up to me for body warmth. She's cold; so am I. My mother keeps the house like an igloo; the alcohol in her bloodstream seems to anaesthetise her against sub-zero temperatures.

I glance at my watch. It's time I got moving. If I leave by 8 p.m. I can get to Emily in time to give her a quick drink and some breakfast before my first meeting.

'Important clients today, Ginger. Could be worth a lot of commission to me. Can't afford to be late.'

But there's something I must do first; check Emily's phone and reply to any incoming messages. Sandie's given me no choice but to keep up this pretence. God knows what possessed her to switch on the phone and reply as if she was Emily. I was annoyed at first, until I realised it was a masterstroke on her part. She doesn't know it, but she's protecting my secret because it's buying me some time before anybody gets suspicious about not hearing from Emily. I can't risk that, especially interference from loud, opinionated friend Liz. I can sense she doesn't like me, and I haven't felt comfortable around her from the moment we met. She's everything I dislike in a woman.

She barely took her eyes off me during the wedding rehearsal, and I could feel her distrust boring into my back whenever it was turned. I wouldn't be surprised if she was the brains behind Emily installing the tracker app on my phone; that sounds like Liz's style. I can't afford her to start snooping around or to turn up at number 12 where she might bump into Sandie and start filling her head with ideas. Not until this nightmare is over, I keep my promise to Annabel, and finish what I've started.

Sandie. I smile at the thought of her. I missed being with her last night, but I need to protect her from all this. 'We need to get home to her, don't we Ginger? I know you miss her too.'

It all seems so right; Sandie's like Annabel in lots of ways. I know our life together can be perfect. The sort of perfect I thought I'd never find again. But this time I won't let anything get in the way.

I switch the phone on and check the new message notifications. There are fewer than I feared, mostly marketing updates. There's only one personal message and predictably it's from Liz.

Hi Em. When r u coming back? I want to see u & check you're ok. Whatever's
going on, we can sort it out. I assume this all has something to do
with HIM. Sorry, but you know my opinion. Better off without the
bastard. Ur strong & u don't need him. Call me, Miss u.
xxxxx

I glare at the screen and shudder at her text speak. And the message is typical of her; automatically assuming I'm the bad guy. I could tell her a few home truths about her precious "strong" Emily. But everybody will know those eventually.

For now, I need to send the best response I can, and remember who I'm meant to be. I hit reply and start typing.

Liz. Please don't worry about me. I know I took off in a hurry, but I had to. I ended things
with Garrie and now I need space. I couldn't deal with staying in the house or having
to see him, so I'm staying with my Aunt Anna. You were right all along, and I should

have listened to you. I know you always thought Garrie was
a mistake. I'll be in
touch when I feel up to coming back there. No idea when
that will be.
Miss you too. Love. E xxxx

I read over it again and hit send; it sounds like
Emily and hopefully it'll shut Liz up for a while. If she does
happen to bump into Sandie and they compare notes, at
least they both have the same story about Emily's fictional
aunt.

I scribble a quick note to my mother which I doubt
she'll even bother to read, I put an excited Ginger on her
lead, and let myself quietly out of the house.

Chapter 58

EMILY

Focus, Emily. Concentrate. Take deep breaths.

I inhale and exhale; three times, and slowly. I need to recharge my system with as many kilowatts of energy as I can breathe into it.

You can do this. Do it now. Work it out before he realises he's made a mistake and comes back.

Garrie was in a rush this morning and looked like he'd barely slept. I suspected there'd been trouble in paradise between him and Sandie, but I knew better than to ask. He was typing frenzied texts with one hand while he held the water bottle to my mouth with the other. I gulped it down in dehydrated desperation and it spilled, but he was too preoccupied to notice. He shovelled breakfast cereal into me at a speed that almost made me gag before he untied my arms and hands and walked me to the loo.

He told me to hurry up and ordered me back to my usual position on the sofa. 'Hands behind your back and don't move.' He pushed my feet apart and tied each of my ankles to a sofa leg. 'One arm forward Emily. You know the routine. Be quick.'

I held my right arm out to be tied in the same way but as he grabbed my wrist, his phone rang. He yelled into it. 'Twenty minutes. Give them coffee and schmooze them till I'm there.'

With a muttered 'Change of plan. Less time than I thought' he grabbed my other arm from behind my back and bound my wrists together. I winced at the rough coarseness of the rope as he pulled it tighter. He stood up, tossed the unused length of rope across the room, and sneered at me.

'Sorry it's a quick visit today, sweetie, but duty calls. Back later.'

As he rushes off, I realise he's given me my first chance to escape. I take another deep breath. The rope is cutting into my wrists and my fingers are going numb. But without my arms tied to the sofa I have some manoeuvrability I didn't have before; I should be able to stand up. I allow myself a glimmer of hope that I might find a way to escape this nightmare. I may never get a chance like this again. I wiggle my fingers to keep the circulation going and pull myself unsteadily to my feet. I look round the room for something that might cut the rope. There's a fireplace to my left with a slate hearth and two glass vases on the mantelpiece above it. If I can shatter one of them, I might be able to cut the ropes and untie myself. But my legs are tied to the sofa legs. I can't move.

Think Emily. For God's sake think. This is your chance to escape.

I drop down on to my knees. If I use my full body length, I should almost reach the hearth. I stretch my bound wrists out and throw myself forward until I'm flat on the floor. Pain shoots through my ankles but I tell myself to ignore it. I'm parallel to the fireplace and shuffle my body round towards it. I cry out as the rope tightens and twists around my ankle and take another long deep breath against the pain.

I look up at the two vases which are tantalizingly out of reach. But there's an antique set of brass fire tools on the hearth which look heavy. Perhaps I can use those to bring the vases crashing down. I stretch my arms out, but I can't reach; I need to get closer. I brace myself against the pain in my right ankle and count to three. In one move I use my elbows to propel me further to the left, stretch my arms to their limit and hit the fire set with my bound hands. It topples towards me. I grab the coal shovel in both hands, roll my body over as far to my left as I can, then prise myself up and take a swing at the vases. I miss. I try to aim better the second time and miss again. I yell in frustration before making a third attempt. My scream superpowers the strength in my arms and I hit one of the vases. It crashes down onto the slate and smashes. I whoop as if I've won an Olympic gold medal.

I grab the most jagged shard I can see and wedge it upright against the edge of the hearth with the shovel. Energy and momentum pulse through my veins as adrenaline surges through my body. I rub my bound wrists across the jagged edge until my hands bleed; but the bloodied rope gets looser. The pain is almost too much to bear but I know I must keep going. I pray I've weakened the rope enough and I try to pull my wrists apart. I shout in exhausted triumph as the rope breaks.

I'm halfway to freedom, but my feet are still tied. I try to think past the pain of my raw ankles. My skin shivers against the cold through the thin material of my shirt. Garrie never did bring me a change of clothes. It's been so cold here that some days I've thought I would freeze to death before I starved. I see condensation as I breathe out into the chill of this room, but somehow being so cold focuses me. I lean forward, reach for my feet, and start to untie the knot with my trembling fingers.

It seems to take forever but finally my legs are free. I'm too weak with pain and exhaustion to stand so I drag myself across the room, into the hallway, and to the front door. I reach up to open it, but it's locked.

I sink backwards, defeated, and let out a scream.

Chapter 59

GARRIE

I press my foot on the accelerator. I'll go and give Emily another quick drink and head straight back to Sandie. This morning's meeting went well, the final completion of a major sale. My boss is delighted, and I know this will probably guarantee me an equity partnership in the firm.

The clients loved Ginger too, and I give her a pat.

'Great job, Ginger, you're hired. You've helped me to earn the best commission I've ever had; and I could use the money.'

Annabel had savings which she put into our joint account, but I've been paying the rent on Emily's house as well as maintaining the home I shared with Annabel, and the money's been dwindling. This deal has landed at the right time for me. I need to keep paying the bills at number 12 because Emily's house isn't actually 'To Let'. I decided it would create less suspicion if it had a sign in the front garden to convince everybody that she's moved on permanently. I put one of my estate agency's 'To Let' signs into the back of my car and once it was dark, I installed it in the front garden.

It's doing its job although it's creating more work because I'm having to deal with any enquiries that come in. It's helped to reassure Sandie, and even nosey Linda seems convinced Emily's gone.

But I can't maintain this pretence forever. I need to move forward with the next stage of my plan.

Chapter 60

EMILY

My screams echo around the empty hallway.

I stare at the locked door and frantically search for a key. I'm seeing the house in more detail for the first time. It's old, with bare stone walls and a hardwood floor. There's a pretty rug that extends across the hallway floor so the house must have been loved at some stage.

There's a telephone on the windowsill, but there's no plug on the end. It's one of those retro phones with a circular dial and numbers. It must have worked at some stage, but the wire has been cut and I'm left with no choice but to smash a window. I need to act quickly because I've no idea how long I've got before Garrie makes his next appearance.

At least smashing the window will give me a clean getaway without getting the police involved. I've got a bit of history with the police and that's probably on record, so I don't want them sniffing around. Not that any of it was my fault.

I know I had started treating Katie like my own child, but that was because I loved her, and she was special. She needed me and I was a woman grieving the loss of my own child, so I needed her too.

I suppose I got things a bit out of balance and people got the wrong idea. Annabel became distant and Martin started calling me obsessed. He thought it was all unhealthy and wanted me to see the doctor again.

But I never had any intention of hurting anyone, and I was heartbroken when Katie was taken away from me. I can't bear to confront the memory of that.

And I need to focus on getting away from here before Garrie gets back.

Chapter 61

GARRIE

I'm nearly at the house. I remember when I used to feel a rush of excitement as I turned into this street, knowing that Annabel was at home waiting for me. In the early days of our romance, when it was just the two of us; before it all went horribly wrong. Before 'she' came into our lives and destroyed what Annabel and I had together.

It was Annabel who bought this house. I remember how she glowed when she first showed it to me, clutching my hand as she took me round every room and proudly described every feature. She'd radiated with excitement and said she had dreamed of the day when she could build a beautiful home and family with the man she loved. I felt like the luckiest man alive.

She would sit on the small upstairs balcony that overlooks the street and wait for me to come home. I'd run upstairs to greet her, and we'd sink into each other's arms. We'd drink wine and sit for hours watching the world.

The two of us. It was perfect.

Now all I have left are my memories as I pull up outside a house that looks tired and rundown. It lost its energy the day I lost Annabel. But I've kept the house because I can still feel her presence inside.

I glance around before I put Ginger on the lead and walk up to the front door. I'm not in the mood to answer anybody's questions about why I haven't sold or let the house yet. I feel the weight of my backpack pressing on my shoulders as I turn the key in the lock and prepare for another conversation with the monster inside. I'm giving food and water to Emily but I'm not sure how much longer I can keep it up.

I want her gone so that I can be alone here to enjoy the spirit of my wife once more.

Chapter 62

EMILY

I'm having a panic attack; Garrie's outside and I don't know what the hell to do. I can't escape through the front of the house because he'll see me. I take a deep slow breath and talk myself back to calmness.

Think, Emily. Focus. You've come this far. Find another way out.

I run back into the room that was my prison cell, grab the poker from the fireplace and run back through the hallway to the rear of the house. I smash the kitchen window. I'm not sure I have the energy to climb through it, but I have no choice. I scrape the poker along the edge of the window frame to remove any sharp pieces, then I try to pull myself up so I can roll through the gap.

I'm so weak that my first attempt fails but I can hear him opening the front door, so I need to keep trying. I drag a wooden chair across to the window so that I can get more height and I'm about to leap to freedom when I hear Ginger barking. I don't look back, but I think she's already in the kitchen, and Garrie's now inside the house.

I hyperventilate as I fall onto the grass below the window. My legs hurt and I slide myself along the ground because I can no longer stand. The window must be too high for Ginger because she hasn't followed me, but I know it's only a matter of time before she does.

Chapter 63

GARRIE

Ginger runs straight into the kitchen, and I make my way up the stairs. It's the first thing I do whenever I enter the house, before I deal with Emily. She doesn't belong here. This house used to be filled with Annabel's love and light, until Emily took it away from me and extinguished it. But this was the only place I could bring her when I had to bring my plan forward. Now I hate her even more for invading the space I shared with Annabel.

I didn't have much time this morning because of the meeting but now I'm back, I can't miss an opportunity to stand on our beautiful balcony that opens off our bedroom. It brings me close to Annabel again. I look out onto the neighbouring fields beyond the houses and imagine she's here with me. She chose this house because of the stunning views and autumn was always her favourite time of year. I breathe her in along with the crisp smells of the autumnal air.

'I can't stay long today, my love. I must get back to Sandie, after I've dealt with the monster, but I'll be back tonight. Beautiful Annabel, I know you're here with me. I love you my darling.'

As I'm blowing her a kiss, I hear Ginger barking. I don't want her attracting attention outside, so I run downstairs. I immediately see what's got her agitated; the door to the room Emily should be in is open and she's not there. *Shit. Where the hell is she?*

I feel a gush of wind blowing through the house and notice a gap where the kitchen window should be. Emily must have found a way to smash it but I'm sure she won't get far in her weakened state. I was careless and sloppy for the first time this morning because I was in a rush but now, I'm almost looking forward to overpowering her again and punishing her for trying to escape. I won't let her do that again.

But she's made the game more interesting.

Chapter 64

EMILY

There's no way out. I'm trapped; surrounded by tall trees and hedges. There are no gaps. I'm sandwiched between a painted summer house and a willow tree. Then Ginger comes bounding towards me. Her tiny paws scrape playfully at my legs because I'm not responding. She wonders why I'm ignoring her.

A moment later I hear Garrie. Calling out in his soft, elongated teasing voice. It's all a game to him.

'Ooh Emilyyyyy. I'm coming to find youuuuu.'

I can't believe I made such a bad choice. I should have smashed the front window and got away before he arrived. I should have acted sooner and made my bid for freedom. But instead, I'm cowering behind a tree fearing for my life, hiding from a man who thinks playing hide and seek is fun.

'Ten, nine, eight, seven…oh dear, what a stupid mistake to make. Jumping out of the back window. Not one of your best decisions.' He laughs. 'We can play this game all day if you want or you can step out now from behind that tree.'

Even Ginger's scared. She cowers as he appears in front of me.

'Boo.'

I shrink back, too weak to try and run. I want to scream but it comes out as a hoarse rasp. Once again, I'm at the mercy this madman.

He sneers at me with mock concern. 'Look at that pretty little face. Such a shame that no one will ever see it again. But never mind; these things happen. You win some you lose some. You understand what I mean don't you

Emily? None of us really knows another person, do we? You walk past someone in the street; smile, say hello, pat their dog, that sort of thing. But you don't know them. You have no idea what they might be capable of.'

I inject as much venom into my response as my strength will allow. 'Oh, I know exactly what you're capable of. You're a monster.'

He leans closer, pure hatred etched into his features. 'That could really hurt my feelings, Emily. But I know you don't mean it. You were going to marry me, remember? I used to lie in your bed, and you couldn't get enough of me, could you? I used to watch your cute little face fall asleep afterwards. You always looked so cute dreaming of our beautiful wedding that was never going to happen.'

He's doing everything he can to make my skin crawl and it's working.

'You see, I'd already had a wonderful wife, and you were never exactly marriage material. Annabel was the most beautiful, perfect woman I could ever wish for. Our life was perfect until you showed up. Your obsession with my daughter destroyed everything.'

I clutch the tree for support as he spits the words at me. I ache with exhaustion and fear of the knowledge he wants me dead. He edges closer; wearing a victory smile as he watches me shrinking in front of him. 'But I'm a decent type of guy. I think you've suffered enough today so let's go inside and I'll make you a nice cup of tea. I'll even open the back door so you can walk through instead of climbing through the window. How does that sound?'

I have no choice. I've blown my escape plan and I follow him towards the house, but I see the jagged pieces of glass scattered across the lawn. As he turns to unlock the door, I grab a small shard and clench it in my right hand. Inside, I follow his instructions. I sit defeated as he ties my wrists and feet to the sofa, even more tightly than before. I drink water. I eat two protein bars. And with an exhausted slump I prepare myself for more discomfort because I realise he's about to tape my mouth shut. There's a look of pure evil and excitement on his face as he cuts the first piece of tape with his teeth.

'I didn't want to do this Emily, but you've given me no choice. I'll be late getting home today because of your unsuccessful Houdini performance. This is the price you pay for trying to get the better of me.'

He closes the door and he's gone. I want to weep, and I almost want to give up the fight. But I picture his evil expression and I know I can't give up. Instead, I press the fingers of my right hand against the piece of glass that is now my only hope of survival.

Chapter 65

SANDIE

Discovering Katie's toybox, and hearing Martha's revelation that Katie also had her own room, has left me feeling disturbed and uncomfortable. I feel guilty that I've trespassed on Emily's grief but learning about both girls' rooms has made me glad she's no longer living opposite us. I will be relieved when someone new moves into her house, but I haven't noticed anyone coming to view it. I'll ask Garrie for an update when he gets home.

For now, I need a happy, normal distraction from thinking about the strange basement at number 12. I spend an hour surfing nursery décor sites, listening to my favourite Spotify playlist, and exploring colour schemes. I want my daughter to be cocooned by happiness and warm sunshine, so I've settled on yellow. I'm convinced she's a girl as I smile down at her and pat my baby bump. I always used to wonder why expectant mothers made that gesture, as if they were reminding the world they were pregnant. Now I understand; it's a primal instinct to protect a new life.

I wander into the kitchen, make tea, and open a pack of custard creams. I have a sudden craving to devour the entire pack; another pregnancy quirk I never understood before. I have course work to catch up on and an assignment to submit in a week, so I grab my books from the shelf by the window and automatically look across at number 12. A man is in the front garden staring up at the house. Finally, someone there to view it. He's now looking furtively through the front window, and I wonder why someone from Garrie's agency isn't with him.

Linda rushes past my house carrying supermarket bags and pulling her wheel-along shopping trolley which is bulging at the seams. She's panting as she quickens her pace so I'm guessing she must have noticed the stranger; she doesn't miss much. I smile at the thought that whatever there is to find out about our potential new neighbour, Chief Inspector Linda will discover it within a few minutes of interrogation.

She's now at Emily's garden gate and I'm crossing the road towards them. She's already laying the groundwork for her questions.

'Hello. Can I help you?'

'I'm here to see Emily.'

'Oh. I assumed you were here to view the house. Emily's away and we don't know where she's gone. Do you mind if I ask who you are?'

As I get closer, I instantly recognise the stranger's face; he's the man in the photograph on Emily's mantelpiece. 'My name's Martin.'

I decide to interject. I'm keen to talk to him and I need to rescue him from Linda's clutches. 'Hi Linda. I'm here to feed Hoppy. Do you want some help with those shopping bags?'

Her exasperated expression tells me she isn't pleased at me showing up at this precise moment. Linda prefers to keep her interrogations private so she can gossip to the neighbours. 'Thanks, Sandie, but I can manage. I need to help this gentleman first. He's called round to see Emily and I've told him she's away and we don't know where she's gone.'

Linda clearly has no idea who the man is. I turn to him and choose my words carefully. 'She's visiting family; her Aunt, I think. I'm housesitting while she's gone. Do you mind if we ask how you know Emily?'

He walks towards us, smiles a slightly shy smile, and extends a hand to me. He's exactly as Emily described him. I feel his nervousness in his handshake.

'I'm Emily's ex-husband. I'm a little concerned about her, as are several of her friends. We've hardly heard from her recently and that's not like Emily...'

Linda cuts across his sentence. 'I've never heard her mention an ex-husband.' She raises an accusing eyebrow at me. 'Did you know about this?'

'Actually, yes, I did.'

I ignore her look of irritation and return Martin's smile, but my mind's racing. I need to find a way of being alone with him. This is the best opportunity I'll ever get to learn more about Emily's past and her connection to Garrie.

'It's lovely to meet you, Martin, why don't you come inside with me? I'm sure you could use a cup of tea and I'll tell you what I know about Emily. Hopefully, it will put your mind at rest. I'm Sandie, by the way. And this is Linda.'

I see a flicker of recognition at the mention of my name, and he glances down at my stomach. 'Thank you. And yes, we should talk.'

I turn to Linda whose glare is now commuting between her shopping bags and me. She clearly doesn't like the idea of missing out on this conversation. 'I'll take my shopping home then come back and join you. I'd like to know what's going on too.'

I don't need to reply to her because Martin does it for me as he shakes Linda's hand. 'It's been nice to meet you, Linda, but I'd prefer to keep this conversation between Sandie and myself.'

He looks back at me and gestures towards Emily's house. 'Shall we?'

I nod at him and smile at an open-mouthed Linda as I turn the key in the front door and wonder what I'm about to hear on the other side.

Chapter 66

SANDIE

I'm staring at Martin and he's staring back. It's clear we're both apprehensive, not knowing where to start the conversation, or how much each of us knows about the other. Since I've been looking through Emily's private diaries, I know more than he probably realises. I'm sitting at her kitchen table opposite the man who featured on every page; staring at a stranger who feels oddly familiar. A pang of guilt hits me because in my quest to discover more about Emily, I invaded his privacy too.

I'm relieved when he finally breaks the awkward silence.

'Thank you for agreeing to talk with me, Sandie.'

'It's good to meet you, Martin.'

'I saw Emily's friend, Liz, recently in the supermarket. She's been keeping in touch and telling me about Emily's new partner and how it affected you. I don't suppose you've got much reason to care about her welfare since she got involved with your fiancé, but I'm here because I'm genuinely worried about her. I'm hoping you can tell me where she is.'

'I would if I could, Martin, but the truth is I don't know where she is.'

He looks disappointed. 'We're divorced, as you probably know, but I still care deeply about her. We went through a lot together. And I know it doesn't make things right from your point of view, but she's been through some particularly difficult times. I'm not convinced she's ever really recovered from them, and I suspect she needs help.' He pauses for a moment. 'I'm sorry. This must all sound terribly garbled, but Emily got herself into a complicated mess.'

I give him an encouraging nod. None of this can be easy for him, but I need to choose my words carefully. 'I'll help as much as I can, Martin. I can see how concerned you are. But the truth is I know very little about Emily's past. I'm back with my fiancé now and he told me that the two of them share some history, but I don't know the details. When they split up, she went to stay with her family to clear her head. I assume she's still there.'

Martin raises his eyebrows. 'Family?'

'Yes, she's gone to stay with an aunt.'

'Emily hasn't got any family so there's no way she can be staying with an aunt.'

I pause because Martin's her ex-husband so I'm pretty sure he would know if she had family or not. But Garrie clearly told me she's gone to stay with an aunt.

'I haven't seen her since the day they split up and she left. She left in a hurry, which is understandable. We're looking after her dog, and I've been coming across here to feed her rabbit. She left it in the garden without any instructions to look after it but luckily, I realised before it was too late. She didn't even tell Linda next door she was leaving. But I suppose she was upset in the circumstances and just wanted to get away quickly.'

'Maybe, but something doesn't seem right. She's barely been in touch with her friends, and we've been wondering if there's some problem with her phone.'

I look down at my hands and try not to think about those fake texts I sent from her mobile. I change the subject. 'It's obvious you care for her, Martin. Do you mind if I ask what drove you two apart?'

He smiles but his sadness shows through it. 'I'll never stop caring for her, Sandie. She's a beautiful person but grief took hold of her after we lost a baby. It really took root, especially when the doctors had to tell her she'd never conceive again. It destroyed Emily. I tried so hard to support her, but she withdrew from me. And from life for a while. She blocked me out because she didn't want to accept what had happened and I suppose I became a constant reminder of the life she had wanted. She was in complete denial and started acting out of character and having blackouts. It broke my heart, and it was the beginning of the end for our marriage.'

I see the genuine look of concern on Martin's face and feel the same strange rush of sympathy for Emily that I did when I read her diary. She seems to wear a brave face but underneath her perfected exterior is a troubled soul.

'I'm so sorry, Martin, and I understand your concern, but Emily seems very organised. She'll be somewhere figuring everything out.'

'I hope so, but it doesn't sound like she organised her departure terribly well. She must have been in an emotional state to walk out like that. And that's dangerous for someone like Emily. It could trigger all sorts of things. Was the house tidy when she left?'

It seems like an odd question, but I try to answer as honestly as I can. 'She left in a hurry and didn't take her laptop. When I came into the house everything was a bit all over the place. Although my fiancé might have contributed to some of that after Emily left. He's not the tidiest. But there was a wineglass that still had her lipstick on it.'

'That's not like Emily. She never left anything unwashed. She likes everything to be in order.'

'I don't know her well, but I've been inside her house, and it's always looked meticulous. Almost…too meticulous.'

He nods. 'She became like that after she lost the baby. She was broken inside but trying to hold everything together on the surface. It was her only way of regaining some control. She felt like a failure and grasped onto anything she could to survive the hurt. Her obsessive need for order after the emotional chaos she'd gone through was part of that, I think. But her obsessions also became unhealthy. And you need to know this too, Sandie.'

He pauses for a moment as if he's trying to think how to continue.

'She became obsessed with someone else's child. She put an advert in the local newspaper offering private tuition for young children and a lady called Annabel replied, which was ironic because that's the name we'd chosen for the baby daughter we lost. She brought her daughter, Katie, to the house and Emily instantly loved her. She also became good friends with Annabel, and I think the name coincidence made the relationship especially important to Emily. Her time with Katie gave her a new lease of life for a while and the arrangement seemed to work. Katie had some special needs which were challenging but having Emily's help meant Annabel could spend time with her husband.' He looks up at me. 'But Emily took things a step too far and started fantasising that Katie was hers. I warned her she needed to stop, and I was in the process of getting her help, even though by that time we'd split up. But before I could, Annabel stopped bringing Katie. I don't know everything that happened, but clearly things got very bad.'

My hand flies to my mouth. 'Oh my God.'

'I know. It all seemed to push Emily over the edge. I guess she felt like she had lost a child she loved all over again once Katie disappeared out of her life. She missed seeing her friend Annabel too. And tragically, Annabel was killed soon afterwards in a freak traffic accident. Her car hit a tree. That was the final straw for Emily. She pretty much went into a complete breakdown. She obviously got better and moved here, but I honestly don't know how much better. And I'm worried that all this recent trauma might retrigger all the bad memories she tried to shut out.'

Martin's chilling words shock me. He may not know the connection but now I know exactly what history Emily and Garrie share.

'We need to find her, Sandie. She certainly isn't with an aunt. We need to know where she's really gone. She shouldn't be alone; God knows what that could drive her to. She needs support and...'

He presses a card with his contact numbers into my hand, looks down at my stomach and then into my eyes.

'You need to protect your baby.'

Chapter 67

SANDIE

Since Martin left, all I can think about are those chilling final words and I shiver as I glance around Emily's cold, clinical kitchen. I'm yearning to get back to the safe sanctuary of my cosy home. And I need to talk to Garrie. I want the truth about where Emily is, and why he lied about it.

I call him, but it goes straight to voicemail. I leave a message.

'Garrie, please get home as soon as you can. Long story but I bumped into Emily's ex, and I now know so much more than I did. But I'm worried. I need to see you.'

I'm on autopilot as I set Emily's alarm and escape the cloying atmosphere of her house. As soon as I'm outside I gulp deep, welcome breaths of fresh air and I see Garrie speeding down the street. He smiles a gigantic smile, winds down his window, and blows me a kiss.

'Is everything OK, Sandie?'

'I've sent you a text message.'

'I heard it bleep but I haven't read it yet. I'm sorry, Sandie. I shouldn't have left you alone last night. I…I barely know what I'm doing. I…'

'Garrie, stop, you're home now, and we can deal with all this together. Emily's ex-husband Martin has explained a lot to me. It's helped me to understand what you and Annabel went through because of her. I wish you'd told me this sooner.'

We enter the house and I lead him to the sofa, sit him down and take his hand.

'I know all about her obsession with Katie.'

He nods but doesn't speak. I squeeze his hand.

'She made your life hell, and you wanted her to pay for that…I get it Garrie, I really do…You might not have gone about it the right way, but I can see why everything got so confused in your head.'

'I'm so sorry, Sandie. I know I messed up. I did want to make her pay but I didn't know how to do it. I was stupid and I can't bear how much I hurt you in the process. I know I should have told you everything.'

'I know now, and we can find a way to sort this out. But it frightens me, knowing she's out there, she's unpredictable, and I'm expecting your child. We must find her, Garrie.'

He lets go of my hand, walks to the window, and looks across the road. But he doesn't speak.

'Garrie, I know she isn't with an Aunt; Martin says she has no family. So, either you really don't know where she is and made that story up to appease me. Or…and I need to ask you this…you know exactly where she is and you're choosing not to tell me. I know how much you hate her, but I'm frightened for her. And for you. So, please, tell me the truth.'

He turns to me. His face is etched with pain and confusion. 'I don't know how to tell you what I've done. You'll think I'm crazy.'

'Garrie. Tell me. Please. You've no choice now.'

'I know. And yes, I lied to you. She isn't with an aunt; or anybody else for that matter.'

Waves of fear ripple in my stomach. 'Then where is she, Garrie?'

He turns away and stares through the window again; transfixed by Emily's house. 'I couldn't bear for her to be at number 12 any longer. I didn't want her to be anywhere near us. Remember she destroyed my life, Sandie. Annabel died because of her.'

I shiver and stammer out the only question I can ask, as icy panic grips me at the thought of what his answer might be. 'What have you done?'

He's crying now and almost screams his answer. 'I didn't know what to do, Sandie, I panicked.'

'Garrie, you're frightening me. Please God, tell me what you've done. I can't help if you don't.'

He doesn't reply. I walk over to him, turn him round to face me and try to speak with a calmness I don't feel.

'Tell me where she is, and we can sort this out.'

'She's at our house, mine, and Annabel's.

'You've got a house?'

'Yes, mine and Annabel's house. I couldn't bear to get rid of it. I took Emily there...I tied her up, and...'

I don't allow myself time to think about why he has a house he hasn't told me about. My priority is to know exactly what he's done with Emily.

I can barely believe the question I start to ask next. 'You've been keeping her a prisoner all this time? How? She's not...?' I can't finish the sentence. I can hardly breathe let alone speak the word in my head.

His face contorts into an expression I've never seen before. 'Dead? Is that what you were going to ask me? No. She isn't dead. But God help me, Sandie, I wish she was.'

I allow myself to breathe again. 'We must go to her, Garrie. We'll take her to Martin; he'll know what to do. He still loves her, and he'll take care of her.'

He stares down at my swollen stomach. There's no expression in his voice when he speaks. 'I'm sorry, Sandie, but it's too late and I'm in too deep. I didn't mean for things to go this far, but it all got out of hand and...'

I don't hear the rest of his words. I try to reach out to him, but my arms refuse to move.

His face, and the room, spin out of control.

Chapter 68

EMILY

My hands shake and shiver against the cold as I keep the tightest grip I can on my precious shard of glass. The rope is becoming wet and sticky with blood from my wrists as I continue my exhausting mission to cut through it. I'm almost sawing at my own raw skin now, but I have no choice but to ignore the pain and break the last few strands of the rope. This is my final chance because I know Garrie won't want to keep me alive much longer after my failed escape bid. So, I either succeed this time or my life's over.

I make one final cut and the rope breaks. My hands are free, and I cry out in pain as I rip the tape from my mouth. I use a combination of my trembling fingers and my piece of glass to untie my feet. I allow myself a sigh of relief; I'm almost free but not quite. I still need to break out of the locked prison that I can barely believe was once my friend Annabel's home. It has no homely warmth to it, but I assume it once did, before Garrie turned it into a cold, abandoned vacuum, and used it to try to break me.

But he's shown me that I'm strong. Stronger than I ever realised. Being locked inside here has put everything into perspective. When your freedom is removed you have nothing left but the passing of time and yourself. You must face your own demons because that's your only chance of freedom. I've had a lot of hours in here to think and I've stared the demons down and now I know I can finally face the future without being haunted by my past.

I sense it's barely evening but it's already dusk. Rain patters against the front window and wind is howling through the house because Garrie never bothered to block the window after I broke it. I know I must get out of here before evening turns to night; before he does his secret walk with Ginger. His late-night visits have become a distressing indicator of time.

I decide my best option is to break the front window but there's something I must do first, something I need to know. I grip the bannister rail to steady myself. Garrie goes upstairs every time he enters the house and stays up there a while so there must be a reason. I can't leave without discovering what it is.

I tread carefully so the pain in my feet is more bearable. I tighten my grip on the handrail to haul myself up step-by-step. I barely have enough strength to lift my legs. I look down at the thin layer of pink carpet that matches the flowery wallpaper. I reach the top stair and the house looks quite pleasant up here. Garrie clearly still pays the electricity bill because the lights all work. I sink my toes into the thicker pile carpet on the landing and look at the photographs of Garrie and Annabel sprawled over the walls. They look so happy. But there are none of Katie with them.

I open each door in turn. A bathroom; an airing cupboard; a bedroom. There's a large wardrobe and the doors are open, so I grab the first item of clothing I see. I remember it was Annabel's favourite dress; its bold red colour suited her, and she always looked stunning in it. I quickly slip it over my head; now it's my escape dress. I can walk through the streets without people staring at me.

I know I should leave soon, but I'm driven on by my curiosity and make my way towards the final room. It's up a set of steps that lead to an attic. A small window to the side of the doorway tells me the light outside is fading fast, but I want to see what's up here for my own peace of mind. My hand slides onto the silver doorknob which seems to have been polished recently; it's gleaming.

I open the door and gasp at what confronts me. I've walked into my worst nightmare.

Chapter 69

SANDIE

I'm sitting in the back seat of the car. It's almost dark and Garrie's driving over the speed bumps so erratically that the car feels it's about to take off.

'Garrie, I wouldn't have agreed to be in the car with you if I knew you were going to act like this.'

My stomach's vibrating in sync with my heartbeat and I clasp my hands over my baby bump in fear I'm about to be induced into early labour.

'Garrie, for goodness sake, please slow down. This isn't safe. Stop the car and let me drive.'

He grips the steering wheel and the tension in his hands matches the stern expression on his face. He ignores my pleas and his next words hit me like a sharp punch.

'You need to get rid of the baby.'

'What?'

'You can't keep the baby.'

I can't believe what I'm hearing. 'Garrie, where's this coming from?'

His response is matter of fact and robotic. 'It's for the best.'

I want to scream at him, but I'm petrified, and frightened it will make him speed up even more and kill all of us. 'Garrie, stop the car so we can talk.'

He doesn't listen and continues speeding through the streets.

'You're not thinking straight. I'm not getting rid of our baby. Please, stop the car. You're scaring me.'

I watch his every move from the back seat. It's where I prefer to sit now I'm pregnant; it feels safer, but not tonight because his knuckles are white from his grip on the steering wheel and he's driving as if he's possessed.

He overtakes on a blind corner and swerves to avoid an oncoming car that flashes its lights and blasts its horn. 'Calm down, Garrie, for goodness sake. You're going to cause an accident. Think of the baby, please. She's what matters. Everything else will be OK. We can sort this mess out.'

I stare at his reflection in the front mirror and see tears sliding down his face. He pulls over and slams on the brakes.

'I can't do this, Sandie. I'm scared.'

Relief floods through my veins as the car halts. I assume he's about to tell me he can't face taking me to Emily, but instead his next words puncture my heart as if he'd driven a stake into it. 'I mean it. You need to get rid of the baby. I can't take the risk.'

I lean as much as the seatbelt will allow and touch his shoulder. 'Nothing is going to go wrong, Garrie. The baby's fine.'

He spins round to face me. 'That's not what I mean. You don't understand. That's what Annabel said, those exact words, but it all went horribly wrong and I lost her.'

He's crying uncontrollably now so I get out of the car, and I walk towards the driver's side and open the door. I need to calm him down. He could speed off again at any moment and I can't let that happen; not while he's in this state.

He grabs my hand and squeezes it hard until the knuckles hurt. 'I can't lose you too, Sandie.'

I wince as I put my other hand on his. 'Garrie, you need to calm down.'

'I mean it. You must never leave me, Sandie. I'm worried the baby will come between us.'

'It won't, but I can't have this crazy behaviour, Garrie. It has to stop now if we are to have any kind of relationship. I'm going to drive, and you have to tell me where the house is because we can't leave Emily in there.'

He looks into my eyes with an urgent intensity I've never seen before. 'But I need you to love me like you've never loved anyone.'

I give him the only response I can to avoid this situation getting any worse. My only priority is to make sure Emily is safe. I hardly recognise the man in front of me but I can't afford to make any mistakes so I say the one thing that I know will calm him down.

'I love you like I've never loved anyone, Garrie.'

I can barely look at him because I don't feel love at all. He's not the person I thought he was. He's got a woman trapped in the home he once shared with his wife. A house I didn't even know about until recently. He's told me Emily destroyed his marriage and contributed to his wife's death. They're big statements and I truly don't know what went on. It must have really hurt him but he's now torturing her and that's downright cruel and twisted. It frightens me to think he's capable of doing something like that. That's not the man I want to spend my life with and it's certainly not the man I want to be the father of my child.

He continues to stare without blinking. 'But you won't love me the same when the baby comes along.'

'Having a child doesn't change anything, Garrie.'

'That's what Annabel said but the baby needed so much care.'

'Our baby is healthy. I've had all the check-ups, and everything is fine.'

'I lost Annabel.'

I'm struggling to keep the aggravation out of my voice, but as long as he's sitting in the driver's seat, I don't have a choice. 'You're not going to lose me, but you have to do what I ask. I'm going to get into the driver's seat and you're going to direct me to the house. Then we can focus on us.'

'Do you mean that?'

'Yes.'

'Just the two of us?'

'Yes.'

'Without the baby?'

'Yes.'

Self-reproach grips my entire body as I swallow down the acid that has risen from the pit of my stomach. There's no way I would ever get rid of my baby, but I must keep him onside and convince him he's the only person who matters, if I'm to get out of this situation. He releases his grip on my hand, and we hug awkwardly between the open car door and I feel sick. He looks fragile as he tries to rest his head on me.

'Let's go, Garrie. We can do this together.'

He takes hold of my hand again and slowly gets out of the car. I watch him make his way towards the passenger side and take a deep breath before sitting next to him. He yanks his seatbelt into position and stares absently out of the window. I'm uncertain about getting back into the car with him but I have no choice and at least I'm in the driver's seat.

We sit in silence while I attach the Satnav to the windscreen.

'What's the postcode?'

His expression is blank. 'What?'

I'm rapidly losing patience with him. 'I need the address.'

'I think we should go home, Sandie.'

'If we go home then we are finished.'

He lifts his head and speaks the address with slow precision. He contemplates every syllable as I sit poised in position for the next chapter of our journey.

I start the engine and follow the monotone instructions that pervade the silence inside the car. I drive into the unknown, fearful of what I'm about to find. I'm going to have to summon all my strength to get through this. My priority is making sure Emily is alive.

Chapter 70

EMILY

I'm overwhelmed by the vision in front of me and I pause in the doorway as the overpowering scent of lilies assaults and threatens to choke me. I know I should run, but this room is pulling me in. The faint sound of music mingles with the air inside this room. It's barely audible and yet I can hear it; *Lady in Red* is playing from a small CD player on the windowsill.

The scent of the lilies masks another underlying smell. It's musty and acrid and I shudder because it's an aroma that reminds me of death. I feel sick as I breathe it in, and it invades my empty stomach.

I'm relieved to see the foot of a bed as I walk further into the room; I'm desperate to escape this cloying atmosphere but I need to sit and regain some energy before I do. But what I see next makes me recoil from the bed in horror and rush to the window. I hurl it open and immediately start to retch. The uncontrollable spasms are unrelenting, until I'm exhausted trying to vomit from an empty stomach. My mouth tastes sour and metallic and I grip the windowsill. I can't allow myself to pass out. Not here, in this room. I take a few deep gulps of fresh air before I turn around. They say solitary confinement can make a person delusional but I'm not imagining this.

Because I'm confronted by the unimaginable. The bed is festooned in white lilies and resting on top of them is the cold, stark, ultimate symbol of death. A coffin. Dark mahogany, highly polished, with gleaming brass handles. A single red rose sits on top of it, flanked by two pillar candles. Melted wax has dripped down their sides which suggests they're being burned regularly. A silver picture frame sits behind the rose with an ornate letter A engraved into it. I pick it up and stare in sick horror at the photograph. It's Annabel smiling on her wedding day and she's wearing the dress Garrie gave to me and holding up her left hand to display the blue topaz ring on her wedding finger. I drop the silver frame with a scream that pierces the sinister silence of this room and Annabel's fractured image stares back at me through shattered glass.

I turn away from it and see the walls are full of images of her and Garrie. There are hundreds of photos but not a single photo of their daughter, Katie.

I'm standing in a shrine to Garrie's dead wife.

I step closer to the coffin and see another small photograph of Annabel interwoven between the shiny mahogany veneer and the pristine brass handles. I think about my beautiful friend, and how things used to be before I lost her. Annabel and Katie were a massive part of my life until everything got confused, broken, and ripped apart. I want to recall every detail about the last time I saw her, but it's always hazy and blurred in my head. I wish I could remember it more clearly, but my brain seems to have blotted out big chunks.

I force myself to touch the coffin lid. The wood is cold and hard against my fingers, and I begin to contemplate the possibility that my vibrant, once so alive, friend Annabel is lying still and cold inside. I can hardly breathe.

'Dear God, Garrie, what have you done?'

I whisper the question into the cloying atmosphere of the room. Even with the window open the air hangs heavily around me. I'm horrified at the possibility that Annabel's body is inside the coffin. I wouldn't put anything past Garrie after what he's done to me. I run my trembling fingers across the coffin lid. I know I have to open it and see with my own eyes, and I don't have long before the light completely fades outside. I stare at the mahogany lid before sliding my fingers to lift it, shuddering at the thought of what I'm about to find inside.

I'm almost relieved when the silk-laden lid opens to reveal a small urn, and strangely comforted that I've found the resting place of Annabel's ashes. I couldn't attend her funeral, but at least Garrie's lunacy has given me the opportunity to finally say goodbye to my friend.

'I'm sorry Annabel. For the way I dealt with things, I'm so terribly sorry. I should never have treated Katie like my own daughter, I realise that now. But I was desperate to feel a mother's bond and that was the closest I was ever going to get. I truly cared and loved her like my own so I would have never hurt her. I understand why you took her away from me and I'm so sorry for making you feel the need to do that. But after it happened, I seemed to relive all the painful memories of losing my own child. It was another hole in my heart and when I lost you too, I couldn't face it. I hope you can find a way to forgive me for all the things I did wrong. I've hidden the memories of everything that happened in the deepest recesses of my mind, but I truly regret my actions...'

I'm interrupted by a loud bang downstairs, and I jump back from the coffin in shock. It's my signal to get out of this room and out of this house. I can't allow my escape to fail. I carefully open the attic door in case Garrie is standing on the other side. My heart is pounding but the house is silent apart from the wind howling through it from the kitchen window I smashed in my earlier attempt to escape. It's making me nervous.

I don't look back as I run downstairs, once again recoiling at the pain in my ankles. The shock of the coffin made it disappear but now it's back and my entire body aches from exhaustion. I stumble halfway down the last set of steps to the hallway and wince as I feel my ankle twist. I hop the remainder of the way and try to open the front door but of course it's locked. My next move is to take the poker from the fireplace and swing it against the hall window. It takes three attempts before I smash enough glass to create a space I can climb out of. I pull down the decorative floral curtain from above the window and use it to cover the sharp edges before I slowly ease myself out as carefully as possible.

I land on the front garden grass in a crumpled heap. Pain shoots through my leg as if a knife is slicing through every tendon. But I ignore it and force myself to stand up. I have no choice. I toss the poker away, and I run. I'm running for my life, desperate to put as much distance between me and the awful place he's been holding me prisoner. I can taste the freshness of the air around me and day finally turns to night, and I can see the moon sparkling brightly in the sky. I'm finally free.

I can barely see as tears stream down my face from the pain in my leg which grows more intense with every step. I have no idea where I am or what direction I'm heading. And I don't care. I keep moving, blindly, because I know one thing. When I finally stop running, wherever I am will be better than where I've been.

I've escaped from a nightmare.

Chapter 71

SANDIE

'Garrie, this is such a beautiful house.' I look up at the home he once shared with Annabel and wonder why he's never mentioned it. It's large and detached in one of the best areas of town; and only a few streets away from ours. We could have walked here and avoided Garrie almost killing us. I can't believe all of this has been happening so close to my own doorstep and I knew nothing about it.

He's too preoccupied to reply as we make our way up the path towards the front door. I notice a small window that's broken: Garrie spots it too, and has panic written all over his face as he fumbles to unlock the door.

'No, no, no, no…' He's frantically trying to open the door with no success.

'Calm down, Garrie, for goodness sake.'

He's all fingers and thumbs and doesn't seem able to coordinate his fingers with the door lock. He's trembling with rage. 'She'd better be here.'

His statement gives me hope she's still alive. He finally opens the door, runs through the hallway and into the first room on the right, and yells. 'Christ! She's gone. Shit, Sandie, she's escaped.'

'You really need to calm down, Garrie.'

He spins round. 'Calm down? Are you fucking serious?'

I've never seen him like this, and I'm scared. I'm alone with an unstable man who's been holding a woman as his prisoner and is spinning even further out of control. I stare at the sofa where Emily must have been tied up and at the rope and black sticky tape strewn around it. Evidence of the horror she endured at the hands of the man standing in front of me. Icy tingles assault my skin as I imagine her bound and tied all this time; and I did nothing to help her because I didn't know what was happening.

I can hardly bear to look at Garrie. All those midnight walks with Ginger, all those excuses. I should have known something wasn't right. But now isn't the time or place to confront him. Instead, I appease him. 'Let's put something over the cracked window and then we can decide what to do.'

He clenches his fists and presses his lips together as his face twists and contorts with rage. 'How dare she do this to me? How dare she fight back? Where the hell is she?'

'I don't know, Garrie. But she couldn't stay in this house forever, and...' I don't know what else to say to him, but I don't think he's even listening to me.

'I should have killed her.' His eyes flash and he spits the words out with sinister venom. 'I should have killed her before she escaped. Now I can't because she's gone.'

He roars as he punches his fists into the air. I'm now convinced he was going to kill her, and I realise he's capable of it. He's wild and fierce; a man possessed.

The only way I can stay safe is to placate him by telling him what he wants to hear. 'She's a bitch, Garrie. We need to find her and make her pay for what she did.'

His eyes are rolling in his head, but he nods and grabs my shoulders. He thinks I'm on his side. 'She must pay, Sandie. I have to make her pay. I need to find her and kill her. I need you to help me.'

'We'll find her, Garrie.'

'Sandie...you do still love me?'

At this moment, I've never hated anyone so much in my whole life and if I could grab something heavy and hit him over the head right now I would. But again, I placate him. 'Of course, I love you.'

'I need you, Sandie.'

I stare at the man in front of me who I don't know anymore; not the way I thought I did. But does anyone really know anyone? Can we ever be sure of what truly lies at someone's core? We all have our innermost secrets and a past that makes up our present. We're a combination of memories and experience. It's impossible to get inside another person's head and I wouldn't want to be inside Garrie's head right now because it's a dangerous place. I know he's suffered because of what Emily did and I understand his anger and hurt. But I'm perturbed by the extremity of his reaction. He's unbalanced and he needs professional help.

'She made my life hell, Sandie.'

'I know, but you need to tell the police, own up to what you've done before she tells them. You're not a murderer, Garrie. You're a man who is hurting and grieving.'

'There's more you need to know. She was obsessed with my daughter and started to behave as if Katie was hers.'

'You can tell the police that, Garrie.'

'Katie even started calling Emily her second mummy.'

'You can tell the police all this too.'

I really want to get away from here and from him, but he wants to keep talking. I decide to let him. Perhaps the more he talks the more he'll get the anger out and calm down.

'When she realised what Emily was doing, Annabel refused to let Katie visit her anymore and cancelled the lessons. But Emily phoned Annabel constantly, begging for forgiveness, saying she loved Katie and she'd never meant any harm. That's when I convinced Annabel to give her another chance, but it was the worst mistake of my life. I ended up losing my wife.'

'Tell me what happened, Garrie.'

'It was on August 25th at precisely 6 p.m.; a date and time I will never forget. It was a balmy summer evening, perfect for a romantic dinner in the garden; a barbecue for the two of us. I was lighting the coals as Annabel emerged from the patio doors wearing the red dress that I loved seeing her in. I remember her smiling at me across the lawn, looking as beautiful as I'd ever seen her. And she laughed as I posed in the chef's apron she'd bought me for Christmas.'

I can see him reliving the moment as he tells the story through sparkling eyes. I wonder if he even realises I'm here. He's so lost in the memory of his love for Annabel.

'We'd been in a happy, carefree mood all that day. Katie was at Emily's and Annabel had phoned to check everything was OK. They were making biscuits in Emily's kitchen and Katie was giggling and sounding happy. Annabel was reassured and I was thrilled I'd finally got her all to myself again. As our food sizzled on the grill, I pulled her into my arms and planted a kiss on her head. I looked deep into her eyes and told her what a perfect moment it was. We lay on a blanket on the grass, drank chilled Prosecco and ate until we thought our stomachs might burst. When the time came to collect Katie, my heart sank as Annabel kissed me and pulled away. She told me she would be back soon. We'd been locked in the perfect moment, and I hadn't wanted it to end. Not ever.

Annabel arrived at Emily's house and knocked on the door but there was no answer. She kept knocking but there was no sign of Emily or Katie. She looked through the window and shouted through the letterbox. She tried the door, not expecting it to be unlocked, but it was. Emily never left it unlocked. Something didn't feel right. Annabel kept shouting as she walked through the house and out into the back garden, but Emily and Katie were nowhere to be seen. In the garden she noticed more signs of Emily's obsession, little plaques in the flower borders with Katie's name on. Emily had told her Annabel they used to plant flowers together and Katie slowly learned their names as she helped to water them. But there were so many of them; Katie's name was everywhere.

Annabel ran back inside the house, calling out in panic as she went upstairs. She was frantic when her daughter wasn't there. And that's when she saw a bedroom devoted to Katie with a brightly coloured name plaque on the door. The walls were covered with photographs of Emily and Katie together, and paintings by Katie with her name scribbled on them. There was a bedspread embroidered with the word Katie in big bold letters and a toybox with her initial on it. It was too much for Annabel. She called me and through choked tears told me everything she'd seen. Then she turned her anger on me because I'd convinced her to give Emily another chance and now it was clear she was dangerously obsessed with our daughter.'

Garrie suddenly looks fragile as he breaks off from the story and clings on to me for comfort. 'Where the hell has Emily gone, Sandie?'

'Garrie, try to calm down.'

'But I need to find her.'

'And do what, Garrie, lock her up again? This has gone too far already.'

'You have to promise me you won't go to the police, Sandie.'

'I'll only keep that promise if you get help and stop all this hatred you've got towards Emily.'

He says nothing. He gets up and starts pacing the room, aimlessly.

'Listen, Garrie. Let's go home. There's nothing more we can do here. You've had no sleep, so you can get a few hours on the sofa and then we'll figure out what to do. And we'll make an appointment with the doctor to get something to help calm you.'

He spins round again, his eyes a mix of wildness and disbelief. 'What? You think all this is going to be ok because I speak to a doctor?'

'Other than going to the police, it's your only option. You can make them understand you were driven to everything you did by grief. Grief that I don't think you've ever processed properly, and you need to do that.'

'Martin said the same thing about Emily.'

'Martin? You met him?'

He nods. 'Yes. When Katie started calling Emily mummy, I went to her house to have it out with her. But Martin was in the street, told me who he was and asked me to give her some space. That she was still grieving the loss of their child and that's why Katie was so important to her. She didn't mean any harm by it, but he thought it wasn't healthy for Emily to be so close to another child for a while and he thought it was best we left her alone. I had no choice and I walked away like he asked. But I didn't tell Annabel about the conversation I'd had with him.'

'Why not?'

'Because I thought if I let a bit of time pass, I'd be able to convince her to trust Emily again and we could resume the lessons. Free Annabel up a bit. Which of course I did. And you know what that led to.'

'Actually, Garrie, I don't. You still haven't told me what happened the day of your barbecue when Annabel didn't find Emily and Katie in the house.

He looks at me with a blank expression. I'm not sure he remembers what he's told me and what he hasn't. I decide to prompt him. 'What had happened? Where were they?'

'Annabel kept screaming down the phone at me from Emily's house and I said I was on my way over. Then she cut me off. I kept calling her, but she didn't answer. Next thing I know she's calling me from the hospital. Apparently, Katie had fallen off a stool in Emily's kitchen and Emily had rushed her to the hospital. Katie was OK but Annabel was even angrier than before. She said it was all my fault for convincing her to give Emily another chance. She told me Emily was trying to convince her it was an accident. I tried to tell her that maybe it was.'

He pauses and I watch him clutch both hands to his head as if he's trying to stop any more painful thoughts and words from escaping. But he keeps talking.

'I made such a mistake, Sandie. If only I hadn't taken Emily's side. Why the hell did I say those words? Maybe it was an accident. Eight syllables that were about to change my life forever. Annabel stopped screaming and her voice went cold. She told me it was over between us and put the phone down. I was devastated, but I couldn't believe she meant it. I jumped straight into my car. I went through every red light and raced full pelt towards the Accident and Emergency Department. I saw Katie and Annabel in a side ward talking to a nurse. Then I saw Emily running down the corridor and out of the hospital. She never saw me.'

'But Katie was OK?"

'Yes. But Annabel wasn't. When I rushed in to see her and Katie, she looked at me as if I was the devil. She grabbed Katie's hand and told me this was all my fault and she'd never trust anything I said again. She wished she'd never listened to me, then she told me she was going to stay in a hotel with Katie, and we were over; she wanted a divorce. I watched her walk away and crumpled against the wall. I loved her so much. I would have done anything for her. She was my entire world. But I never spoke to her again or held her after that day. And I never saw her in the red dress again. She came home the next morning to pick up some things, but she insisted on me not being there. When I got back, she'd thrown the red dress on our bedroom floor, and she never came home again. I tried texting and calling but it was no good. She wanted nothing more to do with me; she obviously wanted to protect Katie all by herself. That was her number one priority, so she walked away from me. I'd lost her.'

He turns his tortured gaze on me. 'I can't go to the police, Sandie. I can't open up the wounds again.'

'It was a horrible combination of circumstances, Garrie.'

'I was wrong to tell Annabel to trust Emily. But it was all Emily's fault. Do you understand?' His anger descends again like rain from a storm cloud.

'You're still bleeding, Garrie, but you can't see the blood. You need to get help before it's too late.'

'It's already too late. If that day had never happened, Annabel would never have left me. And she'd never have had her accident. Don't you see? It's Emily's fault she's dead. She killed my wife.'

Chapter 72

EMILY

I go straight to the bank because I have no money or any other means of paying for things. Luckily, I remember my customer reference number and password. The cashier raises her eyebrows as I sign my signature in bare feet. I mutter 'It's complicated' as she counts my cash, tell her I've lost my bank card and ask her to send a new card to Liz's address. I stop off at a charity shop two doors down from the bank for some old trainers. They're a size too big so they won't rub against my sore feet, and I pull them on with relief.

Now I'm inside a hotel bedroom in the centre of town. I lock the door and check it three times. I close the curtains even though I'm on the top floor then look for a second time inside the wardrobe and underneath the bed before I'm satisfied, I'm truly alone. Being held captive for days does something to your brain. It rewires you to become hypersensitive to the slightest thing. I scan the room with my peripheral vision for any sign of movement. I know it's ridiculous, but I can't help it. Knowing how much Garrie wants me dead is unnerving, and my panic response is in overdrive.

I need to clear my head and make decisions. Garrie taunted me with photographs of the 'To Let' sign in my front garden and took vicious pleasure in telling me about the new family that will be moving in soon, so I'll stay with Liz for a while. She's a good friend and she'll give me space to recover from this ordeal. I remember when everything went wrong, and Annabel stopped bringing Katie to my house; Liz was the one who stood by me. She said people would soon get fed up with the gossip, and they did.

I look down at my body and the red dress that clings to my skin. I know this was Annabel's favourite dress; she always looked radiant in it. I remember it so clearly from the day she stood at my front door and asked me if Katie could stay a while so she could have a quiet dinner with her husband. I was thrilled; she'd forgiven me. I'd missed Katie so much and I'd been preparing something special for her while she'd been away. It had taken my mind off things and helped me to convince myself that one day she'd be back.

≈ ≈ ≈

16 months earlier

I'm painting the room in beautiful pastels and creating a special space for Katie. I'm in the shopping centre and I've spotted a little plaque and a bedspread with her name on so I can't resist. The shop assistant is admiring them as she puts them into a bag.

'These are so pretty. Are they for your daughter?'

'No, a friend's daughter. I look after her.'

I feel the pang of reality as I face up to the truth. She's not my child and she can never be the baby I've lost. I'm no longer able to pretend and I've promised myself I won't get carried away. But I want her to feel comfortable in my home. I walk out of the shop with a smile on my face because today is a new start.

It doesn't take long for me to hammer the name plaque onto the door and place the bedspread into Katie's new room. It's made it feel bright and airy; it's perfect. When Katie the doorbell rings I run downstairs with the same air of lightness. I've been given another chance and I'm going to be extra careful not to do anything wrong.

'Hello, Katie.'

'Can we play puzzle games, Emily?'

'Of course, we can. I've already got them ready.'

Annabel gives her a hug and waves at me as she leaves to get back to her husband. I grab the puzzle blocks and we play Katie's favourite games. She seems to have stopped calling me mummy; I think she's had it drummed into her at home that she must call me Emily. But it doesn't matter to me because I'm looking across at her and she's smiling so I know she's happy.

'Shall we bake some chocolate cookies, Katie?'

'Yes, yes, yes.'

She runs around the living room clapping her hands into the air. She's such a lively, excitable child with so much energy.

'We can put chocolate smarties in them.'

Her face lights up as we make our way into the kitchen. I'm using one of those little pre-packed boxes that contain all the ingredients. We tip them out onto the worktop and Katie grabs the spoon so that she can stir them together.

'Do you know what we put into the bowl first Katie?'

'Butter and egg.'

'Good girl. Those are in the fridge.'

I pour the cake mix, butter and egg into a bowl and Katie starts mixing as the powdered mix puffs up into smoke and splatters over the sides.

'Nice and carefully, Katie.'

The door knocks so I walk away for a moment to answer. It's someone leaving a parcel. I'm about to return to the kitchen when I hear a loud scream.

'Katie?'

She's fallen off the stool and she's lying on the floor screaming.

'Oh, baby girl.' I whisk her up into my arms and carry her to my car. I don't stop to think about anything else. I fasten her into the child's seat, and we go straight to the accident and emergency department. My phone starts ringing as soon as we arrive at the hospital.

'Where is she? Where's my daughter?'

'We're at the hospital, Annabel but...'

'What?'

'Please don't panic. Katie's fine. We're at the hospital in town; it was only a minor accident. She...'

'What kind of accident? What have you done?'

I'm trying to explain but she isn't listening. She's too busy screaming down the phone.

'Why have you got a bedspread with my daughter's name on it?'

I suddenly realise I left in such a hurry for the hospital that I totally forgot to lock up. Annabel must have gone into the house and found the bedroom with Katie's name on it.

'Annabel, it's not what it looks like.'

'Then what the hell is it?'

'Can we discuss this another time? We're in accident and emergency.'

'I'm on my way.'

It doesn't take long before Annabel comes storming through the hospital. She stares at her little girl with a large bandage on her knee. Then she looks across at me with venom in her eyes. 'I should never have given you another chance.'

I stammer my apologetic explanation. 'It was an accident, Annabel. She fell off the stool. I brought her here as a precaution to make sure she's OK and it's just a grazed knee.'

Annabel's having none of it. 'Just go and leave us alone.'

I have no choice but to do what she's asked.

'If you ever go near my daughter again, I'm applying for a restraining order.'

I'm in pieces because I desperately want to be a part of Katie and Annabel's life. But things have gone too far. I've no choice but to stay away.

Chapter 73

GARRIE

Whenever I wake up from sleep, I think of Annabel and the moment that changed everything. It never stops haunting me. Sandie insisted we drive home after I'd finally told her everything, grab some sleep and then decide what to do next. A quick nap on the sofa has plunged me straight into my dreams. Short bursts of sleep always do that to me, and I remember the dream vividly when I wake up. I've opened my eyes and I'm still alone on the sofa and Sandie is nowhere to be seen. I'm glad, because I can relive my memories of Annabel without any distraction; it's a type of catharsis.

My body feels like an empty shell and yet again my tortured thoughts transport me back to the morning of the day my wife walked out of my life. It was the day Katie hurt herself because she fell off a stool.

≈ ≈ ≈

15 months earlier
It's a beautiful, warm day and Annabel is so happy, full of the joys of summer. I want to spend time with her. I want us to be alone.

'I'm going to cook your favourite meal.'
'Garrie, you always burn it when you try.'
She's never impressed with my cooking skills; I know that, but I make up for it in other ways. I want to be romantic, so I put candles on the picnic table and give her the giant bunch of fresh Freesias and Gypsophila I've bought. She loves flowers so I always make sure to stop at the florist on the way back from the supermarket.

I look down at the sweet-smelling pinks and lilacs in my hand and know the bouquet will make her smile. I always love seeing her face light up with happiness. It's the most beautiful sight. When we first got together her face lit up every time I walked into a room. She put me on a pedestal, made me feel invincible. She told me I was perfect in her eyes, and it was the most wonderful feeling.

But things have changed since Katie came along. At first, I was excited; we both were. I remember looking across at Annabel when we watched the positive blue lines appear and thinking how much pregnancy already suited her. She told me I had given her the most precious gift she could ever wish for. For nine months I was her hero, her perfect man, and I wanted it to last forever. But things have changed.

Katie's become the centre of Annabel's world. She took her first breath, and in that moment, I became the side show. Annabel still loves me, I know that, but it's different. I've stopped being the perfect one. I don't feel invincible anymore. Romantic gestures are less romantic, the days and nights are longer, and I watch from the side lines as Katie takes my place.

So today, I simply want us to spend some time together. Surely that isn't too much to ask. I need my wife to be mine again and I don't see any harm in letting Emily look after Katie for a couple of hours.

'We need a break so we can focus on each other.'

'I'm not leaving her too long, Garrie.'

She's started to make me feel second best but I'm planning to put on the charm this afternoon, so she doesn't rush back for Katie.

She does all the "mumsy" tasks like putting on Katie's coat and filling a large bag with things to cover all eventualities. Then I wait impatiently until she returns from Emily's, watching the second hand move around my Cartier until finally she's in my arms and we're staring into each other's eyes.

The day is perfect until disaster strikes. Katie falls off a stool, gets rushed to the local hospital and throws the day into disarray. Annabel phones me in a panic.

'I went to Emily's house to collect Katie and she wasn't there. I've found a room with Katie's name splashed everywhere.'

'What?'

'A bedspread with her name on it.'

'Calm down, Annabel. What's happened?'

'Don't tell me to calm down. Katie's fallen off a stool and she's been to hospital. I'm just leaving there now. Emily says it was an accident.'

'It probably was an accident.'

'Fine. Take her side, because I'm done, Garrie. I'm not coming back home. We'll stay at the Carstone.'

I'm stunned as she rings off before I can respond. And she doesn't come home, despite my constant texts and voice messages.

Come home Annabel. I'm sorry. I need you to come back. I love you so much xx

We belong together, Annabel. We always will xx

Annabel. For goodness sake. Answer my text messages. Let me know you're ok.

Come home. I can't live without you xx

I can't believe you're ignoring me. Annabel? xx

She doesn't reply. I send message after message for two days until I can't take it anymore. She's mad with me because she thinks I'm not on her side. I'm back to those five words, "It probably was an accident." How I wish I hadn't said them. But I did. And now I've no choice but to implement the plan that's been brewing in my head for a while.

I'm driving to Carstone House Hotel on the outskirts of town. When I arrive at the check-in desk it's easy to get the room number because we've stayed here a few times in the past and the receptionist recognises me.

'My wife and I are booked into the hotel. She's already here, but I don't know the room number.'

'It's good to see you again, sir. How are things?'

'Good thanks. My wife is in the room waiting for me, and I want to surprise her.'

She smiles. 'I'll get the key for you.'

She hands me a keycard, but I don't go upstairs straight away. I want to see her and hold her so much, but I must stick to my plan. I position myself at a corner table in the lobby and drink tea for most of the morning hidden behind a newspaper. I've got a perfect view of the elevators and it's only a matter of time before Annabel makes her appearance and heads towards the breakfast room.

I smile when she emerges from the elevator doors a few minutes before 11am. She's never been a morning person and she's left it until the last minute. I knew she would leave Katie in the room so she can collect breakfast and take something back for them both. Katie can be a handful in social situations. It suits my purpose perfectly; as soon as Annabel is busy at the buffet, I make my way to room 157 on the first floor.

Katie's happy to see her daddy. She swings her arms around me, and I tell her I'm taking her for a special treat.

'Is mummy coming?'

'No, this is our special treat.'

Her face lights up as I hold her hand and march her through the hotel. In minutes we are outside and in my car.

'What are we doing daddy?'

'You'll see. It's a surprise.'

I watch her face in my rearview mirror, her eyes wide with anticipation and excitement. She's an adorable little girl and if circumstances were different, I would be a very proud father.

I'm on a tight schedule. I know I've probably got around twenty minutes at the most before Annabel realises Katie is missing. My palms are sweaty against the steering wheel and my pulse is racing in my chest. I speed through the streets and towards Emily's house as adrenaline pumps through my veins.

I know Emily isn't home. It's Tuesday morning and her car is gone as I'd hoped it would be. There's no room for mistakes. I take the front door key out of my pocket; a copy of the spare key she'd given to Annabel. I take Katie's hand and we make our way up the garden path. She's skipping and singing a song that Emily taught her.

I start to execute my plan; I lead her upstairs. 'You need to have a bath to get ready for your surprise.'

'OK, daddy.'

I turn the taps on and watch as the water fills the tub. The moment is almost too good to be true, but things go horribly wrong.

And disaster is hurtling towards me.

≈ ≈ ≈

I realise my fingers have almost locked into position, clenched against my palms as I'm on the verge of recalling the worst moment of my life. I can't deal with any more pain right now. I stretch my fingers and focus back on the here and now.

I make Sandie a cup of tea the way she likes it, a little sugar, milk, and a digestive biscuit on the side. I carry it up to the bedroom, but the bedsheets are neatly tucked in, and the scatter cushions carefully placed over the pillows. She's not inside the room so I rush back downstairs. I have a horrible feeling I know where she's gone. I'm right; the key to Annabel's and my house is missing. Sandie must have taken it and gone back there. My mind is racing. I can't let her discover the beautiful room I've created for Annabel without explaining it to her first, because she won't understand. I don't bother to grab a coat. I let the fresh cold air envelop my body and shudder against the chill and the thought of what Sandie might be doing at this very moment.

I'm on autopilot and I need to get back to the house before Sandie discovers Annabel's resting place.

Chapter 74

SANDIE

We're home and Garrie's fallen asleep on the sofa. I stare across at number 12 and think about everything he's told me. I'm picturing the basement room Emily created for Martha, just like she'd created a room for Katie. It's unnerving that both children had been given their own rooms inside her home. But so is everything that Garrie did to Emily. I turn to look at him. The plan that had made sense to me as we drove home feels less appealing now I'm thinking of actually doing it. But I have no choice.

I grab the key to Annabel's house which Garrie has conveniently tossed into an empty jam jar, then I step outside and give the road a furtive glance, before telling myself not to be stupid. My dark hoodie, leggings and trainers make me look indistinguishable, and who am I expecting to see at this time anyway? It's 4 a.m. Before I can talk myself out of it, I get into my car and drive.

Now I'm standing once again outside Garrie and Annabel's house. It feels much grander than when I was here earlier with Garrie, or maybe because I'm so exhausted, I've shrunk, and it now seems bigger. It really is a stunning house with a white picket fence running around the edges like I imagined I would have one day. It has a beautiful archway that leads towards the front door and the trees and shrubbery look established. It must have been a beautiful home and it certainly doesn't look like a home that belongs to someone capable of murder.

I don't want to be here, but I have no choice. Garrie's been in bad shape since we found Emily gone; he's wound up like a coiled spring. He needs professional help, and I know I can't stay with him, but at least for now I can try to protect him from what he's done for the sake of my unborn daughter. If I can protect her from the stigma of having a kidnapper for a father, I must do it. We've heard nothing from Emily or from the police, so it seems she still hasn't reported that he held her captive. Maybe she wants to disappear and has no desire for her history and her guilty secrets to be dredged up again.

My brain and fingers struggle to coordinate as I shakily turn the key in the front door. But it opens and I'm back inside the hallway smelling its stale emptiness. The air hangs heavy and claustrophobic as if the house has a storm cloud above it, ready to break and rain down its dark secrets.

I step into Emily's prison room with a different mindset. I can see the remnants of her escape, but I find a dustpan and brush to wipe away the debris. It's like I'm witnessing a scene from a movie and I'm standing in the middle staring at disaster from both sides. I can only imagine the beauty that once existed within these walls with an image of Annabel as Garrie's described her to me, breezing in and out in one of her floaty dresses. Then I imagine how Emily's incarceration must have felt, tied up and alone in this cold dark space. The thoughts in my head are exhausting and I haven't had any sleep, so I'm working on autopilot. I talk out loud to myself as I gather up the rope ties and tape and wedge them into the plastic supermarket bag I grabbed from the boot of the car.

'Garrie, I really wish I could understand what was going on inside your head. The Garrie I fell in love with was so loving and gentle.'

I can't comprehend what he did, using these items and his home to create a makeshift prison for his enemy. It's the stuff of nightmares.

I spot a set of fire tools lying on the hearth and replace them upright. I pick up shards of glass from what looks like a broken vase, and I wince as I throw them into the bag and see that several of them are blood-stained. This must have been how Emily cut herself free. The image of that imprints itself on my brain and flashes like lightning in front of my eyes. I rearrange the ornaments on the mantelpiece and find Emily's phone tucked inside a bowl. I should have guessed he'd bring it here. I slot it into the zip pocket of my jacket and scan the room. I see nothing else to suggest Emily was ever a prisoner here. Her fingerprints and DNA must be everywhere, but with her history of stalking she could have discovered the house's existence when she was tracking Garrie, found his key like I did, and let herself in anytime. It would be her word against his.

I check the guest loo and kitchen for anything that could be incriminating but find nothing apart from two refrigerated high protein drinks which I add to the carrier bag before unplugging the fridge. There are two broken windows, but I've taped them up the best I can until Garrie can get them fixed.

My job is done; I can leave. I desperately want to go home, convince Garrie to get the help he needs and make sure he leaves my house. I'm about to step outside and say goodbye to Annabel's home and life and put this craziness behind me when I hear music. It's coming from somewhere upstairs. It's faint but I recognise the song, *Lady in Red.*

I walk up the stairs and I'm confronted by several closed doors, but the music is coming from somewhere above me. There must be another floor, an attic maybe. I walk in the direction of the sound and open a door which leads to another short flight of stairs. There's a door half open at the top of them, and it seems the song is playing on repeat.

There's a strong smell of lilies as I open the attic door and I'm overpowered by the fragrance of death as I freeze with fear at what confronts me. I keep my hand on the door handle to steady my shaking legs. There's a coffin on the bed and the walls are filled with pictures of Annabel. These must have been put there by Garrie, the father of my child, the man who keeps a secret shrine for his dead wife.

A deeper fear rises up from the pit of my stomach as I imagine what might be inside the coffin.

'Surely he's not a killer?'

I can't believe I've said the word.

Killer.

Such a deadly, final word. I stare at the coffin and shiver as my blood runs cold.

I toss the single long-stemmed red rose that adorns the coffin onto the bed. It sits there like a drop of fresh blood among a sea of white lilies. The coffin lid isn't screwed down. I should be fearful but I'm not; I've gone beyond fear. Instead, I'm a spectator, watching in slow motion from above as I see myself push the lid to one side.

I exhale the breath I hadn't realised I was holding when I see it's empty, apart from a gold box that simply says 'ANNABEL' on it. I reach out to touch it because I no longer feel frightened or threatened. I'm connected to this woman. A woman who once loved Garrie like I did. A woman who probably also got caught up in his insane madness.

'It's OK, Annabel; I've found you. And I'll do everything I can to protect your darling Katie from all this. I've seen her photograph and she's beautiful. I'm not staying with Garrie, but I promise to visit her and make sure she's OK. I hope you'll trust me, and I only wish I could have met you.'

I run my fingers over the gold box one more time before I close the coffin lid and that's when I realise there's something underneath it. It's a photograph and I slide it out carefully until I see an image of myself staring back at me. I remember the day it was taken; it was when I told Garrie I was pregnant. My heart pounds as if it might explode as I start to read the inscription on the back.

Annabel, darling. I want you to meet Sandie. She can never replace you, but I've asked her to marry me; I need someone in my life. I know you won't mind that I've promised her your blue topaz ring and the Riki Dalal dress. It will be as if you're standing next to me again. You'd like

Sandie, and she'll be good for Katie. I know you'd want that. And it's almost perfect like we were, except for one thing. She's pregnant. I'm pretending to be happy about it. But I wanted it to be different this time. Please find a way of helping me, Annabel. Please. I love you sweetheart. I always will.

I feel I've been punched in the stomach and automatically reach down to protect my baby from the next blow. I hurl the photograph back into the coffin and close the lid. I stand up and stumble blindly towards the door as angry tears blur my vision. I have to get out of here. But without warning the door slams shut and I hear a key turning in the lock.

I'm trapped.

Chapter 75

EMILY

It's strange how you get clarity when you're not in your own surroundings. I'm sitting in this hotel bedroom enveloped by calm silence and it's perfect; I can think and gather my thoughts. This is the silence of safety. Not the ominous silence that surrounded me in Garrie's house. That was the silence of torture. To think Annabel's spirit lies upstairs in that house like a caged bird. She'll never be free. He won't allow it. He's as obsessed with her dead as he was alive.

I was shocked when I saw the shrine he's created for his dead wife, but not surprised. I now know what he's capable of and I only wish I'd known sooner, then things might have been so different. I wish I'd known Annabel's husband was Garrie, but she always referred to him as hubby or husband, never by his name. He was the mysterious man I never saw but who sounded demanding and almost obsessed with having her to himself. At first, I thought it was romantic but after a while I realised she was always rushing back after she dropped Katie off because she was scared of him. It seemed like a constant juggling act for her to take care of her daughter while trying to keep him happy. It all makes sense now I know it's Garrie. I only wish I'd never got involved with him.

I think back to the day Katie fell off the stool. The day everything began to fall apart again.

≈ ≈ ≈

15 months earlier

It breaks my heart to walk away from the hospital, knowing it's another chapter of my life closed.   The doctor says I did the right thing bringing Katie to be checked out and I thought Annabel would agree, but I guess she's lost confidence in me. She's told me she'll never bring Katie to see me again and I know by the look on her face that she means it. Perhaps I can't blame her for doubting me and being upset. I have been using Katie to block out the pain of losing my own child and I have to let her go. The hardest part is carrying on with life and living with the reality of Annabel's decision. I can't face the world, so I stay in bed and stare at the ceiling. I can barely sleep.

After two days I feel nauseous from hunger and thirst, and I know I can't stay upstairs any longer. I must accept what's happened and try to move on. I take a shower and walk Ginger before driving to the supermarket to do my weekly shop; it's what I always do on a Tuesday.

It's still early when I get back, struggling to carry all the shopping bags in from the car and regretting buying so much. I open my front door, pleased to have made it home, and that's when I hear it. The tiny voice of a child. It sounds like Katie. I pause, convinced my mind is playing tricks. But I hear it again. It's the muffled sound of a child's voice and then a scream. It's coming from upstairs.

I drop the bags so quickly that food spills out across the hallway. I run as fast as I can up the stairs and notice the bathroom door wide open. I am confronted with the nightmare image of Katie floating in the bathtub, her face submerged.

'Oh please, please no.'

I pray I'm not too late as I pull her from the tepid water. Her clothes hang off her skeleton and I wrap my arms around her and lower her to the floor. Her body is limp as her arms and legs dangle helplessly but she's breathing.

'Oh, thank God, my beautiful girl, you're still alive.'

Her eyes are rolling, and I clutch her to me. 'Katie, I'm here baby, stay with me.'

She starts to cough and splutter as I wrap a towel gently around her body. I have no idea why she's in my house or how she got here.

'You're going to be OK, my darling. No one can hurt you now.'

I fumble in my pocket to find my phone and dial Annabel's number in a blind panic.

'Katie's here and she's OK.'

'You've got my daughter?'

'She's at my house and she's…' I pause. I don't know what to say.

I try to catch my breath as Annabel ends the call and my entire body starts to shake. Katie is cradled in my arms, wrapped in the towel I've put around her. She's still breathing, more normally now, and her eyes are open. She seems alert as I hug her.

She whimpers into my neck. 'Katie scared.'

'I know baby, but there's nothing to be scared of now.'

'Love you, Emily.'

'Oh Katie, I love you too.' I hug her again and whisper. 'And thank God, you're OK.'

'Where daddy gone?'

'Your daddy was here?'

'He push me in water.'

My stomach somersaults as I begin to understand the true horror of all this.

'Katie naughty.'

'No baby, Katie's not naughty.'

'Daddy said Katie naughty and push me in water.'

I hold her tightly in my arms, wanting to protect her. But I feel sick because I finally know what Annabel's husband is capable of.

I hear a loud bang at my front door. I look down from the upstairs window to see Annabel standing and hurling her fists at the door like a mad woman. I understand why. Any mother would be frantic; she has no idea why

Katie is at my house. I run downstairs, holding Katie in the towel, to unlock the door.

Annabel takes her from me and screams at me. 'What have you done? You stay away from my child, you hear me?'

'Annabel, I…'

'I thought threatening you with a restraining order was enough, but it clearly wasn't.'

I plead with her. 'Annabel, please. I didn't take Katie. She was here when I arrived home.'

'She magically appeared?'

'She was in my bathroom. Thank God she's OK.'

She cuts across me. 'You're a nutcase and you'd better stay away from my daughter. You come anywhere near her again and I'll report you for assault.'

'Please. I need you to listen to me. I didn't take her. I think your husband did.'

'You need to get help, Emily. Katie isn't your child.'

'I know she isn't. But I love her. And you. You need to protect Katie and yourself. Please listen to me.'

I'm still shouting down the street as Annabel whisks Katie out of the house as fast as she can. I'm trying to warn her, but she won't listen. She thinks I'm obsessed with her daughter. But I'm not. I'm piecing things together. It's her husband who's brought Katie into my home and tried to kill her. I'm assuming if I hadn't come back early today, he would have made it look like I'd done it. And with my history, people might have believed him. It was the perfect set-up to get rid of his daughter and get his wife all to himself.

But it's the ultimate in evil, too.

≈ ≈ ≈

If only I'd known what was about to happen on that fateful day I would never have stepped out of my front door. It's the one day I remember with such clarity because I'd finally made the decision to move on with my life, but it's also the day that stopped me from doing that.

The day when a man I'd never met, but who I fell in love with a year later, walked into my home and destroyed my life.

Chapter 76

GARRIE

It should have been the perfect plan. If Katie was gone, I could have Annabel all to myself. That's all I ever wanted. To be the hero again. To be the perfect man she thought could do no wrong. It's not my fault Katie came along and got in the way. I loved Annabel with all my heart, and I needed her to come back home so the two of us could be a family again.

But Emily saved Katie and destroyed my plan. I hate her for that. I truly despise her for saving my daughter. She was a parasite eating away at my chance of happiness.

When I saw Emily's advert in the newspaper, I knew I'd found my opportunity to get Katie out of the house for a while. Discovering she was grieving the loss of her own child was a bonus. It gave me the perfect solution. A chance to get Katie out of the way permanently and Annabel's love and attention all to myself again. Because Katie had already taken my place. She had become Annabel's world like I used to be.

It's only possible to have that type of love for one person because it takes all your energy. It's overpowering and consumes your entire being so that your thoughts and senses become aligned to making that one person happy. For Annabel, that one person had become Katie. And I didn't stand a chance as long as she was around, so I knew I had to find a way to get rid of my daughter.

Once Emily's obsession with Katie became clear, so did my plan. I'd been watching her for a while, and I knew her routine. She didn't go out much, but she did go to the supermarket every Tuesday and then for a coffee in

town. All I had to do was time it right, so she'd be out of the
way on the day I decided to kill Katie.

I had to put the plan into action sooner than I'd
intended when Annabel took Katie and went to stay in the
hotel. I'd never expected her to leave me, but that's when I
knew I had to act. She was prepared to give our relationship
up completely for Katie. I couldn't let that happen.

When I saw her at the hotel, she looked so beautiful
and any qualms I had about what I was about to do
disappeared. She would always be my beautiful wife and I
was going to make her come back home and never let her
out of my sight again.

≈ ≈ ≈

15 months earlier
Katie has no idea her life is about to come to an end as she
laughs and sings her favourite songs in the backseat of the
car after I rush her out of the hotel. I drive to Emily's but
park around the corner. And I make sure her car is still
missing before taking Katie inside the house.

I fill the bathtub as quickly as possible, and I watch
with delight as Katie follows my every instruction. She
thinks it's funny that I get her into the bathtub while she's
still dressed; it makes her giggle.

I tell her I need to wash her hair and I grab her curly
locks and push her towards the water, but she is stronger
than I think. She's so small and yet has so much strength
and such a deep instinct to survive.

'No daddy, stop. Hurting me.'

'It's OK, sweetheart. It will all be over very soon.
You've been naughty so you need to be punished.'

'No, daddy, I've been good.'

I hear the front door open. Emily is back earlier
than anticipated. I panic and continue trying to push Katie
into the water, but she struggles. She bites my hand and
then screams out. I have no choice but to leave her and get
out of the house. I hide until Emily comes upstairs and

becomes preoccupied with Katie, then I flee to my car. My hand shakes as I fumble with the key. My clever plan has gone horribly wrong.

I drive around for a while. I need to think. I know there will be questions. Far too many questions. Katie will tell Emily I was in the house. And even if Annabel doesn't believe Emily's account of the story, she'll believe it if Katie tells her. They'll piece everything together and I won't stand a chance.

My mind is running on overdrive. All my lies will be exposed. I've made too many mistakes. I finally put my plan into action, and I messed up. I have no choice but to go back home and wait for the police to arrest me.

But that's not what happens when I find myself staring at the two uniformed officers on my doorstep; expecting to hear the standard caution as my wrists are handcuffed behind my back, like I've seen so often on television.

'Are you the husband of Annabel Griffiths?'

'I am.'

'I'm afraid we have some bad news.'

It's not what I expect to hear, and chills run throughout my body. What are they about to tell me?

'Can we come inside, sir? Perhaps you should sit down.'

'Tell me. Please.'

Adrenaline is pumping through my veins. I get excited because I think they're going to tell me Katie is dead. Maybe my plan worked after all.

'Your wife's been involved in a road traffic accident.'

'What?' Time stops. My blood freezes.

'She lost control of her car and hit a tree. We're very sorry to have to inform you she was killed on impact.'

They give me a moment to digest the information before delivering what they think is good news, but for me it's the final blow.

'But we're pleased to tell you that your daughter is safe.'

Chapter 77

SANDIE

I'm still locked inside the attic of Annabel's house. I run to the door and call out.

'Help. Please. I'm in here, open the door.'

I hear nothing. Not even footsteps descending the stairs. I feel sick as I rattle the door handle. It's the lilies; their fragrance seems even stronger than it was. I turn sideways to the door, bend forward, and give in to the nausea. I bang on the heavy wood until my hand hurts and my body heaves with the exhaustion of trying to be sick on an empty stomach.

My mouth fills with the acrid taste of fear but I swallow it back and try to ignore the throbbing pain in my hand, bang harder on the door, and scream as loudly as I can.

'Is that you, Garrie? You've locked me in. I'm here. I came to sort everything out.'

Still nothing. Sobs mix with my screams, and I hear the shrill screech of desperation in my own voice.

'Help, I'm in here…'

I press my forehead into the cold, unforgiving surface of the door as both hands use the last of my strength to deliver intermittent punches at it. But it's hopeless. My hands slide down the coarse wood; my limbs are weak. I sink towards the floor like a floppy rag doll, and I remember the baby. I have the irrational fear I might fall on my stomach against the hard, bare floorboards and hurt her.

I swing my body around and fall instead towards the bed. And the coffin. I crawl to lie alongside it and clutch my stomach.

I stare at Annabel's last resting place and whimper against the horrible realisation that I'm trapped in this empty, lifeless shrine with her.

I can't be here; I need to get out before claustrophobia suffocates me. Why did no one hear me shouting? Someone shut the door and turned the key so they must have heard me shouting.

Lady In Red is still playing on repeat so I grab the CD player and smash it onto the floor. It's a way to release some tension because I need to be out of this room instead of lying next to a mahogany coffin and the ashes of the woman Garrie has obviously never stopped obsessively loving. Now I understand how sick and dangerous he is. I automatically reach into my pocket for my phone and remember I didn't bring it. My fingers are brushing against Emily's phone, and it's dead.

My shocked gasp echoes around the empty attic. Why am I assuming Garrie locked me in here when there's somebody else who could also have done it? Somebody who might be almost as crazy as he is.

A woman who probably now wants payback for her imprisonment at the hands of my child's father.

Emily.

Chapter 78

EMILY

I lie back and sink into the warm water. At last, I can allow myself the comfort of a deep bath to wash the physical traces of Garrie away. I've finally peeled back the layers of guilt that have built up since Katie fell off the stool and events tragically led to Annabel's death; the wrapping paper of my subconscious that kept telling me I was in some way responsible.

But I wasn't. I know that now.

Ironically, it's Garrie's treatment of me - my incarceration at the hands of the man I thought I loved - that has finally cleared the lingering haziness of my memories and allowed me to see clearly. I was his victim. I was weak with the bereavement that continued to engulf me, and I needed help. Instead, he tried to use that weakness against me and make me take the blame. He so nearly succeeded but he didn't, and I'm stronger now.

I open my eyes and shiver against the cold water; I must have drifted off to sleep. I reach for the complimentary bath robe and wrap myself in its comfort. A hotel like this is a luxury I can't really afford but my body still aches as a reminder that my captivity was real, and Garrie did almost kill me. I need this brief time in a place where I'm anonymous and safe, to get my strength back and make decisions for the future. I can't change the past, but I can stop living in its shadow and find a way to move beyond all the pain I've endured.

I look across at the wardrobe where Annabel's red dress is hanging. It's the only item of clothing I have with me since my escape. I think about her and what a wonderful friend she was before everything went so tragically wrong. I should never have become so involved with her and Katie as a diversion from the grief I was trying to deny. If I'd listened to Martin and dealt with it, then we could have got through it together. Martin truly loved me, and I wish I could have seen that at the time.

I lie back on the hotel bed and sink into its five-star luxury. I drift into slumber thinking about Martin and the life we had together. Why couldn't I see that my perfect man, the one man who could have been my salvation, was right in front of me all along? The man who loved me through every moment of the immense joy that became the worst possible pain when we lost our child. My husband. The one person who understood me and the only truly good man I've ever known, until I drove him away.

I wonder whether it's too late to ask him to forgive me. Liz told me recently he'd asked about me. I smile as I think of his lopsided crooked grin and the way he squints against his myopia when he loses his glasses. He's worth fighting for.

It's not long before the door knocks; it's a room service tray with sandwiches, fries and a large bottle of San Pellegrino. I suddenly have an appetite and munch it down while pulling the duvet further over my legs and channel hopping on the flat wide-screen television. I dip the last chip into tomato ketchup and stretch my legs out with the sensation that I'm finally free from the turmoil that has haunted me for so long. I keep myself propped up with pillows and I flick on the bedside lamp because I need plenty of light after spending so long in darkness. I turn the television up louder because I also need to hear a voice that isn't Garrie's.

A blonde female weather girl appears on screen. She reminds me of Sandie. The woman who for so long felt like my nemesis, but who I'd felt a strange connection with when I found out she was pregnant.

I wonder how much of Garrie's past she knows and if she knows what he did to me. I can't imagine her turning a blind eye to my kidnap and imprisonment. She doesn't seem that type of person. I'm guessing he fooled her like he fooled me. It was happening right under her nose but he's a damn good liar. I think we were both blindsided by him. That's Garrie's USP, with women. He believes he can manipulate them into believing whatever he wants. And when it all goes wrong, he blames them and punishes them because he can't see his own faults.

I have no idea how much Sandie knows but every instinct tells me she's in trouble, another victim of Garrie's narcissism. As Annabel was, as I was. And she's pregnant, which puts her at even greater risk.

The silver tray flies across the room as I leap up from the bed. I need to hurry. Why has it taken me so long to join up the dots? A woman and her unborn baby are in danger, and I need to get to her to warn her. I throw the red dress back on and squeeze my feet into a pair of charity shop trainers I picked up on my way from the bank. They were all I could find but I was in agony with my feet. I run out of the door, head to the lift, and press the call button repeatedly, as I hear its doors opening and closing on the floors below me.

Chapter 79

GARRIE

I'm sitting outside in my car. The windows are steamed with condensation, and I can't make up my mind whether to go back into the house or leave her there. I admit it's strange thinking of Sandie locked in that room with Annabel. My two favourite women. I feel pleasantly comforted knowing they are both in the same room and unable to escape. My two little lovebirds nesting together. But I know I can't leave her there. I can't take the risk.

I go back up the stairs and unlock the door. Then I break down in tears as Sandie screams at me. She shouts and yells and screams on the top of her voice. I've never seen her like that.

'Don't you ever…ever…do that to me again.'

'I was scared, Sandie.'

'I mean it. You don't ever lock me in a room. Is that clear?'

I feel her anger piercing my skin. 'I won't, I promise. I panicked.'

'Panic doesn't cut it, Garrie. It's no excuse. You don't lock people in rooms. You don't create shrines for your dead wife, and you certainly don't tie people up in houses as a way of punishing them. That's the stuff of psychos.'

She points to her head as she says it and she looks into my eyes as if I'm mad. But I'm not. I'm perfectly sane. 'Forgive me, Sandie.'

'Forgive you? I don't even know you, Garrie. Not anymore.'

'Yes, you do, I'm still the same Garrie. The man you wanted to marry.'

'Jude was right.'

'Who the hell's Jude?'

'You don't even know who my friends are, Garrie. Coffee shop Jude. She's served you enough times.'

'Oh, that one.'

'Yes, Garrie. The one who told me I deserved better. The one who told me I was mad for trusting you.'

'You can trust me.'

'I should have listened to her.'

'No. Don't say that.'

I can feel her slipping through my fingers. I can't let her leave me. I make my final throw of the dice.

'Sandie, I'm ready to let go of the past and I'm ready to spend the rest of my life with you if you'll give me one more chance. You and the baby.'

The fury in her face mellows at those last four little words. I knew they'd work. That's one of the things I love about Sandie. She can't stay mad at me for long. Even in extreme circumstances like these I know I can win her over with the right words. I repeat them.

'You, me and the baby, forever.'

'You don't mean that, Garrie.'

'I do.'

'I know you don't want our baby.'

'I was scared when I said that but I'm not anymore. And I know I should never have told you to get rid of the baby. It's a part of you. Us. It's our baby, Sandie. We must stick together. I know how much it means to you. I'll never leave you again, or the baby.'

Her face softens at the mention of the baby, as Annabel's always did. Pregnancy does that to women but then the husband slowly gets usurped and becomes invisible. It happened with Annabel, but I'm not going to let Sandie slip through my fingers because she's got something growing inside her. I'll make sure she falls in love with me all over again and then find a way to get rid of the invader.

I smile and place my hand into hers. She tries to pull away, but I grip her fingers even tighter.

'I'm ready to go home, Garrie. I'm so tired now, but I'll walk back.'

'Why do you want to walk? We've got the car.'

'I'd like the fresh air.'

I continue grasping her hand as we walk towards the car. 'We'll open the windows.'

'Stop! Sandie! You need to stay away from him.'

We both spin round at the voice that comes out of nowhere and I see my worst nightmare walking towards us. It's Emily.

'You must leave him, Sandie. He's dangerous.'

I look at Sandie. Our hands are still clasped together. We look like the perfect couple because we are the perfect couple. Sandie wants us to be a family. Her, me, and the baby. She wants that more than anything and she's prepared to overlook my flaws so that we can be a proper family. My beautiful girlfriend blossoming from pregnancy and her hand grasping mine even tighter as Emily approaches.

'You'll regret it if you stay with him. He's unbalanced and dangerous.'

I pull Sandie closer to me and propel her towards the car.

'He kidnapped me. He tortured me and almost killed me. He's deranged. Do you know what he's keeping inside that house?'

I unlock the car as Emily's voice becomes more and more desperate until Sandie responds. 'Go away, Emily. Leave us alone. Please. Let us get on with our lives.'

And that's when I know she's still mine.

Chapter 80

EMILY

I watch in disbelief as Sandie lets Garrie bundle her into the car and they drive away. My head's a mix of anger at her and fear for her. How can she not see who he is and what he's capable of? I make my way up the garden path and into the house. It has the same coldness but there's no sign of my capture. The broken windows have been taped up and the blood has been cleared. The shards of glass have been swept away and the curtains that hung loosely when I was a prisoner are now pulled back neatly with a couple of ornaments on the windowsill. It must be Sandie who did this because Garrie doesn't have the capability. He's too messy and disorganised.

She looked shocked and frightened before he got her into the car. I'm guessing she's only just discovered what he's been up to. But he seems to have worked his magic once again with his manipulation tactics. Or he's threatened her and she's playing along to keep herself safe. Either that or he's made all this out to be my fault; he's a master at twisting the truth. I make my way up the stairs towards the room of horror. I take a deep breath before I enter. Then I walk towards the coffin, open the lid and remove Annabel's ashes. I want to keep them safe, away from this sinister sanctuary he's kept her in. As much a prisoner of his deranged mind as I was.

I also need to find a way to help Sandie. I have to see her. Surely, she must realise by now how dangerous he is, but if she doesn't, I need to convince her. Between us we can decide what to tell the police. I'm scared to call them on my own. Everything will get twisted by my past.

The day I found Katie floating in my bathtub was one of the worst moments of my life. I had held her in my arms and told her everything would be ok, that nothing bad would ever happen again. I had promised I would always protect her. But Annabel arrived and snatched her away. She thought I'd taken her daughter and she didn't give me a chance to explain. Or to warn her that I was scared for them. I knew her husband was evil, and I knew it was only a matter of time before he would try and hurt Katie again.

≈ ≈ ≈

15 months earlier

I get into my car and follow them. It's a hazy day with condensation running down the windows of my car. My breath is causing too much steam and I'm squinting my eyes as I try to follow Annabel through the traffic lights and down the lanes. I drive like a mad woman and so does she. She knows I'm following, and she puts her foot down. We both do. Racing like idiots down a narrow winding lane.

I'm flashing my lights and pipping my horn because I want her to stop. I want us to talk properly because she needs protecting from the man who has tried to kill her child. My blood is boiling, and my mind is racing as fast as we are both racing our cars.

Then it happens. I see her car spin out of control. There is nothing I can do as I watch it swerve and collide with an oncoming vehicle, the high-pitched screech of metal on metal. Then nothing but deadly silence. I slam on my brakes and skid to a stop behind her for a moment but then make a split-second decision. My life seems to flash before my eyes as I make a choice. I know she can't have survived the crash and I can't cope with it. I choose to drive away.

≈ ≈ ≈

That's why I can't walk away from Sandie now. I know she's in danger and I won't let Garrie's actions hurt anyone else.

Chapter 81

SANDIE

Garrie's hardly spoken since we got home. God knows what's going on in his head. He's barely taken his eyes off me but now he's making a pot of tea. Ginger is jumping up his leg, but he doesn't seem to notice. He stirs the tea more times than is necessary; he seems lost in his own world as he carries it through to the sofa.

I grab the key to number 12 and call out to him as I open the front door. 'I'll drink the tea when I come back. I'll go over and quickly feed the rabbit and we can talk when I come back.'

I walk across the road hoping Linda isn't around and luckily, she isn't. Both cars are missing from her drive. I want to feed Hoppy and then get out of here. I don't want anything more to do with this house but some time alone in the garden will help me. I have to get Garrie out of my home and out of my life as soon as possible. He's totally unbalanced and dangerous and the obvious solution is to go to the police, but that thought frightens me. I've stupidly involved myself in this whole mess in my attempt to protect him by covering up for him. I need to think.

I'll phone Jude. I'll go and stay with her until I can safely come back home. I reach into my pocket for my phone and remember it's still at home. Shit. The one I have with me is Emily's and it's dead. I wonder if there's a spare charger here somewhere. I run back inside and pull open kitchen drawers at random. Eventually I find one full of cables and grab a charger. I plug it in, connect the phone and the battery charging signal appears.

I walk back out to the garden and take some long, slow breaths. Today I make a fresh start with a new life that can never again include Garrie. He terrifies me now. But he can't know what I'm planning. If he senses anything, he won't let me go and he'll do to me what he did to Emily. I'll pack my bags and leave while he's at work tomorrow. I have no choice now but to go home, convince him I still love him, and that we need each other. It's the only way I'll be safe. He's full of anger and revenge and I daren't tip him over the edge; he needs to think I'm on his side. He's so self-centred and certain I'm besotted with him, that it'll be easy to make him believe it.

I put Emily's phone and charger in my zip pockets and walk across the road. I'm confronted by a note on the kitchen table. It's the standard "Garrie gone missing" note.

I'll be back soon. You know I love you. And the baby.

Garrie xx

I breathe a sigh of relief. I only have one more night to get through and the less of it I have to spend with him the better. I wish I knew how long he's going to be out, but his note is typical and doesn't give any information. But it does suggest he trusts me, so I'm safe. I look around the house and make a mental note of the essentials I'll take when I make my escape tomorrow.

I start to walk upstairs when I hear a knock at the door and Ginger starts barking like crazy. My heart sinks at the thought that it's Garrie and he's forgotten his key. I make my way downstairs as the knock becomes more frantic. It's Emily's face behind the frosted glass. For the first time I'm relieved to see her as I open the door.

'Sandie, it's not safe.' Her voice is a whisper. 'You need to get away from him. He's dangerous.'

I see the sincerity in her eyes. It must be hard for her to come back here after what he's done to her. She's not the bitter ex or someone trying to cause trouble. She's a kindred spirit who's suffered at the hands of Garrie, pleading with me to escape him. I open the door wider, but she doesn't step any closer.

'I saw him leave and you need to get away before he comes back.'

'Emily, I'm not staying with him, but I need to leave when he's at work. He could be back any moment. I'll go tomorrow.'

'I'm frightened for you, Sandie.'

I want to give her a hug, but I have no idea where Garrie's gone or if he's watching

'Emily, I'm so sorry for what you went through. I didn't know you were tied up inside that house until it was too late. Please believe me. And I didn't realise how unstable Garrie was…I only covered up for him because of…'

My apology sounds pathetic after what she's been through, but she glances down at my stomach and takes my hand. 'I know, Sandie. And it's OK. But you must leave tomorrow. Then we can figure out together what to do and how to protect each other.'

We look at each other, in a moment of empathy and understanding. It's the most heartfelt moment we've shared since we first met.

'Emily. I have something of yours. Wait.'

I run to my jacket, pull out her phone and charger and hand them to her. 'Where will you go now?'

She pauses for a moment. 'Do you have the key to number 12?'

I grab it from the hall table and hand it to her.

'Can you bear to walk back in there?'

'I hate the thought, but it keeps me close to you tonight if you need me. Put my number into your phone.'

I grab my phone from my bag and do what she says, as a message lands from Garrie.

'Shit. He's on his way back. Run home, Emily. If he sees you here…'

'I'll be across the road. Be careful, and call if you need me. I'll only be moments away. And Sandie, leave the back door unlocked.' She squeezes my hand, pats Ginger on the head then glances at the road before running across to number 12. She turns and waves before she goes inside.

I close my door, and relief that this nightmare is nearly over washes over me. I'm strangely reassured to know that Emily is close by. If I was left with even the slightest doubt, her visit has extinguished it. I look across at the house plant that I once hated. I give it some water and smile because it's probably the only thing left in this house that's thriving apart from little Ginger, who's running around the hallway chasing her own tail.

I should have seen through Garrie's façade; realised his consummate performances were a polished act. I should have listened to Jude; she tried so hard to warn me. And I shouldn't have jumped to conclusions about Emily. None of this was her fault but hurt and anger still stab me like a knife. Knowing I was a convenience, despite his claims to love me; a way he could observe her from my house before he made his move on her. His attempt to finally destroy her.

And then the cruellest thing; coming back to me and convincing me he loved me. I wanted to believe it because I wanted my baby to have a father, but all the time he was paying secret visits to Annabel. The ultimate cliché; a married man living with another woman and having a clandestine affair with his wife. Which he was, except…

I shiver at the twisted horror of it…

My lover was having his affair with a dead woman.

I run my hands over my baby bump; the growing new life that looks to me for strength. I will have to be mother and father to this child when I take a leap of faith and walk out of Garrie's life. Being a parent starts now; I won't let my child down.

I'll deal with Garrie. I won't let him win.

Chapter 82

EMILY

Maybe I should have insisted Sandie left with me and not left her alone; I feel a growing unease that I did. It's ironic that I stood at her door and felt such a powerful connection to her; the woman I once thought was my nemesis, as she thought I was hers.

I'm frightened for her, but at least here at number 12 I'm close by if she needs me. She knows what Garrie did and about his abhorrent treatment of me, but she may still underestimate what he's capable of. She's made her decision to stay with him tonight and I respect that, but I have a feeling of dread lurking in the pit of my stomach.

My phone's charging and I keep expecting it to ring. I twirl a teaspoon idly in my coffee and stare through the kitchen windows. The rain that started as light drizzle is now a downpour and rolls down them in rivulets as the cold, wet glass mists up from the warmth inside the house; I've switched the heating up to its maximum setting. I stare at the blurred image of the garden, but only my subconscious can see clearly now; three women in sharp focus. The woman I left on her doorstep, pregnant with the child of a monster. The woman whose ashes he keeps in a lily-strewn coffin in a cold, empty attic, who died because of his obsession with her. And my reflection in the misted window; a woman wrongly accused by a man who nearly destroyed her.

Three victims of Garrie.

And worse. Three willing victims.

But that's the power of the man or beast that connects us all. The man we each thought we were in love with.

A master magician who cast his spell over each of us in turn and bewitched us until we felt powerless to resist him. Before the spell was broken and the magician became the manipulator. Chipping away at our hearts and minds; trying to break us, piece by painful piece, to satisfy his narcissism.

And with Annabel he succeeded. The first woman he truly wanted but destroyed. The woman he needed to possess. The woman he eventually broke when his obsession led to her death, as surely as if he'd been behind the wheel of her car when she crashed.

But it's not her death he wants to punish me for; it's saving her daughter Katie because that meant Annabel's love was shared with someone other than him. He couldn't deal with it. He needed Katie out of the way, so I became the enemy because I saved her from the murky waters of the bathtub.

He wanted Annabel to worship him, and he would have done anything to achieve that. When Katie survived, he became the devil in disguise. He made a promise to his dead wife that he would destroy me. In Garrie's eyes I'm the guilty one, and I know he's thinking I haven't yet paid the ultimate price for my crime.

The rain continues its unremitting assault on the glass window; an appropriate parallel with Garrie's unrelenting assault on me. His determination to be judge, jury and executioner; a one-man, unholy trinity, desperate to make me pay. To punish me for a crime I didn't commit. He won't stop until he finishes what he started; his game of madness isn't over.

I know Garrie better than anyone and I'm certain he's planning something. He always is; that's the way he works. I look at my watch; it's been over an hour since I left Sandie in her doorway, assuring me she had everything under control. But I'm frightened she doesn't. He'll never let her escape. Or me. I can't waste any more time thinking. I must do something. Lives depend on me. And one of them isn't even born yet.

I know exactly what I need to do, and I pray Annabel's spirit will give me the strength to do it. I owe this to her memory.

I won't let her down again.

Chapter 83

GARRIE

I feel exhilarated because she has no idea what I have planned for her, but she's going to love it. Her final hours and the perfect last supper. I feel the capillaries expanding as adrenaline pumps blood through my system. A fitting romantic ending for two star-crossed lovers.

She could never have been a substitute for Annabel. To think I tried to convince myself that we could make it work. I guess we could have been happy if she hadn't spoiled it. I could have moulded her into the woman and wife I wanted. A man has his needs so she could have met mine with a bit more practice.

But she had to go and get herself pregnant. Her sweet little eyes staring up at me with an invader growing inside her. Her foolish excitement forcing me to fake happiness. Smiling through gritted teeth and feeling like my insides are about to burst every time she talks about the little miracle growing inside her.

A foreign body that will grow up to become the golden child. So that I fade into the background and have to watch the baby take what is rightfully mine. Like Katie took a piece of Annabel. Then another, and another. Until there was nothing left for me.

I throw the shopping onto the back seat and hurl my anger at the car door as I slam it shut before sending the supermarket trolley skidding across the wet carpark to join the others in the trolley bay.

I lean back in the driver's seat and take deep breaths. The calmness envelops my skin and a grin spreads across my face as I take pleasure in the moment that's about to unfold.

'Sandie my darling, if only you had been a bit more careful, we wouldn't be in this situation. It's your fault that you've lost everything. Not mine. You could have got rid of the baby. Oh well, never mind, you will have a beautiful evening and a beautiful ending. You could never compete with my Annabel anyway.'

I continue talking to myself until I'm aware of a shopper trying to squeeze past. I stare at him as his trolley scrapes the paintwork on my car, but I don't have time for a confrontation, so I ignore it. Rain pounds against the car roof. It's heavier now; it'll slow all the traffic down. I look at my watch. I've made good time so far, but I need to get moving. I don't want to leave Sandie on her own much longer; I don't trust Emily. She might go to the house and start spitting her venom.

I run through the plan in my head once more and pat my jacket pocket to check I've got what I need. Everything's in place. I text Sandie to say I'm on my way, then I put the car in gear and the wipers on top speed.

There's one quick thing I must do on my way home.

I need to see Annabel.

I stop at her favourite florist and buy lilies. She deserves fresh flowers tonight for such a special occasion. I imagine my beautiful Annabel smiling down on me and approving of tonight's festivities.

I drive to the house and let myself in. It feels dark and cold, damp from the rain, and still reeks of Emily's presence. I can smell defeat here and I don't like it. When all this is over, I'll make changes; rid our home of the residue of her presence here and breathe life back into it. For Annabel and for me. We'll be together. Happy, in love and in peace. It'll be like the old days.

I head upstairs to the attic; I need her with me tonight. This is for her too. I push the coffin lid open and reach for her. Then I hear my own scream echo around the attic. I beat the coffin, and then my head, with my fists.

'No! No, no, no!'

The coffin is empty.
Annabel's gone.

Chapter 84

SANDIE

I'm boiling the kettle when I hear his key turn in the door. I turn around as his footsteps head towards me because I can't give him any opportunity to get close or wrap himself around my shoulders like he normally does. I'm confronted with the usual bunch of flowers that is considerably larger than normal. I smile at him through gritted teeth.

'They're beautiful. I'll get a vase.'

I stretch up into the kitchen cupboard then turn on the tap. I feel his closeness as he pushes his body against mine and his lips press against my neck. I'm pinned against the work surface and the man I hate, and I lean my head slightly to the left as water drips against my fingers and into the vase. I'm desperate to pull away but I can't because then he would know I'm pretending, and it would be game over. He continues planting tiny kisses along my neck as the hairs stand to attention with trepidation. I'm unable to speak or move as his hands slide over my shoulders, the same hands that tied Emily to a chair and the same man who was capable of capturing a woman and torturing her. I pray with all my being for him to pull away until he finally does.

'The flowers are beautiful, Garrie. I'm glad we've managed to sort things out.'

I hold the vase between myself and the monster in front of me.

He smiles back. 'I've been shopping my love. I'm going to surprise you with a special dinner.'

Every word he says makes my skin tingle with apprehension. He's delusional. He seems to think I can forget everything he's said and done and have a romantic meal as if everything's totally normal.

I remind myself what I'm dealing with; I must keep my wits about me so I can get through tonight and make my bid for freedom. 'Perfect. I've walked Ginger and fed the rabbit, so we have the evening to ourselves.'

He doesn't answer. He's clearly preoccupied, which is nothing unusual. I've come to expect it with him. There's always something lurking in the background. A secret layer that bubbles away underneath the surface. And today is no different. He walks towards the fridge and starts to unload his bags. Then he decides to speak. 'Go and relax on the sofa, darling, while I start preparing dinner.'

His words are matter of fact and without feeling, but I don't argue. I grab my phone from my bag, open Emily's contact page, then slip it into my pocket as he clatters around in the kitchen. I ignore the sound of a glass smashing and his 'Sorry, clumsy me. I'll clear it up.'

I know he'll try every trick in the Garrie charm book tonight. The same cycle that's replayed itself over and over throughout our relationship. Now I never want to hear them, or see him, ever again.

Chapter 85

GARRIE

I look across at her exquisitely beautiful face. It's strange how you get a moment of clarity right before the end. I step towards her, slide my fingers through her hair and feel her shiver against my touch. I know she's not sure about me, but tonight I shall make her fall in love with me all over again for one last time. I've always been able to do that with women. I learnt the skills early in life and I've never forgotten them.

'Take a seat, Sandie.'

Ginger hops around excitedly so I fill her bowl with pigs' ears. They should keep her quiet for a while. My perfectly prepared Spotify playlist provides the mood music. I dim the lighting, light candles and place perfectly polished cutlery onto Sandie's placemat. I even got out the special ones. I can't help but smile at my own brilliance. I feel like I could walk on air.

'You've gone to a lot of trouble Garrie.'

She noticed. I'm already winning her round. I know it. 'Only the best for my perfect girlfriend.'

I watch her eyes following my every move. I look at her pretty face and wonder if she's capable of stealing my dead wife's ashes and I don't think so; it's not her style. But just in case, I make a beautiful cocktail of pineapple, grenadine, and poison. Something I keep in the back of my man cupboard; it should do the job. I won't use it unless I have to, but it's good to have a back-up plan. One of the few sensible things my mum taught me; always have a back-up plan in case something goes wrong.

But I've planned something much more exciting. I think Sandie will be impressed with my choice of ending.

I feel inside my pocket. The single earring is safely wrapped in cellophane and the blue topaz ring is alongside it, both ready for their moment. They'll be the perfect evidence that Emily was here. I took them both from her when I tied her up. It's ironic she was still wearing the ring when she became my prisoner. I saw the heartbreak in her eyes when I removed it. Of course, she still loved me, bless her; totally besotted with me. If she hadn't been the enemy, she could probably have made a decent wife with practice, too.

I look across at Sandie and I can see she's trying so hard to be on her best behaviour and smile in all the right places. She's doing exactly as I tell her, and my plan is running to perfection.

After our main course I pour wine for me and sparkling water for her and we clink glasses again. Then I get down on one knee and propose. I know Annabel will be looking down with the biggest smile knowing that this gesture is the beginning of the end. I smile too at Sandie's shocked expression. She wasn't expecting this.

'What are you doing, Garrie?'

I'm perched on one knee with the topaz ring glistening against the candlelight. 'Precious Sandie.'

'Don't Garrie.'

I see the panic in her eyes. 'Beautiful, flawless, Sandie.'

'Not now, Garrie.'

'Listen Sandie, you've made me realise the value of true love. You've made me realise that love has no boundaries. Marry me.'

She goes silent as I slide the ring onto her finger. 'We haven't had a wedding, but tonight we dine as husband and wife.'

She stares at the blue topaz. The moment is perfect.

Chapter 86

SANDIE

His eyes are glinting with deranged excitement and I'm desperate to get out of here. My blood's boiling beneath my skin and the walls are closing in on me. Why didn't I run away earlier when I had the chance?

I look at the ring glistening once again on my finger. A ring that has been worn by Annabel and Emily. To think I once loved it and now it's spine-chilling because I know the depths of his warped obsession and depravity.

'A glass of wine, my love?'

He speaks in a soft whispered tone as he opens another bottle and I wish I could smash it over his head.

'I can't, Garrie. But you should. Just water for me, please.'

I watch the red lava flow like warm blood into the neck of his glass before he picks it up and holds it towards me.

'Here's to the future, my beautiful lady.'

He hands me my water glass. 'Let's drink to our perfect evening.'

I have no idea what part of his warped mind makes him think this is perfect. I hear Ginger lapping up her water in noisy gulps. She's thirsty because she's had so many pigs' ears. It's a strange bit of normality during Garrie's disturbed intensity.

He reaches for the cheese and biscuits, and I tremble at the sight of the cheeseboard. Our names are a little faded, but they are still there as a reminder that I loved him once. Garrie and Sandie without the Y.

'Mature Cheddar?'

'Not for me, thanks.'

'It's your favourite.'

He stares at me without blinking and I know it's the cue to change my mind and agree with whatever he asks.

'I'll have two crackers with the Cheddar, please.'

He prepares them as if for an operation then pops each cracker into my mouth.

'Sandie, this is the most magnificent evening of my life.' He pulls me to my feet. 'And now we dance.'

Our shadows form silhouettes behind the net curtains. The ones I used to stand behind, waiting for him to walk past my house.

'It's time my love.'

He turns up the speaker volume and pulls me closer as his eyes darken and his lips curl.

'Sandie, we were meant to meet. Annabel brought us together and I know she's looking down on us now. Watching us dance to her favourite song.'

The opening bars of *Lady in Red* begin to play, and he closes his eyes, swaying to the music as if he's in a trance. I reach into my pocket and my fingers frantically try to locate the call button on my phone.

'My Annabel. You are the light of my soul, the essence of pure love. I can feel your soul weep with happiness as your tears fall onto us with your blessing.'

He pulls me closer to him. 'The moment has arrived, Sandie. Annabel's beautiful spirit is all around us. Feel her presence.'

He grasps my body tighter. 'Beautiful Annabel. I'm doing this for you my darling. I love you, Annabel.'

He tilts his head upwards as if he's breathing in her spirit. Fear rips through me and I desperately try to push him away as I scream. 'Garrie! Please. Stop. This isn't what Annabel wants.'

His hands close their grip on my neck.

'It's all your fault. You got yourself pregnant. You should have been more careful instead of being greedy. Wanting to love another person. I should have been enough. Me. The man who would have spent his life with you. But now I have to get rid of you. Because I would sooner kill you than risk losing your love to that thing inside your stomach. Because as soon as it comes along your love will be split and I won't matter anymore.'

I can't breathe. He's tightening his grip on my neck. I push against him with my fists as hard as I can, but I don't have any strength to fight as his hands continue to suck the air out of me. His face twists into a contorted smile as if he's savouring this moment and, in his trance, he temporarily relaxes his grip.

I gasp and scream out. 'Please God, Emily, help me.' Where is she?

And then everything happens so fast.

Garrie's eyes fly open as he senses someone behind him. I stare into them and hope he sees Emily's reflection in mine. I want him to know that this is the moment. That this is how it ends. And he no longer has control over it.

Over his shoulder I see the glint of the cheese knife's serrated blade in Emily's raised hand. She pauses for a split second, and I nod my head.

'Do it!'

She plunges the knife between his shoulder blades. He screams a tortured 'No!' as his face contorts with pain. I feel a spasm shake his body before he releases his hold on my neck and staggers away from me. I push against his chest as hard as I can, and he falls backwards onto the knife still sitting snug in his back. It presses against the floor creating a gushing pool of blood.

Ginger makes her way towards him and starts licking the sticky red liquid, her tail wagging excitedly. I pull her away as quickly as I can and shut her inside the downstairs loo.

Emily hasn't moved. She's frozen to the spot. I take hold of her hand and we stare in silence at Garrie. His eyelids flicker and his limbs shake as he gasps against imminent death. I speak into the agony of his dying moments.

'It's all your fault, Garrie. I would sooner kill you than risk losing the beautiful baby inside me. Because I already love her more than I could ever have loved you.'

Emily and I clutch hands as he stares back at us in disbelief. And then a word. One whispered word which he must know will be his last.

'ANNABEL...'

We watch as he writhes around on the floor, railing against death.

Emily reaches into her jacket pocket and looks at me, then back at Garrie as she holds the small urn containing Annabel's ashes above his horrified face.

'I brought her with me, Garrie. She needed to be a part of this; just like you intended her to be. But not quite how you planned it. And don't worry. We'll give her the send-off she always deserved. And this time I'll be there but thank God you won't be. She died because of you. Now you've paid the ultimate price for that.'

He tries to pull himself from the floor, but he can't. He wants to hold Annabel in his dying moment. Now we both hold her above his head, out of his reach.

'You left us no choice, Garrie. This was the only way this could end. With Emily and me finishing this together.'

Finally, he stops moving.

There is only stillness.

And a pair of cold, unseeing eyes staring at a tableau of three women. Two who survived, clinging to each other; and the remains of the woman who didn't.

It's over.

Chapter 87

EMILY

We hold on to each other. Two women who finally fought back and won. Then Sandie pulls back.

'Thank God, you made it in time. I thought I'd left the call too late. I really thought he was going to kill me.'

I smile at her. 'I was already outside. Waiting. As soon as I heard *Lady in Red* playing, I knew he'd try something.'

'You saved my life, Emily.'

'We saved each other. And your baby.'

I watch Sandie carefully place Annabel's ashes onto the table. Then she calls the police. We certainly have a lot to tell them, but we were acting in self-defence. She's got the marks on her neck from his hands and I'm still full of cuts to my wrists and ankles from being tied up by him. We hug each other again and make a pact to never let any man hurt us again.

'I'll drink to that.'

Sandie raises her glass and gulps down the remainder of her sparkling water. She smiles.

'Here's to Garrie's perfect evening. Not quite how he expected it to end.'

I see two cocktails on the side table that Garrie must have made earlier, and I pick up a glass. I want to celebrate, and I can't think of a more perfect way to do it than with one of the fancy concoctions he used to love to show off with.

I feel elated.

We beat the enemy.

Sandie and me. Together. I raise my glass to her. 'To us, my friend. We did it. We slayed the monster. We didn't let him win.'

Then I down the cocktail in one go, barely tasting it. And the world stops.

Sandie's cradling me in her arms.

'Emily. Please. Stay with me. Breathe. The ambulance is on its way.'

I know life's ebbing away from me. But I smile at her because I want her to know it's OK.

Because in the last hours of my life I was finally in control. We made Garrie suffer like he made us suffer. Squirming on the kitchen floor while we held his dead wife's ashes above his head. And I wore his wife's dress, the one he loved her in, which will now haunt him through eternity. The dress I took on the night I escaped from him. An immaculate ending because Sandie and I chose it. Not him.

And because he'll never know that I'm dead. And that, unlike him I can be at peace because I'm with my beautiful baby girl.

My Annabel.

Chapter 88

SANDIE

It's been almost a year and I still can't believe Emily's dead. When the paramedics arrived, they felt for a pulse but there wasn't one, and they couldn't revive her. The police confirmed one of the cocktails was poisoned. Garrie had obviously prepared it for me. It was more evidence against him. I still feel numb when I remember how the colour had drained from Emily's face as she collapsed and lay motionless next to the enemy.

Everybody now knows the truth about Garrie and the extent of his evil narcissism. The police never questioned my involvement in covering up Emily's kidnapping; to them I was another of his victims. The only one who survived. Perhaps his mother mourns the loss of her son, but nobody else does. And it turned out that he was plain Gary Jones; the elaborate Garrie Paisley-Jonas was his pretentious invention to impress, and to hide his past.

I made the decision to move away from my home, because of everything that happened there. My mother bought a smaller house closer to town and I'm happy here. I decorated the nursery in exactly the sunshine yellow I'd planned. And Samantha Emily was born; my beautiful six-pound, six-ounce baby girl. I love her so much. And she loves her sister Katie who we visit every week. I arranged to move her to a top-class facility that specialises in her condition. There couldn't be a better way to use some of the proceeds from the sale of Annabel and Garrie's home, which are being held in trust for her. She's getting better all the time, and it shouldn't be long before she can come and live with Samantha and me. We're her family now.

I haven't seen Martin since Emily's funeral. He was devastated and he's gone away for a while but he's keeping in touch. We've started to grow close. I think we both feel something's developing between us, and we're to going meet up when he gets back, which he tells me will be soon.

I still work at the coffee shop with Jude who now insists on being known as Auntie Jude. She loves Samantha and the feeling is mutual. I hear them giggling in my kitchen when Jude looks after her if I have an assignment deadline. And Ginger still loves her walks, but they're not at midnight anymore.

I think about Emily every day. I will never forget her. Or Annabel, even though I never met her. Because our fates were inextricably connected; we all shared something. Especially Emily and me. We both loved a monster who tried to destroy us. But we found the strength to destroy him. And I owe Emily my life. So does my daughter, which is why it's only fitting that Emily is her middle name.

I walk into the kitchen, turn on the tap and fill a large glass so I can water the houseplant. It's thriving so much that I moved it into a bigger pot when it arrived in its new home. I touch its strong green leaves and smile.

'Thank you, Emily.'

ACKNOWLEDGMENTS

He Walks Past My House has had an interesting journey from the day we wrote its opening line, to its publication as a full-length novel, and we want to thank the many people who have helped and supported us.

This book was written in a non-conventional way, starting life as a series of short daily episodes that evolved into the first novel produced live on social media. We give huge thanks to everyone on Instagram who liked and followed the story and gave us valuable feedback and encouragement. We have been overwhelmed by the continuing support we've received from the social media community, and we are excited to now share the final published version.

All books that go from inception to publication owe a debt of gratitude to a professional team. Our thanks go to Eve Seymour for reading our initial completed story and giving us valuable input as we began the editing process. We also thank our editor Nicola Bowen Rees who helped us finalise the book for publication. We thank Nick Castle for bringing visual life to the story with his cover design expertise.

When books are being written, edited, and prepared for publication, it's not only the authors who live, eat, and breathe them, but also the people they live with. We both give much love and appreciation to the special people in our lives for their patience and understanding.

As *He Walks Past My House* is our first novel as a writing partnership, we also thank each other for the mutual support, inspiration, encouragement, and laughter that got us to the finishing line.

Charlotte & Amanda
(Valentine & Hopewell)